Thadius

By

Lawrence BoarerPitchford

DEDICATION

To the loving memory of my father, Lawrence Judson Pitchford Jr. A Veteran of World War II, a great leader of men, and my personal hero. May your soul be at peace as you drink wine made from the vineyards of heaven.

Also, dedicated to my wife Julie, without whom all my efforts in life would be for naught. Your tireless work and help I acknowledge; Eternal is our love.

And lastly, dedicated to my family whom has always been a pillar of support. My love to you all.

CONTENTS

ACKNOWLEDGMENTS

Cover Artist ~ Lawrence BoarerPitchford

Editor ~ Wendy Schirmer

"Gauisus est vir quisnam has infractus

-------chains quod vulnero meus, quod has desparatus fatigo quondam quid pro totus."

"Happy is the man who has broken the chains

--------which hurt the mind, and has given up worrying once and for all."

Publius Ovidius Naso

Though some persons and places in this book are historical, the situations, and concepts are the sole invention of the author.

BEGINS THE TALE

OF THADIUS

i

CHAPTER 1

Dulviet opened her eyes. Her arms hurt, and she realized her toes were touching grass. She looked down to see a monstrous creature. "Why don't you scream?" the satyr said.

Dulviet's wrists burned as she hung from the thick oak limb, and her heart beat like a war drum. "What do you want from me?" Her tears fell to the dark forest floor with abandon.

The cloaked figure lifted his lantern to examine her bare skin. "You should know, or did Minerva not tell you?" The obscene satyr leered at her with its twisted grin.

"I want to go home!" Dulviet thrashed about for a moment, the leather straps cutting deeper into her wrists as her strength failed her. "My father is—"

"I know who your father is. He knows, doesn't he? He was there… Apollo told me so. That's why you are here, for you carry the message."

The smell of wet grass filled her nose as she watched him walk toward a group of saplings and kneel. "Please… don't hurt me." Panic filled her voice. Straining to see in the darkness, she realized he'd laid out metal items on a white cloth.

"I will begin soon," the satyr said. "There will be much screaming to begin with. Your screams will help to purify you, as will the sweet, sticky blood you will shed. The map…"

The satyr stood and staggered, falling back to his knees. "He searches. After all, it is like the stolen cattle. The gods agreed, and now…" He froze and stared off into the woods, and then clutched

1

his skull. "Not now! I hear you gnawing within my head." He clawed at his face, knocking the mask to the ground. "Why send the hornets to devour my mind? I am doing your will." He convulsed as foam emitted from his clenched jaws. Then he fell to the wet grass and lay still.

Dulviet struggled wildly, twisting her body this way and that until blood dripped down her arms. "Help me!" she screamed into the darkness.

A tall figure in a white robe and wearing a golden sun-mask emerged from the black forest and observed her. "I have come from Olympus at your behest," said a masculine voice.

"Please help me! Cut me down – stop him!" Dulviet cried out.

The satyr slowly got to his knees, groped for the mask, and struggled back to his feet. He had a small curved blade in his hand.

The man in the sun mask turned to the satyr and handed him a cup. "See, you call and I come. What thoughts do you have that anger the gods that they send divine hornets to eat at your brain? Drink, and they will be cast out... for now." He walked around Dulviet, looking her up and down. "I am pleased with your work so far. When this is done, I will give you another container of the gods' powder to defer the pains in your head."

"Yes... the powder is what I need... the gods' powder." The satyr turned his back to Dulviet, lifted his mask and drank, and then replaced his facade. He turned and came at her brandishing the blade only inches from her bare breast. "Do you know what this is for?"

"Please... no," she sobbed.

"A surgeon uses this to cut the flesh around a wound, to drain the stinking puss as putrefaction takes hold."

"Help, help me!" Her voice felt hoarse, as if torn from her throat."

"Your screams will bathe me, and your blood will wash away my tears, and soon you will tell me what your father did and where the map to the Fleece is hidden," said the satyr. "Let us now begin."

*   *   *

Thadius felt the intense Mediterranean sun beating down on his head. The sharp cry of a gull caught his attention, and he shielded his eyes with his hand as he scanned the deep blue sky.

"Thadius, what do you see?" Caldinus walked up beside him.

"Just a gull," Thadius said. "What brings you out in this heat?"

"My wife wants a chicken and a loaf of bread."

"Why not send one of your servants?" Thadius mopped the sweat from his head with the fringe of his toga.

"You've met my wife. It's better that I take every opportunity to stray from the villa " Caldinus chuckled.

"I would never suggest such… but since you mentioned it, I won't argue."

Caldinus inhaled deeply then exhaled. "Well, I'm off. Oh, I didn't ask what you were doing today. Where is it you're going?"

"The bath. Dominus and I are meeting there to take in a steam and have a meal."

"Dominus." Caldinus shook his head. "He's quite the character—gambling to all hours of the night, and staying at the whorehouse for days upon end." He chuckled again. "Some nymph has his name as patron painted over her chamber by now most likely. Nonetheless, I'd better be off or when I return I'll not hear the end of it. Enjoy your day." Caldinus strolled down the alley and into the shadows.

Stepping from the narrow street, Thadius walked under an awning covered in a dark green material. A mangy looking black dog slowly wandered from across the road and sat in front of him. "There, there old Mobius," Thadius said, while reaching into a broad leather pouch on his belt and producing a round wheat biscuit. "I did expect to see you – but not quite so tired." Crouching down he patted the creature on the head and placed the treat in front of its mouth. "As neighbor, we shall keep thee as friend… Pax Romanus Mobius."

Taking the biscuit, the dog sat in the street and began to slowly eat. Glancing up, he blinked his bluish gray eyes, then with a huff, lay down and went to sleep.

"He was up all night barking at deer and rabbits." A dark haired man with an ample belly came from across the way. "He is far too old for such sport, and as you know when Mobius is barking none within a Roman mile can sleep." He stopped and scratched the dog's head. "At least I see that Mobius is pleased with your gift. Where have you been keeping yourself of recent?"

"At home," Thadius said. He patted the man's stomach. "I see the business of fish keeps you well fed, Gaius."

"Well fed, well clothed, and well satisfied," Gaius said. "And seeing you in good spirits and humor fills my heart with joy. So, where are you off to?"

"To the bath to relieve some tired muscles."

"What of those young servants you so heartily keep – surely a few of those lovelies could massage that old back of yours?"

"Custom dictates that I meet Dominus at the bath today regardless of tired muscles or poor state of mind."

"Custom? Dominus?" Gaius chuckled. "That old pirate, he owes me money from a game of dice we played last evening. He seems to conveniently forget his coin pouch from time to time."

Mobius suddenly snorted and looked at the two men. "Perhaps you should take Mobius with you. He could use a good steam, scraping, strong drink, and some rich food, wouldn't you say?"

Thadius patted the dog on the head. "I think he's happy where he is. Nonetheless, it's good to see that Jupiter is smiling upon you both."

"Jupiter is a kindly old spirit, but his brother Neptune can be a fickle master. The last few days our bounty has not been as full, but stop by on your way home, and Neptune willing, I'll have some fresh catch to sell you."

Thadius stepped back into the street. "I'll do so. You're a good friend, Gaius."

"We've known each other for many years now," Gaius said. "And I know the loss of your wife weighs heavy on your heart. You are welcome at my home anytime – and I'm not speaking from pity."

"Be it pity or compassion, you are a good friend."

The bakery has just opened if you wish to buy a loaf and take it with you to the bath," Gaius called to him as he walked away.

"We plan on eating at the bath triclinium," Thadius added. Looking down the street at the corner shop, he could see the blood-red doors of the Dionysius Bakery propped open.

"Where do you think the visitors are today?" the baker asked from beneath the awning.

Thadius wiped the sweat from his brow with the fringe of his toga again. "You know the tourists— they can't wait to get here, coming by boat, cart, and horse, and then when the heat of summer is upon them, they hide in their rented villas and inns until evening."

The baker smiled and went back to pounding dough on a long wooden table. Thadius passed the bakery all the while observing the flowerbeds bursting with sweet white lilacs growing in manicured rows and climbing up the walls and columns. "I love the smell of lilacs mixed with the aroma of baking bread. It's a good day to be alive," Thadius mused aloud.

Pulling down on his white tunic, he felt the garment sticking against his sweaty skin. His beige cotton toga hung down to just above his knees, and he looked down on the simple harpy-shaped brass broach that pinned the fabric at the shoulder. It was a gift from his wife, and it reminded him of happier days—her light laughter, and her glowing smile.

His summer sandals slapped out a cadence on the rectangular cobblestones as he moved beyond the bakery and past the Forum. A slight ocean breeze caressed his face as he turned down the street that led to the bath and gymnasium. A street vendor and two shop owners waved as he passed. In turn, he waved back with a smile. "Tiberius, Pliny, and Victanious."

Pliny came towards him holding a small leather sack filled with coins. "Thadius, this is yours from the last shipment of Egyptian cotton."

"Bring it to my home later. I'm off to meet Dominus at the bath now."

Pliny laughed. "Dominus? Good god, that man is insufferable."

"He is incorrigible," Thadius added.

Victanious approached. "For you my friend," he said as he handed Thadius a cup of wine. "Our new wine was pressed only two months ago."

Taking the cup, Thadius tipped it up to his lips and drank down the contents. "Delicious. Is it from your personal amphora?"

"Of course. If you are in need of some, just let me know and I'll have it delivered to your cellar-larder."

Tiberius stayed in the shade and waved. "Thadius, do you have some time to talk?"

"I must be on my way. You know Dominus, if he is kept waiting he'll bend my ear with a story about other times he was kept waiting."

"Yes, be on your way. We'll speak later," Tiberius said.

The street came to a T intersection. Thadius turned onto a wide street and looked up to see a horse drawn cart slowly meandering towards him. Stepping to the side, he noted the many slabs of beef stacked in the back.

The man leading the cart smiled. "Thadius," he said, "I have some meat from a recent butchering for you. If you like, I can have it cured before I send it. Come by and sample some of my wine too this eve, and we will talk business."

"Belenius, I am engaged and will not have the time," Thadius stated as he continued to walk.

"You never visit when I ask you. Come to my house, I'll take good care of you. As good as your wife did."

Smiling, Thadius passed without glancing over. "Such a fine offer, Belenius, but I am inclined to women not men as I have told you before."

"Suit yourself. But maybe you could bring by that servant of yours to visit? I will treat him well."

Chuckling, Thadius waved his hand dismissing the comment. Ahead of him was the town's large marble fountain—horses held in check by the powerful white marble hands of Neptune. Some women were fetching buckets of water, and several children were splashing one another as he walked by. Just beyond he could see the wrought-iron gate, the hedgerows with hanging grapes, and bright flower gardens of the magnificent bath complex.

Walking up to the entry, he saw his old friend Peresius Albas Dominus standing near the gate, beneath a blue tiled roof. His friend yawned and looked up, saluted, then laughed loudly. "Ah, here comes the great Moras Tiberius Thadius, all hail he in triumph!"

Three men walking past him stopped and stared, first at Dominus then at Thadius. They made no word, but looked annoyed and proceeded inside. Chortling, Thadius approached and bowed low. He patted his leather pouch on his belt. "I've brought enough for lunch, and some wine."

"And a woman or two?" Dominus asked.

Thadius shook his head. "There is little fire left in these loins, my friend."

"Come now... the fire is not in our loins, but in our heart."

"It is too soon for me. I might even give up women altogether."

Dominus laughed and shook his head. "I might give up libation, gambling and stray women, but you'd be wise not to bet your life on it."

"Was that sarcasm?" Thadius asked.

"That is optimism and not the former, my good Thadius. And if you ask me, you could do with a dose of it." He pointed toward the bath entrance. "Shall we steam and scrape?"

"I can do with a good steaming." Thadius walked to the gate. Large columns on either sides rose twenty feet high supporting the roof. To one side, a small gatehouse was constructed of red brick and mortar.

"Well, if it isn't Thadius and Dominus. How fair thee this fine day?" The guard came from the doorway limping and squinting as he stepped into the light.

"Well and good," Dominus stated. "And you?"

"Not well." The guard rubbed the sweat from his balding head with a yellow rag. "It's the old wound, the spear point in my back, and I've not a decent sleep since I was struck down."

"The surgeons still can't remove it?" Dominus said.

"As skilled as they are, the answer is no."

Handing the gate guard the admission of two coins, Thadius grabbed the man on the arm. "I wish you some peace, my friend. Perhaps you'll join us for wine on next Saturni at the Cyclops Tavern?"

The man looked at him and frowned. "My wife says I shouldn't drink so much, it makes me unreasonable."

"She sounds wiser than Apollo," Thadius said and stepped past.

A fine gray gravel path met his sandals as he walked into the garden. The crunching of his footfalls seemed muted by the lush and pristine vegetation on either side. He took the left path at a fork, all the while discussing snippets of news from the public postings. "I'm dismayed at the political ranker being published."

"Ranker? Entertaining more like it," Dominus said.

"So why did Caesar abandon Britannia?" Thadius asked.

Dominus grinned. "Some uprising in Gaul or such. And it would seem that Julius is also again at odds with Pompey. One moment they are the best of friends, the next they are trying to murder one another. But there is more urgent news to be had."

"Is this gossip or news?"

"It's real news of our times. The wine production might be delayed this year for reasons of a terrible blight on the vineyards in Tuscany."

"What?" Thadius stopped at a vaulted doorway. "I make about a hundred and sixty thousand denarii annually from my vineyards there."

"You'll probably lose some money this year."

"Why should I care? I make plenty of coin on other ventures," Thadius said. "It won't be the end of my life. At my age I should be concerned with drinking wine, eating fine food, and having fun."

"No wiser words were ever spoken," Dominus smiled.

Thadius shook his head. "You may be right." He turned and went inside.

Several oil lamps illuminated the room. The floor was tiled with wide yellow squares, light red paint on the ceiling set a mood of adventure, and the walls were covered in frescos. Along one side, was a wooden hutch with small cubbies, and Thadius took off his sandals and put them on one of the shelves. Disrobing, he folded and placed his toga, belt, and sandals in the hutch, then did the same with his tunic. Wrapping his white cotton towel around his waist, he took his straw bathing sandals from his pouch and slipped them on his feet. "This steam will do the trick."

"I can't wait," Dominus said.

Opening the wooden door, he and Dominus stepped into a short vaulted hallway. The air was filled with moisture and billowy puffs of white steam. The wooden handle was warm to the touch, but not scalding, and Thadius lifted the latch and stepped into a thick hot fog.

Sitting on the marble steps nearest the steam pipe, Dominus reclined. Every few minutes scalding hot steam would erupt into the room. A dozen gray-haired men also wrapped in white towels sat around conversing and laughing. "What of your tin mine? Are you still making money?" Dominus inquired.

"Tin is a good business, but I wished I owned more grain lands," Thadius responded.

"Regret is a fool's game," Dominus said.

"All I regret is that I have outlived my beloved Althea," Thadius stated.

"The gods must have more in store for you yet." Dominus scraped his brow and wiped the blade on his towel. "Don't get my meaning wrong my friend. I've no intention of letting your melancholy mood bubble out of you here. You've done great things and have been generously honored in days past."

"True," Thadius said wiping the dirty sweat on his towel. "I don't suppose it would matter that I'm just a foolish old man?"

"Not in the least," Dominus said. "Everyone knows that old men are the worst of fools – just ask any kid in his twenties." He raised an eyebrow. "They know little of the world, but never tire of telling you how much more they know of it than you."

"But, they do have ambition."

"So did we once." Dominus stood. "Shall we go to the caldarium?"

"I don't see why not," Thadius said, getting to his feet.

A dozen men milled about within the thirty foot long, twenty foot wide pool. Others sat on benches along the water's edge.

Thadius set down his sandals and towel and climbed in. His muscles relaxed as he sank up to his neck in the hot water. He could hear the other men discussing the day's events, issues of commerce, and their wives and mistresses.

"Althea was a beautiful woman," Dominus said as he ran an ivory comb through his graying hair. "She's gone now a year– since she crossed into paradise. Why haven't you remarried?"

"Dominus, how many times do I have to tell you? My wife was the one woman for me. I want and need no other. And when I cross into the next world, I will find her and love her there too."

"A case of Orpheus' love I see." Dominus shook his head. "What a romantic you are, Thadius. I'm not talking of the one love in your life; I'm talking about keeping warm in the winter and having someone soft in your bed."

"I know of what you speak, and you're a good friend for wanting that for me. But my servants keep me in good company."

"Okay, that's the last time I'll bring it up."

"You said that before," Thadius stated. "So don't be disappointed if I expect you to mention it again." He submerged then came back up.

Dominus pointed with his thumb toward the opposite side of the caldarium. "Look, there's a group of old bastards more interested in lining their own strongboxes with gold then doing good for the town."

"Do you mean the council men? You're just angry over the council's rejection of your park design," Thadius said.

Frowning, Dominus waved his hand dismissing the remark. "They should have loved my idea. I even suggested a magnificent bronze statue of one of our most respected citizens."

"Who's the citizen?"

"Me!" Dominus splashed water over his face. "I wonder where all that extra money went?"

"You know the way in which things work," Thadius stated.

"I do, but I don't have to like it." Dominus stepped out and reached for his towel. "Let's take a dip in the frigidarium and finish up; I feel the pains of hunger gnawing at me."

"Very well."

Separated by a wide arch and a hall, the much smaller frigidarium was tiled in bright yellow. Light streaming in from four windows and an oculus made the room glow with a golden hue. Climbing into the frigid pool, Thadius took a deep breath and dunked under the water then came up.

Dominus shook his head slinging water out onto the tiled floor. "Who wouldn't love a lavish party along a beach attended by divine beasts of the old world? I could be one of those carefree satyrs dancing about playing a pipe and lyre."

Thadius followed Dominus to the bench and put on his sandals. "I hope they have that soda bread."

"I was craving that lemon water they make. I think it has just a hint of beat-sugar in it, but I'm not sure."

"Hard to say. No matter, whatever we get it'll be good," Thadius stated.

"To the courtyard." Dominus stood, pointed, and headed out.

"With haste," Thadius added.

Moving into the courtyard, the two men sat on a marble bench covered with long colorful pillows. Patrons wandered about gazing admiringly at the finery of the statues and the tall granite monolith imported from Egypt. Thadius could see a child and his parents standing along an artificial brook that wound its way through the garden; the boy grabbed at the fish that swam in its waters.

"What can we prepare for you today?" A young man in his early twenties, clean shaven with curly black hair stood before them.

"Greetings, Joseph," Thadius said smiling. "I'll have fresh squeezed lemon-water, goat cheese baked in honey, pine nuts and dates, soda bread, and a pitcher of wine."

"And you sir?"

"I'll have the same," Dominus said.

Turning, Joseph quickly walked to the kitchen.

"It's too bad that he's a *servus*," Dominus said, reclining on the bench. "He truly deserves to be a freeman."

"Servus est homo est non persona..." Thadius said softly.

"I know he's a man and not a person," Dominus retorted. "I'm just saying he should be a freeman to live at his own wits, not bought and sold in the market."

"Then what, to starve in the streets?" Thadius said irritated. "Not all are born to privilege as we, Dominus. You strayed to the countryside after your service to the Legion, while I lived in the heart of Rome. I saw freemen begging in the streets for food and money... they barely made shadows on the ground for lack of food, and survived only on the daily bread given them by the Senate."

Grinning, Dominus spoke softly, "That is what I appreciate about you, Thadius, all that frank honesty. Well, there is no accounting for my behavior which will turn most foul if our food does not arrive soon!"

"It appears that I stayed in Rome far too long. Forgive me for my outburst. I must be over hungry; I only had tea this morning in preparation for this meal," Thadius said.

"Ah, here it comes now." Dominus sat up. Two young boys carried an oblong platter filled with food. Close behind was Joseph, who stopped and quickly set out the plates, goblets, and two earthen pitchers of wine.

"Would either of you care for anything else?" he asked.

"Not for me." Dominus quickly tore off a piece of bread, and dipped the hunk into his wine.

Thadius shook his head. "Nothing else, thank you." Delving into his repast, Thadius savored the burst of flavors; the cheese mixed with the sweetness of mountain honey, the tart contrast of lemon water. Picking out a roasted date, he bit off a quarter and spit the seed into his hand.

"So, what wonders have you been thinking of, of recent?" Dominus gulped down some wine.

"Nothing of any real importance... a toy, actually."

"A toy? The great Thadius working on a toy? How quaint."

"It's for my grandson," Thadius said.

What is it?"

"A boat that moves via steam."

"Thadius, you are a man of madness," Dominus laughed. "What does this steam machine look like?"

"I fashioned it after the steam machine from Ctesibius treatise on the power of steam. The engine turns a small gear, which turns a large gear that drives a cam that causes two tillers to waggle opposite one another at the aft of the boat."

"Interesting – I mean, really, Thadius, what folly. What practical purpose could this serve?"

"None, it's a toy."

"But if I know you, and I do, you have grander schemes in mind for that toy."

"Perhaps," Thadius said with a smirk. "But nonetheless, it's a toy for my grandson and I shall give it to him when I see him in the month of Quintilis next year, somewhere between Dies Lunae and Dies Veneris. My son and his family want to arrive on one of those days to fit in with their trip to Pompeii."

"Seems to fall on the month of your birthday, will you be sober enough to receive them?" Dominus laughed.

"Probably not," Thadius said chuckling.

Finishing his meal, Thadius put down a silver *sestertius* on the table. He waved to Joseph and pointed at the money. Dominus picked up a slice of bread, dipped it into a bowl of spiced olive oil and popped it into his mouth.

"If I could live here I would," Dominus said. "What do you think? Shall we go to the gym?"

"I don't think it'll do us any good, but okay," Thadius replied.

Walking down the path, they passed under an arbor. Droplets fell as they walked, and Thadius could smell the sweet scent from the grape leaves. Stepping into the cool and dark gymnasium he sat down on a wooden bench, and watched some young men doing pull-ups. He thought of his own youth and his days in the Legion.

"Some dumbbells," Dominus said shoving one towards him.

"I think I'll just relax for now."

"Suit yourself. I intend on keeping my physique all the way to my elaborate and costly pyre."

"And who's going to give you an expensive and elaborate pyre?" Thadius said.

"Well, you of course."

"And what makes you think you're going to die before me?" Thadius looked skeptical.

"For one, I gamble and you don't. Two, I have four lovers, two of which are married, and you have none. And lastly, I hunt still, while you tend your garden. Unless you fall victim to a pesky weed or take it upon yourself to...you know...do it yourself despite me, I have a much greater chance of demise than you."

"And why would the gods allow such a thing? After all, I was a consul of Rome. I paid for the welfare of Romans, provided grain, an aqueduct, rebuilt part of the western wall. And you? If the gods decided to take anyone first, it should be me. I deserve to enter paradise well ahead of you." He smiled a cagy grin.

"You didn't seem to have such aristocratic views the day I carried you from the field at the battle of Aquae Sextiae."

"True, but in my defense I was still capable of striking with a gladius and covering with a scutum. You were premature in removing me," Thadius protested.

"Premature? Your leg was broken, and I carried you to the surgeon who set it. Afterwards we got drunk and you took some poppy resin and slept through the next day."

"Okay, what's your point?" Thadius said.

"You need more adventure in your life."

"If I had more adventure in my life, I'd die early like you most likely will."

Booming a tremendous laugh, Dominus knew he was had. "Okay, you win; you are cleverer than I! And your wit is superior." He pulled each dumbbell up to his chest in turn. "Live your life as you will

and not as your friend wills you to."

CHAPTER 2

The afternoon heat fell heavily upon Thadius and Dominus as they walked through the town. Other pedestrians crowded under awnings and in the cool stucco buildings along the street. "Seems our little town is ready to burst," Thadius commented.

"They're not accustomed to our sweet autumn heat," Dominus stated.

"True," said Thadius.

"They'll shrug off all their sweaty worries though when the afternoon gaming begins – and half a jar of wine has filled their veins." Dominus yawned.

"Thadius!" a voice from across the street assailed them. Emerging from a dark tavern doorway, a familiar young man stumbled toward them.

Dominus rolled his eyes. "Fool thy name is Crandalum."

"Thadius, I've been looking all over for you…" Crandalum stopped and finished the bowl of wine in his hand. "Now where was I?"

"You wanted to see me for something."

"Ah yes, a messenger has come to your home."

"A messenger?" Thadius looked thoughtful. "From where?"

"I don't know." Crandalum swayed slightly. "Your servant asked me to find you."

Thadius shook his head. "So you immediately went to the wine bar? Is the messenger still there now?"

"How should I know? Hey, I have an idea…come in and have a cup of wine with me." Crandalum beckoned. "I hate to drink alone."

"You, drink alone?" Dominus shook his head. "Crandalum, you never drink alone, because if you were alone, no one would be there to buy you wine. How old are you now?"

"Twenty and five years," Crandalum said standing to his full height.

"When Thadius and I were twenty and five years we had steeped our hands in much blood, amassed great fortunes in gold and land, and were well respected. Why don't you do something productive and join one of the legions?"

Crandalum regarded Dominus with a wary eye, and then shrugged his shoulders. "I'd rather make a fortune selling silk along the eastern trade roads, instead of being cut in two by a barbarian sword!".

"Since when have you had silk to sell?" Dominus's voice carried a sarcastic tone.

"I might one day," Crandalum said with a sneer.

Thadius grabbed the drunk by his tunic. "The messenger…".

Seemingly not hearing the question, Crandalum blurted, "Come on you two old war dogs, have a drink with me."

"When you have some silk to sell, come see me." Thadius gave up trying to speak to the man and began walking away towards his home.

"I fear that there is not enough wine in that tiny tavern to sate both you and me, young Crandalum," Dominus chuckled. "Therefore, I too shall bid you a farewell."

"I can drink like a hero also," Crandalum shouted after them.

"Which one?" Dominus asked over his shoulder. Catching up to Thadius Dominus added, "Did we ever drink like that?"

"Not until we became retired." Thadius chortled. Walking briskly, he felt sweat trickling down his neck. The sun now marked the midday, and there was no shade to be found along the road leading to his home. Passing the great cement water tanks that fed the town, he admired the structures.

"You did a splendid job of reengineering the cisterns after the quake," Dominus said.

Thadius smiled. "It's an old Greek design with some Roman modifications."

"All I know is we had very little water pressure before, and now I can wash down my privy without any worry."

"Or any worries by your neighbors," Thadius said.

"Oh, I think they've grown accustom to my scent."

"The word stench I think is more accurate," Thadius said.

"Well, stench, smells, or scents... I have had little complaint thus far."

Coming around a bend, Thadius could see the wall and hedges that marked the edge of his estate. "They're just afraid to tell you what they really think," Thadius stated.

"And well they should be afraid," Dominus said. "After twenty-five years they know my reputation for being caustic, in all respects."

Thadius came to a side-gate, lifted the latch and opened it. He bowed low to Dominus. "Enter if you dare." He motioned with his hand. "Assassins may be waiting to strike, and as you so astutely put it, you'll be called to Styx before I."

Frowning, Dominus shook his head. "Gladly... For a friend such as you, I'd go to Styx and return with Persephone herself... and a sack of pomegranates." He stepped through.

"Hades may have something to say about that," stated Thadius.

"I'd be in and out before he knew what happened." Dominus followed a wide flagstone path that wound its way through dense vegetation. He admired the beautiful garden and patches of dark green grass. A small brook passed lazily along the stones then turned abruptly and meandered into a grove of fruit trees. "It is quite remarkable what you've done here, my friend."

"Just good planning and the amazing soil." Thadius stepped past Dominus and into a clearing. He led the way up to his front door. The villa loomed beneath the shad of five large mature pecan trees.

Dominus exhaled loudly as he walked up the stone steps to the green and yellow colonnades supporting the portico roof. "By Jupiter, that was a fast pace."

"Simon," Thadius called as they entered the main hallway. "Simon, where are you?"

Simon dashed from a darkened corridor and slid on the marble floor, halted, and brushed his gray tunic with his hands. "How may I serve you, my lord?" he asked, looking at Thadius.

"Did a messenger come to see me?"

"Yes, that fellow Crandalum brought him here from the marina. I offered him refreshment and food then asked Crandalum to find you while I kept an eye on the stranger."

"You did well, Simon," Thadius said. "Where is he now?"

"He is reclining at the Venus pool. May I get you and Lord Dominus refreshments?"

"Yes, bring it to the pool."

"I must tell you, master..." Simon trailed off looking nervous.

"Tell me what?"

"He is a rather large fellow – a Gaul, I think. Don't be surprised when you see him."

Thadius patted Simon on the shoulder. "See, Dominus, no man could have a better servant than I. He has the caring and compassion for my safety, more so than even you."

Dominus looked bemused. "I think you have overrated my concern for you, my friend. Truth be told, if you were to be killed, where would I turn for free wine, bread, and company?"

Thadius shook his head at the comment. "So you say. Come let's have a talk with this Gaul." Walking through the hall he turned and passed through the atrium into the gardens. Stopping in the doorway to the courtyard, he turned to face Simon. "You did say a Gaul?"

Simon nodded his head. "He is large and fair of hair."

"Curious indeed. Coming, Dominus?"

"I'll go, but only to make sure the Gaul doesn't turn you into a martius lepus for supper." Dominus raised both eyebrows twice.

"With you by my side, how could this be?" Shielding his eyes with his hand, Thadius walked out into the wide and long peristylium. He wound his way to a small bridge over a narrow stream, past the peach trees, through some hedges, and past the olive trees to the pool. The emerald blue of a large pool came into view, and at the furthest end, near a mature hedgerow, he could see a great muscular giant of a man reclining on a couch eating fruits and meats from a marble table. Thadius watched as the man glanced their way. Slowly he rose to his feet, finished his cup of wine, and looked down at them.

Thadius approached. "I am Moras Tiberius Thadius , your host here at Villa de Moras. I understand you have a message for me?"

"I do," the man stated while passing his fingers through his white-blond hair.

Thadius studied the man's face. "You are not from Gaul and speak my language very well."

"My name is Eilifr Blodriner, Lord of Iron Hill. I am not from the place you Romans call Gaul, but much further to the north beyond Germania. I was sent here by a friend of yours to seek your help." Eilifr smiled as he looked about the peristylium. "You little Romans live well." He leveled his gaze upon Thadius again. "Your friend needs your help with a matter of the utmost importance, and if you are willing to come, I am to take you straight away." He handed Thadius a folded waxed papyrus note. "It has traveled a weary distance, but as you can see it is unopened."

CHAPTER 3

My Dear Thadius,

Since the meeting of our great leaders in Gaul at the villa of Sertorius Marco, I have thought of you and the carefree days in which we made sport and drank good wine.

I do admit that in sooth I have missed your company and often wished to renew our friendship now dormant these many years.

I had heard rumors that you married and fathered several children. A grand achievement for a man who desired no children at all. I have a wife but we were not blessed with children.

Unfortunately, I write to you under a guise of grief.

I was given a great responsibility on the island of Britannia. My wife's brother in Rome asked me to take his oldest daughter for sake of her health. It was a sad blow to his family that she was not chosen to keep the eternal fires burning at the Vesta Temple. She was a lovely girl.

But grief has charged me with ill news — for her life was taken of recent by villainous foes that lurk about these dark and foreboding lands.

I am unable to agree with the official inquiry and report. I am not convinced that the natives are at fault. The local king to favor Rome has executed one of his subjects and in doing so has not made our purpose here any easier.

I now must beseech you to come with all haste for I remember well your proof of innocence you showed, while Tribunal over a slave regarding the death of his master. Your powers of thought are unmatched and your heart of the purest for justice for which I have ever been a witness too.

I have much detail that was overlooked in the official report. I have conducted a thorough examination of the body and the site where the body was found. Further, I have recorded the manner in which facilitated her death.

If you ever called me brother, come at once to the Island of Britannia. My reputation and that of my wife's family, will be subject to your action.

Your loving friend,

Marcus Maruscinus Gnaeus

Sitting down on the marble bench next to the table, Thadius let the letter hang in his hand. Fluttering slightly from a gentle breeze, the paper bent and folded along its creases.

Looking up, he noted the bemused expression on the Northman's face.

"Fearful news, I expect..." Eilifr stated.

"Strange news to be sure." Thadius set the letter on the table and weighed it down with a bowl of mutton. Pouring himself a cup of wine, he sat and thought.

"Well, do we have to beat it out of you, or is it none of our business?" Dominus said reaching past him and tearing off a greasy hunk of lamb and popping it into his mouth.

Thadius took a sip of his wine. "This letter is a call for assistance by an old friend, whom I've not seen in many years."

"Always the juiciest gossip and news is best when it's been long for the telling," Dominus said.

"Seems no gossip, my friend, but terrible news of murder."

"Far away?" Dominus looked interested.

"Very," Thadius replied.

"Should we make plans to travel?" Dominus quipped. "Shall I pack my shield and sword?"

"We'd be going to investigate a murder, not commit one," Thadius said.

Dominus formed a crooked grin. "Well, I guess I'll have to come along and make sure you don't take advantage of the man's good nature, nor his good daughters."

"If I had any daughters, you could have them all. Women are expensive to keep," Eilifr stated with a laugh.

"I see this will be a trip of some humor," Thadius said as he rose to his feet. "That's good, for I think we're going to need all the humor we can get. By what mode of transportation will you take us?"

Eilifr took on a serious air. "By boat. It will take four, maybe five weeks."

"Is there a brothel on the boat?" Dominus said.

"No room, and a woman on the boat would only lead to bloodshed and the loss of a man to pull the oars."

Dominus sat down. "Pull oars? So you possess a galley of some sort?"

"No," Eilifr stated. "How soon can you be ready to travel?"

Thadius thought for a moment. "Tomorrow at the tide we should be ready. How large is your boat?"

"Sixty feet long, and twenty wide."

"What in great Hade's name?" Dominus said loudly. "Is it a fishing boat we are to take?"

"A boat built for trade, and war," Eilifr said.

"If you say so; a nice Trireme would do me better, though."

"My ship is fast and has a shallow draft. I can go places that war ships and pirates cannot."

"Dine with us tonight. We will discuss this voyage and what is needed," Thadius said.

CHAPTER 4

Laughter echoed throughout the villa late into the night. Dominus gripped his sides and fought to stay in his chair. "Thadius, you're one of the best storytellers I've ever had the pleasure of knowing." He wiped tears from his eyes. "Now tell me again why you and this Gnaeus fellow hid the sheep in the centurion's quarters?"

"Centurion Maligius was having an affair with one of the girls in the small village not far from our garrison. He would slip out of his quarters and meet his lover in the bathhouse north of the fort."

Pausing for a moment, Thadius took a sip of his wine and a mouthful of stuffed grape-leaves. "So we decided to hide and slaughter the sheep in his room, knowing that he would not be back until morning. Gnaeus grabbed a bucket and placed it below the sheep's neck ,then he gripped it by its wooly main and held it fast. I swiftly cut its throat – but remember, we were rather drunk. Clumsily Gnaeus let the sheep slip free. All around the centurion's room the sheep bolted – knocking over his table, breaking his pitcher, up-turning his luggage, and jumping on his bed. Then, groaning, the sheep fell over dead."

Booming with laughter Dominus coughed several times trying to catch his breath.

"Please, please my friend, take a drink to quell your dry throat," said Thadius. "Now, where was I? Oh yes. We gathered up the sheep and slipped it into the stables and butchered it. Taking the quartered parts to the kitchen, we kindled the fires and prepared to bake the parts in one of the ovens. We made sure none but the watch lurked about." He winked at his company. "Then, we seasoned the meat and put it in to bake. Once in the oven, Gnaeus and I settled in for a bit of rest while it cooked, but we forgot ourselves and overslept."

"Thadius, you were a rascal." Dominus chuckled loudly.

"Maybe so," Thadius said filling his cup with wine. Drinking deeply he set the cup down and cleared his throat. "In the morning there is this terrible ruckus coming from the courtyard. *The Centurion of the Watch has been murdered,* echoed the panicked cries from the centurion's pet legionnaire, Tamius.

"Gnaeus and I woke suddenly and fumbled to pull the mutton from the oven. It had baked crispy and we each took a quick mouth full before heading outside. The rest of our barracks were filing out onto the parade ground to see what all the fuss was. Gnaeus and I stepped out from the kitchen. Tamius was wide-eyed, pale; shaking in fear while holding up the bloodied bed sheets. He shouted, *Maligius has been murdered!*"

Falling from his chair, Dominus rolled about on the floor gripping his sides. Simon rushed in, and Thadius waved him back with a laugh. "No need to worry, Simon, all is well here."

"I – can – hardly – breathe!" Dominus said in between gasps.

Simon turned to go.

"Simon," Thadius called. "You may take your liberties with the wine if you'd like."

"Thank you, my lord," Simon said boasting a smile.

"I mean all of the servants may take their fill as well," Thadius added.

Simon nodded and left the room. Thadius watched Dominus slowly climb back into his chair. "Then what?" Dominus asked while pouring some wine into his cup.

"Well, the whole post was in an uproar. Soldiers ran to secure the gate, officers ran to keep control of their soldiers, and Gnaeus and I sat back with bemused expressions on our faces." Thadius leaned forward in his chair and picked some grapes from a plate on the table next to him. Popping them into his mouth, he smiled. "*Fire and brimstone of Hades,* I said to Gnaeus. *You're right about that,* he said to me." Some soldiers on the ramparts blasted their horns calling in the patrols. It was as if someone struck a hive and all the angry hornets buzzed around looking for a victim to bite. Finally the commander of the garrison called all soldiers, including the officers, into the courtyard to assemble."

"Let's get to the bottom of this, shouted the Legatus Legionis. *Who's been murdered and by whom!* Tamius came forward and told his story of going to wake Maligius for his morning run and found the room, tossed, and covered in blood with the centurion nowhere to be found. Tamius handed the bloody bed linens to the Legatus Legionis and everyone – except me and Gnaeus gasped. The commander was furious and ordered an investigation, but then a battering at the gate captured all our attention. *Open these gates! Hearing the call-to-arms I have come!* And, yes, it is our friend Maligius rushing back from his lover's hut to the call of the horns."

Jumping to his feet, Thadius pantomimed the throwing open of the gate. "There, in plain view of all, the chalk white form of the centurion came to view. Truly, he was the ashen gray of death standing there between the posts of the great gate.

"Gnaeus and I jumped at the sight – as did all the soldiers and officers. *What is the order, my captain?* he shouted. In response the Legatis yelled back, *Be gone, ghost."*

"Be – gone – ghost," burst Dominus, laughter pouring from him.

"Well, the centurion notices us all looking as if he were Medusa in the flesh. *Don't you recognize me? It's me, Maligius your centurion, the Hastatus Prior of the fifth Centuri second Cohort.* But all remains quiet, except for the cawing of a host of ravens. Then Gnaeus shouts, *if he bleeds, he's not a ghost; shoot 'em with an arrow and see if he bleeds!"*

Sitting back down, Thadius hooked a footstool with his feet and pulled it close while he sipped his wine.

"How many arrows did they stick in him?" Dominus asked.

"None. The centurion turned on his sandaled heels and ran for all he was worth back out the gate. Several soldiers followed with bows notched, but they were not able to catch him. Several days later the commander uncovered the mystery and found the centurion hiding at his lover's modest hut. I found out later that when the centurion heard the call of the horns he dashed back to the garrison, but in his haste in the early morning hours he stumbled into the camp's ash pit near the forest fence."

"Did they ever find out if it was you and Gnaeus who caused that entire ruckus?" Dominus wiped tears from his eyes.

Unpinning and removing his toga, Thadius pulled up his tunic and turned his back to Dominus.

"I see," Dominus said, "and I always thought you got those scars in a brothel battling off the busy hands of several maidens." He frowned. "So dies the admiration for our heroes."

Thadius laughed. "Neither of us complained though. The whole event was well worth the ten lashes."

Eilifr shifted in his chair and put his feet on a footstool. "Most entertaining."

"I'll get more wine," Thadius said standing. He could feel the ground swaying beneath him with each step as he moved down the hall. Taking an earthen pitcher and a small oil lamp, he moved down the passageway to a staircase. Going down, he stepped lightly as he passed the servant's quarters. The small bedrooms ran the length of the villa, and he could hear the murmurings from within. While they were non-citizens, they were good hardworking people, and he felt responsible to keep them contented. He made it a point to treat them well, so by example the Roman way could be impressed upon them; the way of civility, honesty, and honor. Simon he liked most of all; a man of integrity and honor, educated and shrewd. He was almost another son to Thadius.

He staggered to the end of the hallway and a solid oaken door with a brass latch. Opening the door he descended another set of stairs some ten feet more coming to a cold room with a stone floor. He stood for a moment swaying slightly, then walked to a heavy wooden center beam and hung his lamp on a hook. Looking for an open barrel of wine, he found Simon's wax tablet and stylus hanging from a nail. He examined the tablet; the man was detailed and kept good records. The third amphora from the end was marked on the tablet as being open, and he staggered to it. Finding the cap open, he dipped a pewter ladle in and slowly filled the pitcher. Stopping at the last set of stairs he straightened his tunic and rose to the master's level of the house.

"Here is more wine," he announced while entering the room. Glancing over, he saw Dominus sleeping soundly in his chair. Eilifr held out his empty pitcher.

"When your affairs here are in order, we shall sail," Eilifr said.

"I'll be ready by tomorrow eve at the latest. I trust it will be good sailing?" Thadius poured some wine into Eilifr's pitcher.

"It will be the best sailing. Cast no fears; I'll not let the monsters of the sea have you for sup." Eilifr's laughter came bubbling out of him. "Besides, your god, Jupiter, will watch over you."

"Perhaps," Thadius said, "if he cares to cast his eye upon this unworthy mortal."

CHAPTER 5

Rolling over in bed, Thadius looked out his bedroom window. The beautiful lilacs blooming outside waved back and forth in the cool morning breeze. Yawning, he sat up and glanced over at the mirror on his vanity table. "You look like you've climbed from the bowels of Tartarus," he said to his reflection.

"And why should you look any different?" Dominus stated, walking into the room and handing Thadius a cup of strong willow-bark tea. "Now what? Are you still planning on going to help this friend of yours?"

"Of course. You don't have to go, if this all scares you," Thadius goaded with a smile.

"If I don't go, who will carry you around if you break your leg?" Dominus countered. "Besides, this is an adventure isn't it?"

"I suppose it is," said Thadius. "You may want to bring some warm clothes. It gets pretty cold up north I hear."

"You do me a disservice, my friend. Who was it that lent you his fur-lined cloak in Germania?" Dominus walked to the window. "I'm fully aware of the conditions where we're going."

Thadius chuckled. "I'm not sure if you remember or not." Standing, he went to the vanity and poured water from a pitcher into a basin and washed his face. Quickly dressing he walked to the window, drew in a deep breath and spoke somberly. "I've grown fairly old, my friend."

Dominus waved his hand in dismissal and grunted. "Then what does that make me?"

Thadius put his hand on the shoulder of his friend. "Almost as old, but not as refined," he said. "I want you to know that I would think no less of you if you chose not to come."

Dominus looked amused. "My dear Thadius, I don't think you could think any less of me than you already do."

Smiling warmly, Thadius clapped his hands together. "Then let's get started." Turning he headed for the door. "Let's eat in town and gather what we need for the trip. Tis the slow rabbit that makes the easiest meal."

A grin grew across Dominus' face betraying a wicked thought. "But, the slow rabbit is the only one that is ever caught. Oh, I forgot to ask, do we get to take a woman along to keep warm?"

Thadius made it to the path. "You'll have to move faster than that, Dominus, if you wish to not get lost," Thadius hollered back, as he disappeared into the garden.

Dominus doubled his pace as he pursued his friend into the woods.

"Perhaps we should stop at the brothels first – to make sure there is no temptation on the boat later," he shouted.

Thadius headed to the market to purchase dried meats, fruits, nuts, grains, cereals, wine, amphorae of fresh water and boxes of salt. Dominus went to the manufacturing side of town and purchased cold weather clothing, back packs and sacks, small pots and pans, jars of lamp oil, blankets, and sacks of coal. By late afternoon the two men were exhausted.

As the darkness approached, the lamplighter slowly strolled down the street that led to the taverns and brothels. Thadius, Simon, and Dominus approached the marina. At the docks a strange looking boat was moored, and many large men moved about. "It seems that in the north giants are reared," Dominus said pointing at a dozen large blond, red, and dark-haired men loading the long shallow drafted boat with supplies.

"I have never seen such large men before," Simon said surprised.

Eilifr saw the men approaching and called to them. "You and Dominus will ride in the back with me." He looked at Simon, "We have no room for more passengers."

"He is my servant. He's not coming with us. He has duties here to keep my estate well and managed," Thadius said.

"Good," Eilifr nodded. "Our room is limited and your friend Dominus was not expected as a passenger when we were dispatched."

Dominus looked bemused. "Well, the world is full of surprises."

"True," said Eilifr as he loaded a sack of grain. "What is also amusing will be seeing you two pulling at the oars," he chuckled.

"Surely you're not serious? Our passage is paid; we've provided provisions for you and your men. How can you expect us to labor also?" Dominus looked indignant.

Eilifr smiled. "You soft Romans," he said laughing. "On this boat any man who is not able to do another's job is worth putting over the side. This will be a dangerous trip and all hands, including yours, will be needed."

"When can we board?" Thadius said.

Looking thoughtful, Eilifr replied, "Within the hour all my trade goods and the supplies you sent will be loaded. You must board then."

"Will we be sailing tonight?" Dominus asked, peeking into the boat.

"We try not to travel at night. We will sail at first light with the tide. But we all will sleep on the boat tonight. No man starts a long voyage that has stayed on land the night before. It is our way."

"As you wish. But I must say that a night in my own bed would be far nicer than being wrapped in a fur on a wooden plank," grumbled Dominus.

"It is our way, and no other way will do," stated Eilifr.

"Very well," Thadius said. "We will sleep on the boat."

Dominus shrugged his shoulders. "At least we'll be used to the roll of the waves by morning, and sleeping on this contraption."

"Eilifr?"

"Yes?"

"Where you come from, do all your boats look this way?" Thadius asked.

"Some smaller and some larger, but the shape is the same."

"Interesting…" Thadius pulled out a papyrus roll and rod of charcoal from his backpack. He quickly sketched the boat, wrote some comments, and handed the paper to Simon. "Take this back with you and put it in my study. Also, as we discussed, if I do not return, in three years you are to open the two strong boxes in the cellar and do as the parchments instruct you."

"Of course, my lord. But you will return. I prayed for your safety and safe return of you and Dominus last night."

"You have no worries, for if I am lost at sea or killed in my journeys you and all the servants will be well cared for." He placed his hand on the young man's shoulder.

"We will watch over the villa and keep it well in your absence," Simon said.

Thadius smiled. "Now off with you, or I'll be weeping like a baby."

Simon walked towards the port gates. He felt ashamed by a sudden rush of emotion.

Ahead, two sentries stood by. At the gate he turned and looked at the many ships anchored in the harbor, then looked down at his master's ship and sighed softly.

"Fear not, Simon," the sentry said. "Thadius is made of much stronger stuff than you give him credit for."

"I know," Simon agreed, "yet I fear for his safety anyway." He turned and walked through the gate.

Returning to the villa, Simon descended into the servant's quarters. He entered his room and disrobed. Lying down in his bed, he looked over all the wonderful items that he'd bought with the money Thadius insisted upon paying him. Remembering back, he had been puzzled when Thadius, his master, came and paid him a silver coin for his first month at the villa. "What is this, master?" he'd asked.

"I pay all my servants, Simon." Thadius calmly put the silver coin in Simon's hand.

"If you are wise, you may do well to save these bits of silver, and one day buy your freedom. Perhaps you might even buy Villa de Moras in due time."

Month after month Simon saved his coins. When he had enough money, he would pay Thadius, then a lawyer, to draw up the documents for his freedom. But his feelings had grown for his master. The man was kind, gentle, and wise, and went to great length to educate Simon by providing him access to a Greek tutor. One day Thadius needed Simon to accompany him to Rome.

Simon found the streets of the *Eternal City* filled with the poor and starving. Beggars and shysters seemed everywhere, and it took little time for Simon to realize that being free could mean starvation, and perhaps brutal death. For two days he contemplated his desire to be free, then he did something one might consider quite mad; instead of freedom, he bought his master a gift. Spending ten silver coins he purchased a ream of paper, a bottle of ink, and a Greek ink-pen with an ivory handle from a vendor in Rome. Returning to the clean and orderly streets of Herculaneum he presented his gift and smiled warmly. "My lord, though I'm only a *servus est homo est non persona*, you've been more a father to me than I have ever known. I am forever in your debt."

Thadius took the present with pleasure. "Even my own son has never been so gracious. I'm without words."

Simon could see the true emotion in the old man's eyes. "No words are needed, sir." Having said that, Simon walked out of the room. Three weeks later, Thadius' wife died in her sleep, and the man became inconsolable. For a month Simon cared for Thadius as he struggled through his pain and loss.

Rolling over in his bed, Simon made ready to blow out the light. For a moment he watched his wife sleeping quietly next to him. He caressed her arm; she rolled over and looked up at him. "What is it?" she asked.

He smiled. "Just thanking the gods for all that you are."

She smiled back at him, laid her hand against his cheek and motioned for him to hold her.

Leaning over he kissed her softly, blew out the lamp, and put his arms around her. Darkness enveloped the room and Simon felt the heat from her loins against his. Sleep would have to wait, at least for a time.

CHAPTER 6

Dominus rolled to one side and fell. He slowly climbed to his knees and looked about. Chuckling, he remembered that he was on a ship. Several large bearded men laughed at him as they pulled against their oars. Glancing around, he noticed Thadius still sleeping in a tangle of rope at the bow. He took in a deep breath of sea air, held it for a second, then exhaled slowly.

"Where are we?"

A large man with a trimmed black beard looked at him as he drew the oar to his chest. "Among the beasts of the sea."

Glancing over his shoulder at the aft, Dominus could see Eilifr maneuvering the rudder. "The wind is against us, so we must row," shouted Eilifr as he made eye contact with Dominus.

Dominus climbed up on a bench next to a sailor, who in turn glanced at him with a queer expression. Looking out over the saxboard on the port side he could see the rise and fall of the sea. Over the other side, he could see the coast and its jagged cliffs.

"How long have we been at sea?" Dominus asked.

"Since just before dawn," Eilifr replied. "You soft Romans do much sleeping." He laughed as he leaned on the rudder adjusting the course of the boat.

Staring out at the cliffs, Dominus could make out the shapes of Roman battlements every few miles along the coast. Suddenly he saw a blue colored flag shoot up from the middle tower and flutter back and forth. Eilifr tied the tiller with a length of coarse rope and jumped to the mast near Dominus. Grabbing a folded bundle of green cloth he tied it with some twine and pulled it up the mast. Like a great battle flag it unfurled and billowed out in the headwind.

"Your people are always concerned about invasion. They like to be comforted."

Dominus wrinkled his brow. "What do you mean?"

"All Roman ports here in your lands require an approaching ship, or retreating ship, to display a colored flag. I was told at your port that green is the color of the merchant for today. They will relax now, and so will their comrades in the other towers as we sail along the coast," Eilifr said.

"I was part of the Roman Legions before," Dominus said. "I'm quite familiar with the signaling standards."

"The army and the navy are allies often, but not the same." Eilifr tied off the flag and made his way back to the platform.

Dominus knew all this—that sailors tended to view those land-based soldiers with distrust, and the army only appreciated the navy when supplies were delivered or transportation was needed.

He found his pack and pulled it out. Digging through his provisions, he found a loaf of bread and a slab of goat cheese. He cut several slices of cheese and broke the bread in half. The barbarian next to him eyed him with some sense of amusement.

"Would you like a slice?" Dominus asked.

The other man shook his head. "We ate long before you woke."

Picking up his wineskin and his food, Dominus moved to the place where Eilifr stood and began to eat his meal. "Do all of your men speak Greek and Latin?"

Eilifr looked down at him, bemused. "No, they all speak, read, and write Greek and Latin, and ten other languages."

Dominus raised his eyebrows. "Indeed!"

"Be careful at assumptions, Lord Dominus, you will always be unsettled by the truth."

"I see."

"Where we come from, if a man makes a wrong assumption, he can end up dead."

"So much for civility," Dominus quipped.

"Civility?" Eilifr laughed. "We have laws and policies, and protocols, but in our land we do not assume that another man is so weak that he cannot feed himself."

"I think I understand," Dominus stated. "How long should we let Thadius sleep?"

Looking very serious, Eilifr held the rudder steady. "He seems a man not to be disturbed. He will wake when a gull whitens his face." He chuckled again.

Pitching suddenly, the ship drove into a swell. Salt water from the churning sea showered Dominus and he shuddered at the cold. Wrapping up his food in some cloth he tucked it back into his bag Letting the sun warm his face and body, he reclined in the Roman fashion and thought about the day he first met Moras Tiberius Thadius.

"He's been through a lot in his sixty years," Dominus said.

"Any man who reaches sixty must," Eilifr stated.

Pitching to the side, the ship caught the tip of a swell and cool sea water splashed over the bow. Thadius sat up and looked around. He rubbed the sleep from his eyes. Making his way to the aft, he retrieved some food and climbed up beside Dominus. "What are you thinking?"

"I was just thinking of the first time you and I met," Dominus said. "Eilifr," he shouted up, "has Thadius told you of how he and I first met?"

Eilifr moved the rudder. "No, but tell me now," he called down.

Passing a heavy sigh, Thadius swallowed some wine and cleared his throat. "Very well, but I don't think it's entertaining," he warned.

"Tell me anyway," Eilifr said.

"We met after a fierce battle many years ago. Dominus was the Tribunus Laticlavius to the disgraced General, Servilius Caepio. Servilius commanded the army of Rome, and I commanded the Third Legion. I led half my men and trapped the Celts at the gates of a burning fort. My second in command flanked the enemy and cut their remaining forces in two and routed them. By the misty morning as smoke and fog mingled with the sticky blood of Roman and Gaul alike, the stench of death was heavy. I tell you true, twenty thousand of their forces lay burnt or butchered on the field, and only two hundred and twenty two of my command was sent to the gods."

He took another bite of bread and drink of wine. "I was weary as I wandered among the corpses and carrion birds. I turned to the new sun to warm my face when what do you think I should see coming up the road?"

Eilifr shrugged as he angled the rudder.

"Up the valley came Dominus. He was dressed in a red cape, and light armor," Thadius chuckled. "He was truly dressed in the height of fashion for a soldier who advises the army commander. He informed me that Caepio approached."

The spray of the ocean washed up over the side, and Thadius wiped the water from his face. "Two years later after Caepio had been exiled, I enticed Dominus to join my legion. My Tribunus Laticlavius retired from service, and I needed a good man." He shrugged. "I told you it was boring."

Eilifr chuckled, shouted an order to his men, then turned back to Thadius. "You Romans can make any story boring," he said. "And what of the gold?"

Thadius' eyes widened. "You've heard of that?"

"Of course, or I wouldn't have mentioned it," Eilifr said.

"Lost to history... stolen by marauders never to be seen again," Dominus cut in.

The corners of Eilifr's mouth turned up and it grew into a knowing smile. "If you say so. It was said that the train of gold extended for two miles. How could marauders make away with such?"

Thadius leaned back. "I was as surprised as you when I heard the wagons never arrived in Rome." He took a bite of bread and drank some wine. "The Third was dispatched to find the wagons, but we found only bodies littering the woods and no sign of the wagons, gold, or standards… they were all gone. We assumed it was the Celts."

From beyond the bow, dolphins leapt skyward and plunged into the water. The great fish appeared, and to Thadius it seemed as if it were flying. A gray streak passed between Dominus and Eilifr and sailed from starboard side to port side over the oarsmen. Dominus jumped to the side, slipped on some netting, and fell into the bottom of the ship.

"Beasts of Neptune," he cried with his fist in the air.

The crew laughed but kept the cadence of the row in perfect time. Slowly, Dominus climbed up to the benches. His frown turned to a grin and he boasted a tremendous laugh. "Yes – those fish know how to teach an old soldier to dance," he said. "One day this will make for a good story. Just substitute the name Thadius for mine when you tell it."

CHAPTER 7

Thadius leaned back on his elbow watching the oarsmen, the cords in their arms showing like a tangle of rope stretched taunt. He could hear the splashing sounds as the oars dropped into the sea. Standing he yawned, swayed with the ship, and looked over the side. The waves rolled and crested, the tips forming white foam.

"What say you, Captain? Are we making good time or no?" Thadius asked.

Eilifr smiled broadly. "It's nice of you to take an interest in our journey. We're making very good time."

"It's good to take an interest in new things unfamiliar," Thadius countered.

"Stow oars," Eilifr shouted. "Bojon, raise the sail!"

The crew removed the long wooden oars from the iron-shod holes and stored them along the saxboard. Thadius watched the man called Bojon and two others raise the sail. The sheet ballooned out coming full. The ship lurched forward. Thadius maneuvered along a plank to the bow.

"You look like you've been to Tartarus and back along the viadolor," Dominus said.

"I have been many times before…why not now too?" Thadius said. "But the question of the day is, where are we?" He looked at Eilifr, "So, Captain, where are we thus far?"

"Not as far as we need to be, but a considerable ways from where we started," Eilifr said with a grin. "It'll take us several days to get to the place you call the Pillars of Hercules."

A large fellow dressed in furs glanced over at Thadius and Dominus and then up at Eilifr. Saying something in his own tongue, the man motioned with his hand as if throwing something over the side. Bursting out with laughter, Eilifr addressed Thadius.

"My crew thinks you are slowing the ship with your extra weight. They think we should toss you overboard." Eilifr briskly addressed his crew in their own language, and they laughed. "I told them it would only tempt the beasts of the sea to come eat us if we fed such small morsels to them."

Tossing a thin string to Thadius, a red-haired man with a bristly beard spoke. "Make use of your idle hands and tie some hooks to the ends of these lines. If we're lucky, Tuturk will prepare some fish for us to eat."

He eyed the two Romans. "I am called Heragaus Lord of the Nine Valleys, like Eilifr we are all noble of blood." Then he began naming his fellow crew. "That man is Wyglad Blood Eagle, cousin to Eilifr." Pointing to another man, he said, "He is Bojon of Walhal. The one near the oars is Hajlmar Skullsplitter, and the man next to him is Orkning the Fierce. The man with the boy over there is Tuturk the Cook and the boy is Tuk. That man oiling the swords is Sigurd the Wise, and the man tending the arrows is Volund of Rinefall, and the two men down from them are Neri the Small, and Imsigull Lormarker." Turning slightly Heragaus pointed at a group of men near the aft baiting some hooks. "Thorir of Rhol has the long black beard, Melnir the Dark is holding the hooks, and his cousin Thord son of Turod the Honest is bathing his hands in chum."

Heragaus laughed. Turning he stepped down and spoke some strange words to the group of men doing the fishing at the aft.

"I'm glad he's not called Heragaus the Buggerer in his homeland," Dominus whispered.

"Looks as though we're on our way to becoming sailors on this voyage." Thadius smiled. "Soon they'll trust us."

The midday sun moved overhead and the heat was punishing. The men set about doing various tasks that seemed mundane, but Thadius knew them well as the duties of soldiers without wars to fight. Tuk moved about the ship assisting and learning from the men, but seemed to pay the most attention to his father, Tuturk. Helping with the crates of turnips, the boy studied Tuturk's knife work, stripping the skins and putting the vegetables into a pot. Tuturk motioned for Tuk to do the same, and soon both were stripping turnips, parsnip and tubers and dropping them into the pot.

"I'll wager he's very proud of his boy," Dominus stated.

Thadius nodded. "Why not... they are together, the teacher and the student. I missed that with my two sons. They learned from a Greek tutor while I was away." Winding some line around a hook, Thadius looped the string through the eye and tied it up around the shaft.

"Do you regret being away so much?" Dominus said.

Thadius took some chum and put it on the hook. "I would say that's a fair assessment."

Sigurd, his black hair blowing wildly in the wind, came from the bow and handed Thadius and Dominus horn cups. "Drink," he ordered.

Dominus sniffed. "What is it?"

"It is wine made from honey. It will breathe life into your tired limbs." He turned and was handed another horn. This he gave to Eilifr. Raising the cup to his lips, Eilifr drank deeply.

Handing the horn back to Sigurd, Eilifr spat a mouthful of the wine into the sea. "That's for the sea gods," he said. "Drink well, lords of the sea, and give us fair wind and slight distraction." Shifting the angle of the rudder, he directed the ship along the crest of a wave and down another trough. The white of the waves smashed against the side and showered the crew whom did not stray from their various duties.

CHAPTER 8

Thadius looked up at the sky and could see a few large fluffy white clouds moving shoreward. He wondered if a storm would form. Turning his attention toward the shore, he thought they should soon put in for the evening.

"The sun-fall approaches. Maybe another hour till dusk, then we will land at a place I know that will provide safe shelter," Eilifr stated as if reading Thadius' mind. He angled the rudder slightly. "Now, my soft Romans – this night we will rest in comfort."

The evening wind grew in strength propelling the ship towards a crescent shaped cove. Black jagged rocks gave way to cliffs rising two hundred feet high. Barely visible were a few wooden structures on the bluffs. In the craggy cove were several light Corbita ships anchored in the calm waters, and several small rowboats on the beach.

"What is this place?" Thadius said.

"Hidden from your tax collectors, but well known to sailing traders; a sea faring outpost along these cliffs awaits us. It is a place for trade and comfort."

Tapping Thadius on the shoulder, Dominus remarked, "Good thing we're heading in. The mist is growing out to sea and will devour the shore soon." He pointed to the thickening white vale of fog.

Ramming against the beach the stout shallow draft boat embedded into the gray and red pebbles. Thadius saw ten of the largest men leap ashore and tie the ship to two rusted iron rings driven into the sea cliff. Eilifr directed Thadius and Dominus to disembark. Landing on the pebble laden shore Thadius took in a deep breath. The salty air mixed with the acrid odor of bird guano, brine, and sea life filled his lungs.

"Now help with the supplies," Eilifr shouted down at them as two small barrels fell to the rocks with a thud. "Take these barrels with you. They will make us a pretty trade for this night."

"Are we expecting a fight?" Dominus asked pointing at Ivar's armor and weapons.

"No. A man separated from his arms when in need is worthy of little more than his own death, thus, we keep them always close at hand," Ivar said.

"We shall stay the night on the hill. The chief of this trading post and his family I know well. We will bring them these treasures, and they will give us shelter and good food. Our ship will also be well protected in this cove," stated Eilifr.

Looking up, Thadius could see the crumbling rock walls and a narrow trail leading from the beach up along the cliffs. Ten men dressed in armor carrying shields and torches slowly came down the path.

"Is that you, Eilifr?" shouted a burly fellow with a torch in hand from atop the high cliff. "Come up, come up!"

Eilifr waved at the man. "Barnabus, I hope you have stocked your larders, for we have a powerful hunger and thirst!"

"Come and enjoy my hospitality," shouted back the man. "Bring up your crew!" He called down to the soldiers on the trail, "They are welcome, escort them up."

The soldiers marched in single file in front of the party. Once around an outcropping, the path leveled out into a lush green field. Thadius could see chimneys churning out white smoke from the many small buildings. He could smell the unmistakable fragrance of roasting meats. Lanterns, torches, and braziers illuminated the area. The door to the blacksmith shop was wide open, and he could see two large and burly fellows laying hammers on red hot iron.

The two men illuminated by the forge stopped briefly to look at the newcomers. Turning back to their work, the sharp clang of iron upon iron rang into the air again.

Carrying one of the small kegs, Thadius kept pace with the others. Ahead, a large villa loomed. Smoke billowed up from four chimneys and quickly vanished into the windy dark sky.

"I smell burning oak and the baking of bread," Dominus said and nodded to the barrel. "I hope a feast is part of our reward for bringing this treasure."

Marching ahead of the two men, Eilifr said loudly. "This area is a much forgotten old Roman outpost long abandoned. Our host sailed into this cove some twenty years ago and has occupied it ever since. For trade goods such as we've brought, he will let us feast."

Halfway to the house the dirt path widened and turned into a road paved with cobblestones. Thadius admired the precision of their placement. It was apparent that it was built by legionaries.

"What sort of visitors does this Barnabus host?" Dominus said.

Eilifr again glanced over his shoulder at Thadius and Dominus. "Not just legitimate shipping. You will be well advised to keep your wits about you here."

"Who is this Barnabus?" Dominus asked.

"Some say an old pirate, and others say he's a simple tradesman. The man who owns the land here is as skilled at trade as he is cunning and not to be trusted completely. Make no mistake – watch your guard, or you might lose your possessions to the bones or your life to treachery."

Dominus smiled broadly. "We know your meaning, Eilifr, for we both are experienced at the dice and politics. Wine and women are my only true vices, and both of those can leave a man poor and destitute as any bad roll of the dice."

"True!" Eilifr laughed loudly, as they approached a low stone fence with a broad wooden gate leading to some gardens.

The barbarians moved ahead to the portico and set down their goods on the porch. Each in turn stepped aside and waited while chatting with each other. Walking up, as if in no hurry, several men dressed in brown tunics began to count and record the items. After a few minutes the counting stopped and a portly man emerged from the dark doorway. He stood for a moment with his arms folded as he looked at the cargo, and then at Eilifr.

Eilifr held his arms out. "Barnabus, we see how well you fare these days."

Barnabus stepped down from the doorway and embraced the hulking Eilifr. Stepping back, he laid hands on his own belly and laughed loudly. "It is a wealthy man who can become so fat! How good it is to see you alive, my friend. And I see that along with your crew you bring guests."

He turned his large, beaming face to Thadius and Dominus. "Welcome, welcome! Enter my home and be well cared for. This is my house, Villa de Vitorus, and all that is mine," he paused for effect, "with exception of my beautiful wife," he again paused, "is for you to enjoy."

Turning on his heels he walked to the doorway, stopped, and spun about again, the tails of his toga flying around. He grinned. "Everything can be had for a price, and if you are a betting man, you could even come away with more than you came with."

*   *   *

Night engulfed the villa, shrouding it in a thick wet mist. A fireplace roared with several great logs blazing. From time to time gray smoke belched out into the room.

Many individuals were in the main hall and Thadius noted the feasting table setup with meats, and fowl, brown earthen amphorae of wines and beer. Small iron cauldrons of stews and plates of bread came from the kitchen even as he watched.

Drinking some new wine from a copper goblet, he admired the wealth and generosity of this fast moving and stout host. Walking over to the feasting table, he took a brass plate and piled some roasted chicken on it. He made note that the inside of the manor appeared resplendent. Huge tapestries depicting battles or country scenes hung on several walls. Brightly colored frescos of golden age Greece adorned the other walls, and though the large room lay bustling with guests, it was not crowded; in all, it held a modest charm for Thadius.

As he consumed the fowl, he walked around the room observing the social interaction of the various guests. Getting close to a window, he could hear the howl of the coastal wind hitting the side of the house. A daft of air swirled the smoke in the high timbered roof, and two shaggy dogs lay by the fire. After taking a long draft from his goblet, he set it on a small wooden table and sat down on some pillows on the floor. Gooseflesh rose on his arms as warmth from the fire washed over him. He propped up a pillow near a marble bench in front of the fireplace and watched the orange flames leaping into the blackness of the chimney. *Strange*, he thought, *why isn't he using a furnace? Surely, the furnace would be more efficient.*

Barnabus appeared and sat next to him. "I do so enjoy a good open fire. I found them charming when I was in Gaul many years ago."

"I was wondering why you used them instead of a proper furnace," Thadius admitted.

"It is in use too, even as we speak." Barnabus pointed to the floor. "See, it is warm to the touch in here."

Thadius smiled. "Indeed it is."

"Not so barbaric after all." Barnabus stood with a smile and moved quickly off into the crowd.

The giggling of young girls and the laughter of boys came to his ears as the children dashed through the villa. A man shouted, and the trundle of dice clacking on a board filled the air. Hardened men rolled the bones, while bawdy women played a game of a different sort. To Thadius, Barnabus' home seemed more like a bath-resort than a trading post. Slaves and freemen as well as guests interacted with little civil impunity. A young woman came by, and Thadius picked up his cup and held it up to be filled. She poured the wine and then handed him a shard of pottery with the number five on it. "Your room number on the second floor, sir," she said before traveling to the next guest in the crowd.

Yawning, he turned to look at the water clock in the corner of the room. It showed the time as midnight. He stood up, a bit unsteady, and set down his goblet on a small table.

Making his way through the crowd to the stairwell, he climbed slowly to the second floor. The hallway was long and straight and he could see the doors all numbered in red paint. He came to room five near the end of the hallway and opened the door. His travel bag was sitting on the raised bed, a small oil lamp rested in a brass slot near the window giving just enough light to see clearly.

He moved to the bed and undressed. Shivering, he quickly climbed in between the sheets and pulled the blankets up high. The wind, moaned softly outside, lulling him into a deep sleep.

*　　　*　　　*

There were torches to light the tunnel. Thadius felt a sudden fear of being buried alive. He took a few steps; dark holes loomed from the sides. The smell of fresh turned earth filled his senses.

"She awaits you by the river," a voice said.

"Who are you?" he asked.

"You don't know me?" replied the voice.
"Are you god?"
A gentle laugh filled the air. "She awaits you. Go to her."
"Althea?" he said, his heart suddenly racing.
He ran down the jagged tunnel and emerged from the mouth of a cave.
Just ahead Althea waited. Her creamy skin shone in the early light. Her
dark hair looked like raven's feathers shimmering in the pale sun. But no sun
could be seen from the valley floor, and yet a streak of blue sky overhead was so
crisp and clear it set his heart pounding. She ran ahead of him along a flagstone
road that followed the shore of a black glassy river. He caught her and she
wrapped her arms around him. She sang into his ear a Greek children's song,
like the ones she did for their children.

Falling to his knees he began to weep. Tears dropped to the polished
stones of the path, then rolled like rain into the river. For how long he remained
on his knees he couldn't tell. Leaning to the side he let his hand fall into the river
and a biting cold took him. The water felt like ice and he lay there shivering as
the current rushed past his hand.

"Thadius," the soft voice echoed, "you must now wake."

The room was dark and cold, and encased him in silence. Glancing to the side he looked at the window, wet with condensation. He stayed silent and listened intently. No wind outside.

He sat there for some time until the faint shimmer of sunlight shone through the beads of water on the inside of the window. Pulling back the covers, he sat on the edge of the bed. A soft knocking at his door roused his attention.

"Yes?"

"Sir, may I come in and light the fire for you?" The timid voice was muffled.

"Yes, yes of course you may – please come in," he said shivering slightly.

A small boy peeked around the door. Wearing wool trousers and a small tunic tied with a belt around the waist, he appeared to be no more than twelve years. Hurrying to the hearth he carried a faggot of wood and quickly stuffed some dried moss and wood shavings into the fireplace. Placing several pieces of pinewood on top he produced a lit lamp, from where Thadius could not tell, and lit the wood.

"Morning meal will be served in an hour. Our lord would like you to join him. May I tell him you will?" the boy said.

"You may tell him I will," Thadius stated. The boy turned on his heels and scampered out the door, closing it behind him.

CHAPTER 9

After dressing, Thadius secured his belongings in his pack and headed down to the ground floor. All the mayhem of the night was gone. Through a wide arched doorway he stepped out onto a stone path that led to a patio made of round stones forming a large half circle. "Thadius my friend," shouted Barnabus with delight, his ample belly shaking. "Sit here with me and eat."

Slowly, Thadius walked to the table and sat down. A young servant boy ran to fill his glass then rushed off to another empty cup.

Barnabus smiled. "What do you think of my hospitality?"

"Your hospitality is not in question, not with me," Thadius said.

Barnabus grunted a laugh. "Showing it is half the fun, my dear General; you are retired I believe."

"Retired," Thadius affirmed.

In no time, several small roast pigs and two large platters of baked fowl were brought and set on a large table. A kettle of steaming soup came next along with bowls and spoons. In the cold morning air the steam from the caldron reminded Thadius of the many hot springs up on the mountain near Herculaneum. He fetched a bowl of soup and sat back down. Taking a wooden spoon he sampled the concoction,.

"This is very good," he stated.

"Of course," Barnabus laughed, "all that is here is always good."

"By chance have you seen—"

"Your companion? He's not come down yet."

Thadius shook his head. "I hope the old brigand isn't dead from too much indulgence?"

Barnabus laughed, and then waved his hand in the air. "He took two females up to his room last night. I think the old dog still has some bite left in him."

"Or so he thinks," Thadius chuckled.

Barnabus signaled his servants. "Bring cheeses, wine and tea," he shouted.

As quick as Jove's lightning came the delights. "Try these," he pointed. "The cheese is from Sicily, the wine from Placentia, and the tea from Tyre."

"Fabulous indeed," Thadius said taking a crumble of cheese and crushing it between his teeth.

"What sort of trip are you on?"

"I'm visiting an old friend. I suspect it will take another six weeks to make landfall at Britannia," Thadius said.

"Britannia?" Barnabus repeated, surprised. He rested his large elbows on the table, cradling his wine in both hands. Looking over the top of the cup he smiled. "With Eilifr's men, I'll wager it will take you four weeks."

Thadius looked thoughtful. "Perhaps."

"In any event, be wary," Barnabus stated flatly. "Watch for pirates who roam the waters just off these shores. They look for unsuspecting fools sailing this sea, and those who make their home along the coast."

Thadius drank down his wine. "You live along the sea."

Booming a great laugh, Barnabus poured both cups with more wine. "'Tis a fair truth you speak – but I have a formidable force, and besides those pirates are my best customers."

Thadius sat staring into his goblet of wine. Looking around, he noted many of the patrons from the night before engaging in discussions of travel and commerce. Barnabus shot to his feet. "My dear friend, it would appear that I am being signaled from the kitchen. A matter of some great importance no doubt. Please forgive me. I truly hope to see you again someday."

He quickly drank down the contents of his cup and shuffled off the patio towards the kitchen. Thadius rose to his feet, and taking a wedge of cheese and piece of bread, he moved out into the garden.

The strong briny sea air assailed his nose, and he looked out on an azure sky. He peered over the edge and down to the beach where the barbarians were working to load the ship. The brawny fellows tossed crates, amphora, and barrels from the shore to some crewmen on the boat.

"Thadius, I'd suggest more drink as an alternative to jumping," Dominus said. Holding a large leg of lamb in one hand, and a tall cow's horn in the other, he strolled towards Thadius. "What's so interesting down there?"

Thadius turned to Dominus. "So the warmth of the two women from last night has worn off?"

Dominus grinned and took a large bite of the greasy lamb. Chewing a few times he swallowed and then took a deep drink from the horn. He wiped his face with the back of his hand and smiled broadly. "A rather harrowing evening. Just when I thought I would falter, I found some way to rally my strength." He laughed. "I suppose I was lucky to have roused my old soldier at all. I'm not sure, but I think all this sea air has been rather good for me."

He moved next to Thadius and looked down at the barbarians on the beach. "Loading the ship I see."

"We'll be on our way soon I trust," Thadius said.

"Look there, our contribution to civilization." Dominus pointed along a low ridge at the ruins of a tower. "How sad that battlement has fallen into disrepair."

"Tis not sad, Dominus, at least they're still standing. That's more than I can say for the soldiers who built them."

"True enough." He paused for a moment. "Looks just like the ones we constructed in Gaul."

"We should gather our things and make ready to set to sea as soon as Eilifr is ready."

"Tis a fair bet he's weak from last night's exploits as I." Dominus took another heaping bite from the lamb and another drink from his horn. "I saw him with four women and he was in the midst of coitus with each."

"At the same time?" Thadius said.

"I think so," Dominus stated with a smirk. "It was difficult to tell where one body started and another one ended. It's safe to say he knows some barbarian ways of pleasing a woman that we should learn."

Thadius stood and began walking toward the villa. "Come, we should make ready to leave."

Thadius and Dominus gathered their belongings and waited in the main hall. Eilifr arrived and said farewell to four young dark-haired women. Turning to Thadius, he laughed. "I have a hearty appetite for food, drink and women!" He grabbed the hilt of his sword. "And battle!"

"When shall we board for sailing?" Thadius asked.

"Now." Eilifr smiled. "We sail as soon as we get to the boat."

They made their way down the cliff and onto the beach. Eilifr handed a heavy chest to one of his men and motioned for Dominus and Thadius to climb aboard. "Come, little Romans... tis time to take our leave of this place."

Thadius looked at the rope-ladder hanging over the saxboard. Grabbing the wooden rungs hanging over the side, he went up first, straddled the saxboard, and then stepped down onto one of the rower benches. Dominus followed suit, and soon both men were onboard.

Eilifr said a few words in his own language then aided in pushing the craft out into the surf. Two men maintained the mooring ropes and held the boat fast in the gentle surf while the others came up the ladder and took their places at the rower benches

"Make ready the oars," Eilifr said his voice booming over the sounds of the sea.

Dominus sat back near the aft of the ship lying against some bundles of rope. Watching, he could see the brawny men untying the long oars and putting them over the side. Drawing the handles through iron-shod holes, the men made ready.

CHAPTER 10

The boat cut through the dark blue water. The noonday sun beat down on Thadius in contrast to the cool breeze of the sea.

"Rack oars," shouted Eilifr from the rudder.

Thadius watched the crew remove their oars and pull them aboard the ship. One by one, from bow to aft, the oars were tied into place. Having completed the task, the men took up their various other duties. Eilifr gave more orders to his men in his brash language. Thadius could see Wyglad and Yngvi hoisting the broad square red sale up the mast. Catching the wind the sail snapped loudly and filled with the sea air, and the vessel lurched forward moving with swift speed along the waves.

The young lad named Tuk rolled up the heavy bow rope, while Thadius pondered the relationship of these hardened men. Retrieving his journal, ink and pen, he noted the events of his trip thus far, and the visit with Barnabus at his villa. Once he'd finished, Thadius took out a thin cylinder of charcoal and quickly sketched the image of Runolf and Raknar using stiff brushes to scrub parts of the boat.

For three weeks the routine remained the same: make landfall before dark, find a place to camp, eat, sleep little, and wake before dawn to sail again. Thadius felt invigorated by the crisp air and being around these free-men of the sea. Dominus seemed to be enjoying the trip, too, as he mingled with the barbarians and tried to speak some of their language. On the fourth week, Eilifr pulled the two men aside and told them that pirates were about.

Dominus said, "If you need us we can fight."

Eilifr laughed loudly. "I'm telling you this so you can stay out of the way."

Dominus did not expect this response and shrugged his shoulders. "I feel it my duty to tell you, the art of war is not unknown to Thadius or me. In fact, that is how I met him, if you remember?"

"Tell me again," Eilifr said.

"Imagine a pristine new fort, with wooden palisade walls twenty feet high, the tips sharpened to a fine point. The fort is just finished, made with an inner wall of stone and artillery elevated along the walls," Dominus began.

Eilifr adjusted the rudder, and the boat flew down a wave, up the other side and into another.

"Now the Helvetii come, those very souls who've revolted and come to throw the Romans out of their lands. It is night, and twenty thousand are massing to take the fort and kill the six thousand Romans there in. But what the Helvetii don't know is that those six thousand—" Dominus pointed with his thumb, "—are commanded by Thadius."

"Then what?" Eilifr asked.

"The old lion has a plan. Knowing he's out numbered, he leaves a contingent of legionnaires inside the walls of the fort, and extricates five thousand six hundred men through a sewer and into the woods not more than two hundred yards to the south where it empties into a wide brook."

Dominus took out a bottle of wine and opened it, drinking down a mouthful. "The battering of the gate started then the fire arrows fell, then the ladders. The four hundred and eighty men inside fought bravely repelling the invaders for a time, but they were soon overwhelmed and fell back to the inner wall. There, some cunning traps were sprung; pits filled with pitch and spikes consumed many Helvetii." Several of Eilifr's men had now taken an interest and took up positions around Dominus.

"The Centurion evacuated the remaining lads through the sewer then bravely threw a fiery lantern into the last trap. The walls were covered in pitch, as were the buildings, and the ground. Sheets had been soaked in it and lightly covered by dirt and gravel. The lantern hit, the fire erupted, and the Helvetii panicked."

"Did they die in the blaze?" Bojon said.

"Some, but the battle was not ended there, for it was Thadius and his First File who came from the forest in two attacks. One, led by the General himself, charged the gate and bottled the enemy within. The First File led his men in a flanking maneuver and split the remaining enemy forces, smashing them and scattering them to the wind. The cries of the enemy were loud from within the fort, as they were consumed by the fire."

Dominus paused and drank more wine. "By morning the field of battle was littered with carrion birds; the dead were piled so thickly that as I approached, I could walk five hundred yards without touching the ground. It was then, and there that I met Thadius; beaten down, tired, the wear of a thousand lifetimes on his face."

"You were not in his legion?" Yngvi asked.

"No. I was with another that was on a march to Gaul."

"A most glorious tale, better than when Thadius first explained it," Eilifr said.

"He doesn't embellish much, but I on the other hand, always do," Dominus stated.

Eilifr looked over at Thadius. Thadius shrugged his shoulders. "He's right." A large hand landed on Thadius' shoulder. Looking over, he noted Tuturk attached to it.

"Will you help with the meal?" he said.

"I will," replied Thadius.

"My son will standby with the dousing-pale. I need you to help with firewood, I will cut the meat," Tuturk stated. Lifting a plank he retrieved several flat stones and five pieces of flat iron plating. His son secured these items on a set of boards making up a temporary platform. Climbing down into the gap, Tuturk handed firewood up to Thadius. Tuk in turn laid it by the iron plates. "We will eat well today," Tuturk said while climbing up and carrying two copper pots.

He laid out the stones like paving blocks. Arranging the iron plates, he laid one down on top of the stones for a base and the others at an angle. He then fastened the iron tightly with hooks made of brass. Putting tinder in the bottom of the makeshift oven, he struck flint to steel. Watching the glowing embers fall into the fuel, he let the sea air fan it into a fire. Tossing a leather bucket attached to a rope over the side Tuk hauled up some seawater. He stood with the bucket ready to douse the blaze if commanded.

Laughter and stories percolated from the men as they drank mead and amused themselves with tales of heroes, dragons, and sea monsters. Dominus could see Thadius eating comfortably near the starboard side. He dipped his bread in his mead and took a bite. Suddenly, Thadius' expression changed from calm to anxious and worried.

"What is it old friend?" Dominus said.

"A ship." Thadius pointed out to sea. "And it's approaching fast!"

Climbing to his feet, Dominus peered over the lip of the port side saxboard. A Corbita styled boat headed their way. He squinted in the bright sun to see its crew. Several gangly fellows stood at the bow, others were lining the sides, weapons in hand.

"A ship off the starboard and it looks aggressive," Bojon said taking notice of Thadius and Dominus.

Eilifr shrugged his shoulders. "They are of little concern," he said. Turning the boat towards the shore the ship caught a wave and pitched heavily to the side then righted. "We will lead them to ground then be on our way. Prepare," Eilifr said.

A wave of water sprayed the crew, and Thadius turned away shielding himself, but his effort was for not as his graying hair fell straight to his shoulders with the dowsing. Several of the crew looked at Thadius with some amusement, but then quickly focused on removing some armor, weapons and shields.

"So we will fight?" Thadius said to Eilifr.

"Not exactly," Eilifr chuckled.

Bojon handed out the weapons, while Wyglad dispensed the shields. Retrieving some iron mail coifs, Rolf handed them out to the men and then carried one to Eilifr. Shouting to his barbaric brethren, Eilifr ordered the sail struck and the oars to be brought out. Looking down at his passengers, Eilifr said, "You there, get Thadius and wait at the bow with the mooring ropes." Pulling hard at the tiller, the ship rode over a wave.

An arrow passed overhead landing several yards beyond the port side of the ship. Eilifr gave no notice of it and again called to his shipmates. The crew of the offending ship shouted and clashed their weapons in aggression. Eilifr reached down, took the coif from his crewman and put it on over his head. "Right forward, left back," he shouted. The ship pitched in the water and turned sharply. "All forward," he yelled. His warriors drew on the oars and the ship moved forward.

Looking over the bow, Thadius could see a reef in shallow water passing just below. Realizing the advantage afforded by Eilifr's boat, he laughed heartily. "The Corbita can't follow us," Thadius said, "Their draft is too deep."

"Wait for my order!" Eilifr shouted to Thadius and Dominus.

"Wait for his signal." Dominus looked over at Thadius.

"Five hundred yards and closing," Thadius said. "Don't break anything on the way over the side," he added to Dominus.

Dominus shrugged. "I'm old not stupid, my friend!"

The men heaved on the oars, their great muscles flexing with each pull, a grim determination on each man's face. They seemed like a machine, functioning with precision and deliberate intent, and none of them seemed now the individual men of the hours before.

Shouts erupted from the pirate's ship as Eilifr's ship raced towards the shore. The Corbita veered away from the reefs and headed up the coast. The captain of the other ship looked angered, and he said something to his men that caused them to whoop and holler louder.

Eilifr ordered his men to slow, causing Thadius to fall against the curved prow. A wave carried the ship towards the shore, as Eilifr's men pointed the oars upward. Glancing at his friend, Thadius prepared to leap over the side and make for shore. "Stay where you are, little Romans!" Eilifr shouted. Hajlmar and Orkning rushed past and leapt from the bow into the surf. Thadius looked just up the beach; the pirate ship had also beached, and the men aboard were getting to the stony ground. Eilifr was outnumbered two to one.

"What do you think Eilifr's game is?" Dominus asked.

"I've no idea. He is shrewd though – and we should arm ourselves."

Gulls appeared overhead in great numbers. "I wonder if god has taken notice of this event," Thadius said. "Killed by pirates is not a fitting end for us."

He saw the brigands running down the beach, thrusting their weapons against their shields and shouting challenges and taunts. Several flaming arrows landed in the boat and were quickly put out with a bucket of water by Tuk. Eilifr stood as if made of marble staring at the pirates. He looked down at Tuturk. The cook struck up some tinder in a pot and fanned it into a flame.

"Now!" Eilifr said. "Little Romans at the bow, throw over the ropes."

Tossing the thick ropes over the side, Thadius watched the two men at the bow lean heavily against the prow shoving the ship back into the surf. The ship lurched backward, breaking free of the beach. The oarsmen extended their oars into the water. Looking over the side, Thadius saw the two men push the ship back past the breakers, then scramble up the ropes onto the ship. Straining against the oars, the men at the oars chanted as the craft lurched with every draw. Dominus watched from the wale as the pirates, their mouth's gaping, stared in disbelief.

"Prepare," called Eilifr. "Right back, left forward!" Coming about, the boat paralleled the shore. "Forward," Eilifr said. Both sets of oars plunged into the cold sea. Drawing hard against the blue waters the men propelled the ship forward. Passing the Corbita, Eilifr held the rudder steady.

"Look," Dominus said to Thadius.

Hajlmar and Orkning stepped to the wale with bows in hand. They dipped their cloth-wrapped arrows into the flaming pot, drew back their strings, and took careful aim. The arrows hissed as they flew. Tuk handed them new arrows and prepared another set. Again the men ignited the missiles and let them fly.

Every arrow landed either in the sail or mid-ship. Flames raced up the canvas and caught the mast on fire. The deck burst into flame. Some of the pirates tried throwing buckets of water up the mast, but the flames began devouring the dry wood. Discipline on the pirate ship came undone as panic set in and some of the sailors jumped into the surf. A thickening black pillar of smoke rose into the air as the sea breeze drove the flames into a frenzy. Angry pirates rushed along the beach shooting arrows and shouting curses. With every pull of the oars Eilifr's ship became further and further afield of the Corbita. Smaller, and smaller the pirate ship became in the distance. Turning, Dominus noticed two other ships off the portside, their crews looking over with some concern.

"Rack oars, raise sail," Eilifr shouted.

*　　*　　*

Thadius leaned over the saxboard. The water was becoming lighter and lighter, and finally he saw the sharp coral reef appear. "The coastline is jagged here," Dominus said coming up beside him.

"And it's not long till darkness settles in," Thadius observed.

"There," said Bojon pointing, "the island of fallen columns."

Eilifr angled the ship towards a chunk of land isolated from the shore. Thadius could see the island was no bigger than fifty acres, and shaped like a teardrop. The sea rose up and down within a great hole cut through the middle. A thin strip of yellow sand extended around the base of the island, and in places columns poked up from under the sea.

"Lower the sail and extend the oars," Eilifr said.

He maneuvered the boat into a shallow channel cut into the reef, sailing with care past jagged rocks. "Last pull," he called as the men raised the oars and the boat plowed into the soft sandy beach. "Disembark!"

Several of the sailors climbed overboard taking the bow ropes with them. Two rusted wrought-iron rings protruded from the stone of the cliff. Tying the boat's mooring ropes to the hoops, the men secured the ship.

"Unload the supplies," Eilifr said. "You – little Romans, carry some supplies too."

"Carry them where?" Thadius asked while lifting a box onto his shoulder.

"There," Eilifr said pointing at a stone stairwell on the cliff. "Up we go little friends."

"Be wary," Rolf motioned at the wet steps. "The soggy stones can be your end."

Dominus' foot slipped and he fell outward, but was caught by Bojon. Gripping him tightly, Bojon pulled him back onto the stair. "Keep your feet, little Roman," he warned.

Cresting the top stair Thadius stumbled onto a long and irregular plateau. The Northmen seemed to know where they were going as they pressed ahead into the growing darkness.

Dominus waited for him. "Come on, you old fool," he said. "One misstep and you'll be bait for the fishes."

"Would you believe that not long ago I was complaining that I was sore from working in my garden?" Thadius said.

"I believe it. Now come on before they've left us in the darkness."

A flash of light appeared ahead. Several torches came to life and they could see the ruins all about them. In the middle of the island, a structure appeared in the dim light. The ground was cut like a ziggurat with each level harboring ruins. They appeared ominous in the orange light. In the foreground vertical columns stood on stone foundations like branchless white marble tree trunks. A cobblestone road made its way past fallen walls, crumbling columns, and a large two-story dome that rose from the second tier. Eilifr and his men headed straight for the dome.

"This structure was built by the feared Therans, a seafaring race that ruled these lands over a thousand years ago," Thadius whispered.

"How could you know this?" Dominus said.

Shrugging his shoulders, Thadius pointed at a collapsed wall. "The blocks of stone, the stucco, and the wooden beams within the walls all tell that tale."

"I am again surprised by what you know," laughed Dominus.

The Northmen went directly into the round structure. Thadius followed, but lingered for a moment at the arched doorway, running his hands along the marble surface.

"Are you coming in?" Dominus asked. "I hear it is the finest accommodations in this area."

In the distance, a haunting sound seemed to be carried by the wind. Thadius took a few steps and listened; it was there, a flute-like sound, then it was gone. He shrugged and walked on.

Eilifr put the end of his torch into the fire pit. The smell of smoke filled the room. The glow of the coals became a light, and the darkness abated. A pit lay in the middle of the room, and he watched as one of Eilifr's men brought a bundle of wood from the darkness and put several pieces on the fire. Soon the room was lit, and Thadius marveled at the elaborate frescos along the walls and the dome.

Bojon walked around placing coal into the wall sconces, while Heragaus followed lighting them until the room became fully illuminated. At the far side, a statue stood more than ten feet high and loomed from the shadows. Setting down his pack, Thadius walked over to the white-marble statue and examined it. The features appeared to have been worn down by the salty air and weather. He could see it appeared to be carved from a single piece of marble, and bore a likeness to Poseidon.

Gray smoke twisted and glided up to the top of the domed roof and found its way out a wide hole at its center. In the clear sky above, Thadius could see the bright stars twinkling in the blackness. "Foreign gods dwelled here once," Eilifr said, while in the distance the fluting sound returned. "From the looks of the ruined land, I'd say that my god smote it with his hammer."

"Do you know this place well?" Thadius asked.

"Well enough to know, if drunk and wandering, one can fall to his death from these heights," Eilifr said. Bojon came and filled Eilifr's drinking horn from a clay jar. He took a swig and began talking in his own language, stopped and addressed Thadius. "I see in your eyes a curiosity – if you go out, stay away from the edges, they are crumbling."

Setting down his travel bag, Thadius exited the temple and walked out into the night. Moving around the building he could feel the cold sea wind on his face. In the darkness he could just make out the shadowy lines of the other buildings. Carefully he made his way along a stone pathway. Crumbling foundations, toppled columns, and half walls were strewn about like so many other places of the ancient world.

Approaching the top tier he stopped; before him laid a simple looking structure. A single story rectangular building extended for a hundred feet along the top plateau. Columns held up a stone portico, and a strange flouting sound came from within.

"You're a fool for wandering out here without a light," Dominus said from behind him. A shimmer of light flickered in the wind as Dominus held aloft a small oil lamp.

Entering the building, Thadius could see a large sculpture in the darkness. The sound was loud here and definitely was the source of the fluting. Approaching the sculpture, he could see it was long with irregular shapes along its surface. "Looks like brass scales," Dominus said over the loud sound. Holding up the lamp, he ran his fingers over it. "A serpent maybe?"

"That's what it is. It's a sea serpent, or maybe a Titan."

The sound changed pitch and gave him a start. Dominus laughed uncomfortably and walked along the curvy statue. At the far end the statue's head appeared bent towards the ceiling.

"Its mouth is large enough for both of us to sit in," Dominus said.

Reaching inside, Thadius ran his hand over the many rows of blunted and faded white teeth. The flame of the lamp bent back towards him, and he could feel the strong wind blowing from the mouth. Putting the lamp into the mouth he could see the red tongue recessed back. "It has a set of gears and some kind of plumbing. I think the teeth are the music pipes, but I could be wrong," he said.

"I'm freezing my own pipes!" Dominus stated. "Let's get back to the fire."

"Very well."

They left the strange sculpture and wound their way back down to the domed building. Moisture was heavy in the air, and Thadius knew it would be a chilly night. Finally, at the building entrance, he gave one last look into the darkness and drank in the haunting melody that carried through the air.

Having opened a large earthen jar topped with wax, Tuturk removed some of the contents. Thadius could see it was salted meat, and watched as Tuturk flattened some with his hands and laid it in a hot iron pan. The roasting meat filled the chamber with such an aroma that Thadius' mouth began to water. Eilifr opened another of the large jars and ladled out liberal amounts of the liquid into each man's drinking vessel. Dominus joined in and indulged, his laughter booming into the room. A meal was prepared, and all sat around the fire to eat.

Thadius watched with quiet humor as Dominus cast off his noble Roman ways and became a surrogate Northman with little shame. And although Thadius desired to follow suit, he felt his sense of propriety outweigh his want of impropriety.

He stood and came to the fire pit. Tuturk removed some large round flat bread and laid a helping of roasted meat on top. Handing one to Thadius, he smiled broadly. "Eat, little Roman, for when we come to the straights we will all need strength."

The revelry lasted late into the night. Eilifr finally fell to the ground and leaned heavily against a large amphora near the fire. The other sailors began finding places to sleep as the fire turned to embers. In the distance, the lone piping of the serpent signaled the end of the evening, and Thadius settled in at the base of the statue. Dominus placed a few logs on the embers rekindling the fire, then lay down and fell fast asleep.

CHAPTER 11

Sunlight filtered through the oculus. Thadius climbed to a sitting position and glanced about. Dominus still slept by the fire, although it was nothing more than charcoal and ashes. Droplets of moisture fell from the open ceiling and hissed as it hit the coals.

Eilifr sat up and gripped his head. Climbing to his feet he took an earthen pitcher and staggered to a wide copper pot. He poured some water into the pitcher and washed his face and hair. Shaking his head, he showered the other men who grumbled loudly at the rude awakening.

"Eilifr, if you wish to prove you are the son of god you need only to provide thunder not rain," Bojon said, as he got to his feet and went to the doorway. After relieving himself, he came to the fire and placed some wood in the coals. "We'll have warmth soon."

Thadius dug into his pack and retrieved a bar of olive oil soap and a rag. He went to the wooden keg that held their drinking water and dipped in his teapot, then walked to the fire pit. Setting the small pot in the coals, he sat patiently waiting for the water to heat.

Once the steam emerged from the container, he poured the hot water onto a rag and wiped himself down. He completed the whore's bath quickly and turned to the bemused expressions of the Northmen crew.

"What strange rituals you Romans have," Runolf said shaking his head.

Dominus pulled back his cloak and glanced up. He scratched his scalp and got to his feet. "I suppose I should be grateful I'm alive – but I'm not." He frowned, clutching his head. "The drink has struck me nearly blind."

Thadius handed him a cornmeal biscuit. "Here, eat this and you'll feel better."

"Eat?" Dominus groaned. "Even the suggestion makes me want to purge."

Thadius walked to his pack and retrieved two mugs and a papyrus cylinder filled with some powder. "I'll make some willow-bark tea," he said. Fetching more water he again put his pot over the fire to heat. Soon the water boiled and he added the powder into the cups, and the hot water too. A strong smell of lavender filled the room.

"Why do you do that?" asked Rolf stroking his long blond beard and mustache.

Thadius made a wry smile. "It's a special tea made of willow bark, sandalwood, and lavender. My surgeon formulated it to help soldiers recover after a night of hard drinking... Would you like to try some?"

"I am Rolf, I need none but strong drink, meat, hard steel, and many – many women to fill my bed," he said, and then turned his back on Thadius.

Dominus sat down and took the cup from Thadius, who laughed. "They think we're barbarians."

"We are," Dominus said grinning. Sipping from his cup he rubbed his head. "These lads are twenty – maybe even thirty years our junior. It's no wonder they don't wish to partake of our tea."

Thadius smiled and shook his head. "Were either of us ever that young?"

"I just remember getting my toga virilis at age fifteen," Dominus said with a laugh.

"Fifteen – seems like a million years ago," Thadius chuckled.

Dominus shrugged. "And a million battles."

"We must get on our way. To get to the next harbor will take us all day," Eilifr said, as he placed his sword belt over his shoulder.

Coming up the cliff was harrowing, but traveling down was more terrifying. The worn stairs were slick with moisture. Ahead of

Thadius was half the crew, and behind him the other half. When he finally stepped onto the sandy shore, he felt like kissing the ground.

"Get aboard," Eilifr said. The ship rested in the shallow surf gently rocking with the tempo of the waves. "We have miles to make."

Thadius stored his pack at the aft then fetched a cup of wine.

"To the oars, make ready," Eilifr shouted.

Slowly the ship moved back into the waters where the shallow reefs dwelt. They maneuvered out between the high rock pillars and into the open water. The wind blew hard from the east, and Eilifr angled the ship parallel to the mainland.

"Rack oars," called Eilifr. "Raise sails."

*   *   *

The late afternoon sun baked the deck. The strong east wind pushed the ship onward at a frightening pace. Ahead Thadius could see the Straits of Hercules. Eilifr navigated the ship closer to shore then turned toward a crescent shaped harbor. "The island of Calpe," he announced. "It's not large, but conducts a lively trade. Drop sail, and prepare for land."

The ship glided into the harbor and Thadius could see the cement piers that jutted out into the water. Two dozen ships were tied to the docks and stacks of crates, sacks of grain and jars of products were stacked on every surface. Eilifr brought the ship into an open birth, and Bojon leapt to the pier with a rope in hand. He secured the bow, while Rolf secured the aft rope. Once the boat was secure, Eilifr went ashore.

Calpe was crowded. Many merchant ships were moored in the harbor. Darkness was settling, and the ship lanterns were being lit. Thadius could see the Corbitas and Galleys, some low and some high, in the waters. Torchbearers came out onto the long cement walls of the marina and lit sconces. The smell of brimstone filled the air as the dockside fires burned providing light.

"I can almost smell the money here," Domirus said.

Thadius nodded toward a crowd of merchants and longshoremen. "Indeed – seems the danariis are exchanging hands here with much haste."

"It is prudent to keep a dagger close at hand," Eilifr said while stepping onto the dock. "We will leave ten men here to guard the ship's cargo. You and Dominus come with me. I have someone I'd like you to meet."

They walked from the birth along a narrow road into the town proper. Many sailors wandered in and out of the wine taverns and brothels. Turning to his men, Eilifr grinned. "Do not bring down the disdain of the gods by your actions tonight. Be back to the ship by the mid of the night."

He began walking along a rectangular slab of cement that led to a cobblestone street. Thadius could see in the darkness the buildings recessed back from the harbor. They resembled structures built along the shores of Numadia. He passed stone warehouses with apartments built above, more wine taverns, and groups of sailors playing dice.

Eilifr turned down a wide avenue. "You Romans call this area a forum," he said.

"How cosmopolitan," Dominus retorted.

Sconces sitting atop wooden poles cast a yellow glow over the street. Approaching a three story stone and timber building, Eilifr stopped, turned and looked at Thadius and Dominus. "This is the shop and home of my friend. Come in and have food and drink while I secure more provisions."

Entering the structure, Eilifr stooped to fit in the door. "What thief dwells within this house?" he called.

"Eilifr, is that you?" answered a deep voice.

"It is none other," replied Eilifr while he approached a wide wooden table.

"Who is that with you? Two old men for a crew?" The man laughed as he came out of the shadows and into the low lamplight.

"Two Romans foolish enough to sail with me," Eilifr chuckled. "We will need some provisions for the next leg of our journey across the Cold Sea."

"I can help. My cousin now has a bakery and dried meat shop."

Smiling, Eilifr placed his palms down on the table. "I have twenty bolts of silk and twice as many jars of Pescarin wine."

"Hmm, you say silk and Pescarin wine?" He drew in a deep breath letting it out slowly. "That's quite a bit of fine wine...I think we can do business."

Eilifr pointed at the man. "This is Burg of La'dor, but we call him Burg the wily." Turning back to Burg, he pointed at Thadius and Dominus. "These two men are traveling to the Island Britannia. Moras Tiberius Thadius and Peresius Albas Dominus—good fellows, and you'd do well to be a friend to them as you have been to me."

Burg came to Thadius. "You were a consul, I remember your name." He turned to Dominus, "Albas Dominus, didn't you serve under Servilius Caepio?"

Dominus looked surprised. "I did." He glanced over at Thadius then back. "How did you know that?"

"I served under him too. I was a centurion in the Fifth," Burg said. "You both will be welcome with or without Eilifr." He turned and fetched an earthen jug on a shelf. "We shall drink to great friends and great wealth." He called a servant from the back room, "Go to my brother and tell him that Eilifr's ship is docked at the harbor. Fill his ship with what he needs, and bring back his trade goods. Tell Carmelius to bring extra guards, for the shipment is pure treasure." He watched the servant leave then poured some cups full of wine. "Now let's drink."

For several hours Thadius and Dominus sat in the little shop drinking with Eilifr and Burg. His servant returned and reported that all the trade goods were delivered, and stocked in his storehouse.

"It is growing late in the hour. Tis good to see you old friend, but now we must go back to the ship." Eilifr stood. "Once we sail into the Cold Sea we will need to make many miles to avoid the pirates that sail those waters."

"Pirates?" Dominus asked. "Perhaps we should mount a couple of scorpions on your boat."

Eilifr chuckled. "You Romans use might when cunning is better." He reached the door and stepped into the dark night. "Have no fear, my boat will protect us."

Dominus turned to Thadius. "His boat will protect us? Then I hope it does more than sail."

CHAPTER 12

The ship came under speed and the sailcloth stretched tight. Thadius watched as a flock of white gulls passed overhead in the new morning light. It would be a blue sky this day, and he thanked the god Neptune. Ahead, he could see the Pillars of Hercules that marked the corner of Gaul and the place where the two seas came together.

"Stand with me, Roman," Neri said while climbing up to the rudder platform.

As the boat shifted, Thadius leaned heavily against the starboard railing where the aft of the ship curled upward. Eilifr maintained the course as they paralleled the shore, and at the bow, Dominus stood.

"Look into the blue waters," Neri said. "We displace only a fraction of what your ships do, and we can glide over coral and stone that would tear the heart from your galleys."

Eilifr shifted the rudder and the boat headed further out to sea. The ship raced up a swell cresting the large dark peak, breaching it, and coasting down the other side. Thadius held on for fear of plunging into the cold waters.

Thadius climbed down into the belly of the boat. Rolf motioned for him to approach. The salt air filled his lungs, and he felt quite good. He took up a spool of string and began helping Rolf and his brother Runolf mend one of the fishing nets. What seemed like minutes turned into hours as Thadius helped the crew do chores. Glancing up he was surprised to see the sun directly overhead.

Tuturk passed by with a pot and pan, and he knew the midday meal would soon be prepared.

The feast was simple— millet bread, boiled meat, and some apples. After they ate, Thadius again assisted members of the crew in their daily tasks.

After a time Runolf looked up. "Night approaches. We will be heading to land soon."

Eilifr turned the ship towards a long white sandy beach. Calling to have the sail struck, he let the waves carry the ship. The craft shuddered once and then settled down on the sand. "To shore," he said.

Over the bow the rope ladders fell and each man climbed over in his turn. Yngvi and Raknar took up the ropes and moved up the beach, unraveling the coil as they went. Each man fastened the rope to a tree then returned to help carry the supplies.

Thadius watched the waves crashing on the sand. The boat rocked up and down. Supplies were lowered, and the men advanced up the beach to the rocky coastline.

After erecting several tents above the high water line Eilifr's men began stacking firewood. A bonfire was lit and all the men sat about pouring cups of mead and wine from earthen jars. Tuturk handed out dried beef with loaves of bread before taking a place by the fire. Consuming the food and quaffing down wine, the men drank and ate long into the night.

"Drink," cried the men to Thadius. "Drink, drink, drink!"

He looked annoyed, but then took up a horn and lifted it to his lips. The honey wine was sweet and went down smoothly. He took another swallow, and then another. Soon he was laughing and telling stories from his past. The men listened with great intensity while he regaled them with tales of war and riches.

Looking up, intoxicated with the mead, Thadius could see the constellations shimmering in the black of the sky. In the distance he heard the cries of the sea birds and the smashing of the waves against the shore. The sea breeze picked up and he pulled his cloak tightly around himself.

"I shall take my rest," he said getting to his feet and looking into the bright firelight.

"Then to good rest you shall go, my friend. Don't let the sand fleas have you for supper." Dominus laughed as he poured more mead into a large cow's horn and quaffed.

Getting to the tent, he could hear voices in the wind as the sounds of men and gods melded into haunting echoes. He laid on his bedroll, tucked his dagger in hand, and pulled his wool blanket about himself.

"Keep us safe," he prayed while closing his eyes. Soon he fell into a deep slumber.

Thadius came awake just as the sun peeked over the horizon. As the sun rose it painted the ship in a ghostly light. Eilifr's men slowly climbed to their feet and began loading the ship, preparing to depart.

Climbing into the ship, Thadius felt strange, a feeling that he had in some way changed. He pulled himself up and over the wale, landed on the prow, then turned and offered a hand to the other crewmen coming up. Each man climbing aboard greeted him with a strange phrase he had not heard before.

"They say you are like a long tooth lion, gray of hair but still strong," Eilifr laughed as he made his way to the aft.

Thadius helped Dominus scramble onboard. "I'm not ready for the jackals to have me yet," he said.

"Thadius," Dominus began, "I can't tell you how this adventure has brought me back to life. I did not know how much an old man I had become until I was reborn over these many weeks."

"Yes," Thadius replied passionately. "Perhaps we should take our place among the oars? Give some of these young fellows a break."

Eilifr smiled. "Bjorn, Tuturk!" he shouted. "Let the Romans relieve you at the oars."

Bjorn looked up, a wry smile on his bearded face. Standing, he and Tuturk held down their respective oars so the flat end rose out of the water.

Eilifr motioned with his hand. "Take your seats, my soft Roman friends. Soon you will be forged from Roman copper into northern steel!"

"We will show you what to do. Watch us and row as we do," said Heragaus, glancing back at them.

To Thadius the oar felt heavy. Eilifr motioned for all oars to be raised. With his hand he signaled for the rowers to begin. All readied themselves. Heragaus pushing his oar forward, Thadius did the same. Dipping the oar in, he pushed against the bench in front of him with his feet and pulled on his handle. It creaked loudly, flexed slightly, and the ship moved into the crashing waves. Thadius repeated the motion in time with the other men. Moving back into the water the ship jolted with the impact of the waves. He saw Ivar, Thord, Imsigull and Volund scramble over the bow and pull up the ladders. The four men, dripping from seawater, moved to the mast and waited. Sweat began dribbling down in rivulets to the end of his nose. Pulling on the oar was not the difficult part, Thadius thought… it was keeping the speed with Heragaus. Keeping his momentum with the other oars-men was not easy, and his old muscles began to feel the strain.

"Halt!" commanded Eilifr. "Up!"

Thadius hoisted his oar so the flat end pointed upward. Seeing Dominus drenched in sweat he laughed. "Not so hard, eh?"

Looking over with a wry smile, Dominus merely shook his head. "Rack oars," Eilifr shouted. "Raise sail."

At times it felt as if the ship was flying through the waves as the powerful wind pushed it forward. Remaining fair and breezy the weather allowed the boat to travel many miles each day. Thadius found himself looking forward to his turn at the oars when the wind failed. With each passing day he felt himself becoming stronger, more fit; he felt himself changing within and without. His respect for his companions grew.

"Look there," he said to Dominus. "More villages on the shore."

"And, fishing boats," Dominus added.

They passed more hamlets and even some large towns as they came around a spit of land. Thadius realized a large town lay directly ahead. Ordering the sail dropped and the oars put out, Eilifr guided the ship toward a dock that jutted out into the water. Ships bobbed in the small bay and some were moored at the dock. Eilifr ordered the oars on the port side to be secured. Using the starboard oars the men maneuvered the boat up against the wooden dock. Thadius made ready to disembark.

"This town you Romans call Itius Portus," Eilifr said.

Jumping down from the ship, Dominus looked up at Thadius. "Are you coming? And, do I have to catch you when you jump?"

Thadius calmly climbed down the ladder and smiled. "I've not been reborn with quite as much youthful vigor as you, my friend."

"'Tis no doubt that I feel ten years younger and in the prime of life. If it's the same for you, you must feel a hundred," Dominus said. Thadius merely gave him a dismissing shake of the head.

"Come, little Romans, tonight we dine and drink at the great home of my friend, Calculis of Dorm."

"Calculis of Dorm? The same man who owns the laundries that do the garments of the lords of Rome?" Dominus asked raising an eyebrow.

"He is very well known, and very well off," Eilifr said smiling. "I have taken goods for him to and from the islands before. He will have something for me to take this time too."

"I always wondered what happened to Calculis." Thadius mused. "How interesting."

"Come with me," Eilifr said turning and striding through the arched gates and into the walled town.

CHAPTER 13

Calculis' home lay just off the town's forum; a four-story stucco building, oddly shaped with a façade of thinly cut white marble. A colonnaded portico surrounded the entrance to the atrium. Thadius could clearly see a wide balcony extending under three of the second story windows. One wide wooden door, painted bright yellow and trimmed in red, was set back from the ornate limestone stairs. To either side were ionic columns that extended up the wall and supported a small ledge that ran above the first floor windowsills. Thadius admired the rich red color of the columns then realized there was a person at the top of the stairs.

"Who are you, and why have you darkened this doorway?" the man said.

"Eilifr and company to see the lord of the house," Eilifr announced.

"Eilifr, you say? Yes, I see now... you have come back to us from many months at sea. Come in, for my master will be delighted to see you again."

Waiting in the atrium, Thadius and Dominus sat on a long white marble bench adorned with cherubs. After sitting for some time, Dominus stood and walked to the fountain. The stone sculpture of a fish spewed water into a tiled basin keeping the chamber cool.

Sitting on the lip of the fountain, Dominus put his hand in the water and swirled it about. "Quite cold and effervescent."

"Artesian," Thadius asked.

"Undoubtedly," Dominus replied.

Approaching in haste from down a hallway, several servants stopped at the room's main portal. Watching the four young men take up positions to either side of the corridor, Thadius knew they were preceding their master. Their well-tailored tunics and togas were impressive, and each boy's hair seemed perfect, clearly the work of methodical preparation. Several young women approached from down the hallway tossing out flower petals. Two younger girls behind them carried incense, filling the room with the pungent, white, smoky scent of sandalwood and myrrh.

Emerging from the darkness of the hallway, two burly men were carrying a sedan car. They stopped and placed the platform near the fountain. Sitting atop the sedan, a shriveled old man stared out. "Eilifr, is that you there?" he said. "Who is that with you?"

Eilifr gave a great belly laugh. "It is two travelers, sailing with my ship from your homeland."

"Romans? Tis not about my brother, is it?" He looked concerned. "Has he gone on to paradise?"

"No, not messengers, Calculis," Eilifr said loudly. "Just two travelers going to the island. They have traveled all the way from Herculaneum."

Seeing the old man shifting in his seat, Thadius could tell he was uncomfortable. For a long moment Calculis sat in silence. He cleared his throat. "They are not here to collect taxes are they?" he asked with some concern.

"No, these men are just travelers," Eilifr assured him.

"Praise the gods then," Calculis stated with a crooked smile. "Eilifr, will you take some things for me to the island? I will need for you to bring some goods back upon your return also."

Eilifr laughed again. "Of course," he said loudly. "Now are you going to keep your guests waiting?"

"You blond warthog, you overstep yourself... but you are a good friend and skillful sailor. I'll over look this breach of civility, and wager you've not brought any villains into my home? So, come in and be my guests," Calculis said with resignation.

He clapped his hands several times, and servants rushed to his side. Whispering something to a boy, Calculis waved his hand in dismissal. "Off with you and do as I bid," he said. "Now move me to the feasting room," he shouted at his servants. Lifting the sedan the two servants turned and slowly walked into the dark hallway.

"Come in – come in," Calculis called behind him.

* * *

The evening grew late as Thadius drank several glasses of dark beer brewed by the host. Fish was prepared with exotic garnish, placed on the table,and quickly devoured. A second course of steamed vegetables, rice, and gravy came. This too was consumed as the third course— pheasant, grouse, pigeon, and goose, prepared and glazed in a honey sauce and trimmed in figs, with walnuts, were brought and laid on the table.

Calculis ate and drank little. Perhaps twenty years senior to Thadius and Dominus, he was a frail man. His wrinkled skin lay about him like an old sack, and his hearing required much repeating of words during a conversation. Eilifr conversed loudly with him in Latin and Greek, and was patient when the old man would fall asleep in the middle of a discussion.

A clock, somewhere in his house, echoed the passing of ten bells. Thadius chewed on a small pheasant leg, savoring the crispy skin, and seasoned meat.

Calculis began chuckling, then turned to address Dominus and Thadius. "Far from home," he stated. "Why?"

"Business on the island," Thadius said.

"Business? Do you mean you are going to make a profit, or that you are on a personal errand?"

"You are a very shrewd man, master Calculis," Dominus said.

"I see it is no point keeping a secret from you, sir," Thadius said.

Guffawing, Calculis ran his bony fingers through his thin, gray hair. "Best to be clear now, than when the wine has stolen our wits."

"True," Thadius said. "I have an old friend residing on the island as a regent. He has asked me to attend him in some matter of a murder."

"Seems a subject best left to the local authorities, wouldn't you say?"

"His fear is that the issue was settled out of hand and he would like my opinion."

"Well," Calculis said lifting a copper cup of wine with some difficulty to his mouth. "Are you a shrewd man?"

"I like to think I am," Thadius said.

"Then, take this from me, beware such requests from old friends. It does not bode well that your friend is a regent, and he discounts his own investigators."

Watching the wine cup quaking as the old man lifted it to his lips, Thadius smiled. "The thought has crossed my mind."

"But?"

Thadius took a sip. "But, it seems a worthy quest for a man longing for adventure."

"Well," Calculis began, "don't let adventure lead your head off its shoulders. Now, enjoy my hospitality this evening. My servants will see to your needs. I must retire now. I may not rise in the morning, but if I do it will be a profitable day." He clapped his hands together and two sedan bearers came, hoisted his chair, and exited through an adjacent hallway. Thadius thanked Jupiter for his own good health.

Late in the evening the last of the beer was set out and Dominus, Eilifr and Thadius finished it along with the remains of a well-roasted suckling boar. Feeling the heaviness of the beer in his belly, he decided to call it a night and head to his sleeping chamber. A young woman, carrying a small oil lamp waited at the hallway to escort him down the long passage. She guided him past several glass windows, all sealed by shutters. Coming to a dark oak door with polished brass hinges, the girl turned and opened it.

A large bed dominated the center of the room, and the floor radiated heat. A heavy cover of quilted silk sat on top and the woman motioned for him to approach. The servant walked to the bed and pulled down the blanket to reveal layers of wool covers and cotton sheets.

Walking over to the side of the bed he sat heavily down to unlace and remove his boots. The woman, whose raven colored hair fell in front of her face, held his hands fast. Through her hair she smiled up at him and shook her head as if to say, *I'll do this*. She quickly unlaced and removed both boots then began helping him to remove his clothes.

"No, no, my wife…" he labored slurred as he pushed her head back and gazed down at her dark brown eyes and full pink lips. "I can't do this. You are lovely, but I must abide to my wife."

She stared mournfully up at him like a person chastised for making a mistake. Taking her face in his hands, he smiled at her. "It's nothing you've done wrong."

His mind drifted to his home and family. A feeling as if falling came over him and the girl grabbed him by the arm. With surprising strength, she brought him to his feet and helped him to the bed. She laid him under the sheets and for a moment stood staring down at him. His eyes became too heavy and he fell into darkness.

Charon used his gnarled wooden staff and shoved Thadius back from the boat. From the other shore his wife called to him. "Thadius, I await you!"

Brandishing two gold coins, Thadius desperately held them aloft shouting again over the din of the assembled dead. "I have the coins! They are gold!"

But the ferryman continued to hold him at the shore. Shoving with the wooden rod, Charon forced him back into the throng of angry souls.

The ferryman listened with deaf ear as Thadius complained. Other souls passed him and climbed aboard the boat. Once full, Charon levered the ferry off the shore and into the dark waters of the Acheron River. "Don't go without me!" Thadius called. "My wife! I must see her again – even just for a moment!"

Thadius sat up feeling as though the room was tilting back and forth. "Are you alright?" a soft voice asked from behind him. He turned, eyes wide. Sitting next to him was the young nymph from the night before.

"It is okay, we did nothing as you bade me," she said apparently reading his thoughts. "But I was told to stay with you for the night, and I could not leave until morning. And two in bed is warmer than one." She coyly smiled.

"Thank you for your kindness," he stated. "It is morning, and I release you from your service."

"I shall do as you wish. If you need me I will be outside the door. You are a kind man," she said. She got up and left, and the portal closed behind her. Once again Thadius was alone with his thoughts. He rubbed his pounding head as he stood and went to the basin. He washed, but his stomach could not be ignored any longer and it cried out from hunger. He dressed and exited the room.

As he walked out the girl stood and motioned for him to follow her. "This way, my lord."

She led the way to an arched opening. Emerging into a large room he gazed in amazement. Constructed of large blocks of gray stone, the walls climbed to thirty feet high. Huge timbers spanned the width of the hall supporting a large roof made of wooden planks.

Dominus and Eilifr sat at a long wooden table. They were helping themselves to chunks of meat and boiled eggs, turnips, parsnip, and roast door mice when Thadius approached. "Good of you to join us, old salt," Dominus said. "Eilifr and I were wondering if we should leave you anything to eat."

"Where's our host?" Thadius asked.

"He's busy with his daily affairs," Eilifr replied.

Taking some food onto a wooden plate, Thadius ate greedily not talking for some time. Finally, he looked up to see the bemused expressions of his friends. "The past days rowing seemed to have built a great hunger within me."

Glancing back at the girl still standing in the entry to the hall, Dominus laughed. "Seems to have built a hunger for more than food."

Thadius glanced back too. "Yes…" he paused, "it seems like my soul is new in many ways."

Pushing his plate back, Eilifr chortled. "Calculis has asked that we take our leave at our convenience. That time is now." He looked down at his companions, then headed towards the doorway.

Thadius and Dominus followed, and soon they were heading back toward the marina.

CHAPTER 14

The island lay just off the starboard bow as the waves were swelling. Dark clouds gathered over the sea as Eilifr navigated the boat towards the land known as Britannia. A mist began to rise and swallow all that was around it. The view of the island slowly vanished, but Eilifr continued on.

"The shore is not far off," Eilifr stated. "Strike the sail, put out the oars."

The mist parted, and Thadius could see the massive white cliffs. They were majestic, and defiant to the sea in which they were captive.

"Julius Caesar had a powerful desire to conquer this island," Dominus said.

"He wrote that it's a wealthy resource for the Republic, but he probably really meant for himself," Thadius said.

"Don't give me that self-righteous foolishness," Dominus said. "You can't fool me, you old salt – you'd pillage this land for your own gain just as fast as Julius, or Pompey, or I would."

"This place is called Portus Dubris," Eilifr said while leaning on the rudder. The ship picked up speed toward the rocky beach. "The sea here is tricky and can at any moment swallow a ship. Just ask your General Caesar. When he tried to land his ships on this coast many were consumed by the cold waters."

Thadius gazed at the looming cliffs. Seagulls flew into the air, circling and diving at the boat. Several huts were visible along the beach as was the road that led into the forest just beyond.

"You'll find the garrison and your fried up that road," Eilifr said.

A wooden tower constructed along a bluff rose three stories in the air. Several carpenters worked securing timbers and planks forming a skeletal framework. Along the shore small fishing boats were beached, and larger ships sat at anchor.

"Looks like the hand of god scooped out a section of the coast," Thadius said.

Eilifr looked at him. "Perhaps he did."

The odor of roasting meats and baking breads became strong. "Rack oars," shouted Eilifr as the boat was lifted by a wave and taken to shore.

Several of Eilifr's men jumped out and secured the ship to some mooring posts as the rest of the crew climbed over the side. Some men along the shore watched with subdued interest then went back to their tasks. Shacks near the shoreline puffed smoke from roof holes, filling the air with smells of burnt oak, while sounds of merriment echoed from all around. Thadius felt strangely at ease.

Dominus walked up and placed his hand on Thadius' shoulder. "We've arrived says I."

"Let's lend a hand," Thadius said.

Dominus and Thadius assisted in the removal of all the goods from the ship, bringing them up above the high water mark. "Rolf," Eilifr called. "Find the merchant Borras and tell him to bring several carts." Rolf nodded then dashed off along the road leading from the shore into the forest.

Eilifr sat down on a crate and scratched his head with both hands. Shaking his blond hair, he yawned widely. "It will be a short time. The merchant lives near the garrison." A moment passed and several men emerged from one of the shacks and came forward, looking at the goods on the beach. "What have we here?"

"Stay your hands, my good fellows," Eilifr warned. "These belong to Borras and his kin." The men from the shack nodded and went back to work. From the forest, men with carts came down the road and Eilifr raised his hand in greeting. "Borras and Grendal!"

"I hope the salt is not wet," Borras said.

"And the cloth is not stained," Grendal shouted after him.

"Tis all well and fine," Eilifr stated and smiled. "Have I ever not delivered quality items and on time?"

Borras and Grendal stopped their carts by the supplies and began to load the crates, boxes, barrels and amphora.

"It'll take us some ten trips, me thinks," Borras said while fingering his dagger at his belt. "I'll see if my cousin can bring his two carts to speed things up."

Eilifr looked unconcerned. "If it will speed things up then do it." Turning he addressed his men. "You stay with the goods." To Borras and Grendal he said, "I'll see you two at the tavern."

"And to some good drink and meat you shall be treated," Grendal added.

Dominus looked at the sky. "A storm comes."

"The cold will bite you like a wolf," Eilifr chuckled. "Bundle yourself for we have a bit of walking to do before we get to Gnaeus."

*   *   *

Thadius watched as the raindrops beaded up on the road and rolled to the side filling the small cement aquifer that paralleled the highway.

"The road is paved well," Dominus said.

"A legion's handiwork," Thadius replied.

Buildings loomed out of the forest along the road. From time to time a face could be seen looking out a window, or they found themselves greeted by a dweller in his yard. People periodically came down the road with carts and goods. Breathing in deeply, Thadius smelled the wet rich soil on either side of the road. They walked into a wide opening where merchants, families, and soldiers alike formed a wide market. Further up the road they came to the walls of a town. The people eyed them, but were not rude.

"This place is a bustling point of commerce," Thadius said.

Dominus nodded. "Coin surely changes hands here, but it's a long way from Roman civility."

Another hundred yards and the men came to the town gate. Several Roman soldiers were standing out in front— one resting his arm on a wooden plaque that read *Legio Septima Claudia Pia Fidelis* just above a carved bull and a lion.

Dominus leaned over to Thadius. "I thought that legion was in Africa."

Thadius shrugged.

Two of the guards leaned against a stone wall under the protection of an awning. Clearly bored, the men watched as Eilifr, Thadius, and Dominus approached.

Pax Romanus," Dominus said.

A dark haired soldier with the helmet of a Prefect came around the corner. "Get to your posts, you dogs!" The two soldiers rushed to either side of the road.

The fair-haired soldier stood like a proper sentinel, his pilum at his right side and his scuta on his left. The other much older legionary stood with his shoulders lower, feet wide, and his scuta resting on the ground. His pilum sat at an angle to his body, and he studied Thadius, Dominus and Eilifr with some suspicion.

The Prefect stepped forward and brushed his dark hair from his face. "You," he said scowling. "What business do you have here?"

"I'm a citizen of Rome and have come to see a friend," Thadius stated.

"The question is to you two as well," the Prefect motioned at Dominus.

Dominus smiled. "I'm a citizen of Rome too."

Folding his arms, Eilifr stood at the front with his feet placed widely and his gaze cast downward at the man.

"You know me, little Roman… I am no citizen of Rome but a friend of Rome, and a friend of Gnaeus delivering these two men to him by his order."

The Prefect looked the party up and down, then spit into the trees that lined the road. Clearing his throat, he scowled. "We'll see about that. Runner!"

A young man age nineteen or twenty rushed up and came to a grinding halt, his sandals barely staying on his feet. "Sir?"

"Find Lord Gnaeus and see if…" He directed his attention back to Eilifr and barked, "Your name?"

Eilifr rolled his eyes. "Eilifr," he calmly said. "You know who I am, Prefect Culdarius."

The Prefect's face relaxed. He turned to the runner, "Tell the Legatus Legionis that Eilifr is here with two men."

"Yes, sir!" the soldier shouted. He turned and dashed through the arched gateway.

"Sit if you like," the Prefect said pointing at some wooden benches set up on either side of the pathway.

"Have you had need to use your weapons of late?" Thadius said.

"No," the youngest guard responded, relaxing a bit. "Since old Cassivellaunus retreated back across the river north of here, we've had no troubles."

"Shut your mouth," the Prefect ordered. "How do you know these men are who they claim to be?"

"Yes, sir," the young man answered.

"It's okay, Fabilius," the other guard said. "The boy is speaking to none other than Tiberius Thadius, former Legetus Ligionis and fellow soldier."

"Do I know you?" Thadius examined the man.

"Yes, sir. We met in Germania Superior many a year ago. The Helvetii had forsaken the reasonable taxation of Rome and chose to blast their war-horn." He took out his canteen and opened it, took a drink and handed it to Thadius. "You rode a brown horse and had the emblem of the house of Moras on your helmet. I grew up near the villa of Moras and told you so. You and I talked of Rome and women and drank some local wine late into the night."

Thadius smiled. "Sadly, in my older age, I do not remember such a day. But I am glad I made an impression on you."

"Moras Tiberius Thadius?" the Prefect said surprised.

Flying around the corner, the young runner skidded to a halt. "Sir, the Legatus Legionis is coming."

"Very well, keep to your posts," stated the Prefect.

The young guard directed his question to Dominus. "What news from Rome?"

"We have lived outside of the city for some twenty years now. The only information I have is snippets of gossip and traveler's opinions."

The young soldier shrugged his shoulders. "Just as well, I suppose. Who cares what's going on there anyway?"

"Who cares?" a jovial voice came from beyond the stone archway. "We all should care what is happing in our beloved Rome?"

Seeing the young man stiffen, Dominus realized Gnaeus approached. He emerged from the archway in a horse-drawn chariot attended by a contubernium of guards and several servants. He looked as if he was in a triumphal precession. Stopping just inside the garrison wall, he climbed out and approached.

"I have been counting down the days, awaiting either your letter or your person." He laughed heartily. "And now, in person you come. You are more welcome than Mars at Troy."

Standing just over five and a half feet tall, he didn't look like a powerful man. His hair was nearly gone save for a wreath of gray hovering just above his large ears. His face was narrow with a beak-like nose, and his slate blue eyes were the only inspiring feature. He licked his lips once as he got down from the chariot.

"Eilifr, you have done very well indeed," he said, happily patting the man on the arm. He turned to Thadius. "You have not aged a day, my friend."

"Nor have you, I see," Thadius said.

"Yes, yes the platitudes are laid and it is time for refreshments and talk. Much drink and food we shall have this night. I'll call for an orgy this evening after you have rested. Now, who is this fellow?" He bowed to Dominus.

"This is Peresius Albas Dominus. He and I met after The Third defeated the Helvetii in Germania. We live in the same town now."

"Is there more here than I see? I thought you preferred women, Thadius?"

"No love here, save for that of a brother-in-arms," Thadius added.

"And, I have heard tell that the sheep near the Villa of Thadius sleep with one eye open," Dominus added with a laugh.

"Well met indeed, my new friend." Gnaeus straightened his leather tunic. "Now, you must all come and enjoy my hospitality." He turned and led the way into the garrison.

CHAPTER 15

"The new garrison will be built on the hill," Gnaeus said while walking along a cobblestone road leading past a small wooden building. "That over there is the bath, gymnasium, and a field for games is behind it." He pointed toward a stone building. "That's our temple to Jupiter and next to it is the temple to Mars."

"How long have you been here?" Thadius asked.

"Since Caesar left two years ago. We have been virtually on our own."

"The trading must be good, though," Thadius observed.

"'Tis so, but not Roman good." Gnaeus laughed. "Yet I have made the best of it to date. Now come and enter my home."

Walking up the steps to the main entry, Thadius admired the thick oak frame. Gnaeus opened the door and went inside. Smoke filtered out into the portico, and braziers appeared along the stone entryway just inside the portal. He could see wall sconces holding oil lamps lining the walls making the room bright.

"You live in grand style," Thadius said.

"Yes, as the unofficial regent here I'm blessed with good fortune." Gnaeus stopped and appeared embarrassed by his candor. "Forgive me, my friend, I've been here long and have no right to boast so freely. Where are my manners?"

"It's quite all right," Thadius said.

"Good, I'm glad you are so forgiving. Let's have some drinks and good food and rejoice, for you've arrived!" Gnaeus motioned for two servants to attend him. "Bring wine and meat, and prepare for a feast in the triclinium."

Entering an aula, Gnaeus paused and pointed at the glass windows. "See, even in the wilderness we are not without our modern conveniences."

"Lovely," Dominus said.

"If it was a bright day you could see my paristylum through these windows. It's filled with some nice plants and several fountains. Come," he said motioning for Thadius and company to follow. "Refreshments have been set out in the triclinium."

Moving into the dining room, the men marveled at the wonderful artwork on the walls. The room was well lit and several tables were laden with bread, cheese, and fish, as well as pitchers of wine and beer. "Please, my friends, help yourselves," Gnaeus said. "When you are ready, take a tour of our bath. I think you'll find it pleasant. Then we'll have dinner."

*   *   *

Thadius stared at the meat filled pastry sitting on a platter in front of him. He'd eaten his fill, and then some. Now, with his belly stretched tightly filled with wine, beer, and food, he loosened his belt and lay back. "The bath was delightful, and the opulence took my breath away," he said.

"Yes, I think that my bones finally warmed," Dominus added. "I feel almost human."

Gnaeus nodded his head. "It is an amazing bit of construction." He sat up and finished drinking a glass of wine. "If you like we can go relax on the portico and take in the cool night air."

They moved outside. Thadius watched as some soldiers lighted the hanging lanterns around Gnaeus' home. Drinking the rich red wine from his copper goblet, he thought of his own garden.

"Dreaming of some soft woman?" Gnaeus asked.

"No, just home."

"That is a sentiment I often have myself. For no matter how many amenities I have here, I still long for those streets and smells."

"The wine is very good," Dominus noted.

"Ah," Gnaeus exclaimed with a grin, "I have it brought over from the mainland. Quite fine wine they make there. Our wine making capacity here has not been without its trials."

"Grapes don't grow here?" Thadius asked.

"No, the problem is not the grapes. They grow well. Seems there are some malcontents who feel that the vineyards will only entice us Romans to come and stay. Those malicious brigands tear up the vineyards, burn barns, smash wine presses and typically make a nuisance."

"Not able to track them down?"

"Well, I must weigh commerce, rule, and diplomacy in one hand and anger, retribution, and vengeance in the other." Gnaeus smiled warmly. "Tis no small matter I assure you, especially here without reinforcements."

"I noticed you left out justice," Thadius commented with a wry smile.

"Yes, I seem to have forgotten that one. Maybe I've been too long here in the wild with barbarians and their brand of justice. As you know, the local chiefs have the authority to mete out local punishments, and to tell the truth I have never needed to dispense or administer Roman punishment or even hold court here. The locals take care of most of it for me."

"This land, while wild, seems like a paradise for an ambitious man hungry for wealth and recognition," Thadius said.

"Paradise? Perhaps to those who love the country? I would trade all this for an appointment in Rome any day. You see, Julius left us behind to keep a Roman root planted, but he seems to have forgotten about me – I mean us."

Thadius poured more wine from a pitcher into his cup. "He has been on a tear of late. The barbarians in Germania give fight to all things Roman, and there are those in the Senate who fear he will be asking for a position as Princep soon."

Gnaeus' eyes narrowed. "Really, to be First Citizen – like a king…"

"King?" Thadius said surprised. "Even the thought turns my blood to ice. No, I think his intent is to be a Consul such as Magnus."

"Pompeius?" Gnaeus took a drink. "That blowhard." Malice dripped from his lips. "I have written the Senate a hundred times since being stranded here, and the only letter was from he – to say obey Caesar and do Rome good service."

Silence followed, as the two men drank. Dominus stood up, adjusted his genitals, and walked to the doorway. "I'm off to use the privy," he declared and went into the house.

Thadius sat forward. "Now, what of this niece you wrote me of?"

"Yes, a lovely girl." Gnaeus pulled up a chair and sat with his back to the wall.

"You mentioned in your letter that you suspected she was murdered. Why?"

"I believe she was murdered by someone other than a local." Gnaeus poured some wine from the pitcher into Thadius' goblet. "When her body was found near the forest, the locals informed the king. He arrived with his men and then sent for me. I took ten men and arrived in midafternoon to a scene of torture and brutality."

"But you don't think it was a native?"

"Her hands and feet were tied to stakes between two buildings. The local noble said he had never seen anything like it in the area. She had clearly been tortured. Her belongings here in the fort were ransacked as if someone was looking for something. My experience is that Druids may torture a criminal, but they don't go to their house and rob them."

Sitting forward in his chair, Gnaeus cradled his cup. He stared down at the floor, pensive. "Further, the torture marks seemed strange to me," he added.

"How?" Thadius swirling his wine.

"Several things bothered me about them. One, they were deliberate, done by someone who knows how to interrogate. Second, I read a report by Caesar about the cult of Druids and it detailed some of the rituals. These rituals were not performed on the victim. And there was the obvious violation of her quarters here on the post. They don't rob and they only torture those who have committed some severe violation of their laws. The girl committed no such violation, and they knew she was protected by Rome."

"Was there anything taken from her room?" Thadius looked curious.

"How should I know," Gnaeus asked.

"How did the Druids become implicated?"

"I was in the midst of the investigation when I was overruled by a guest of mine."

"Who?" Thadius pressed.

I am loath to speak of it, but suffice to say he held authority to take over the investigation and draw up official documents stating that Druids were the cause."

"But you believe different?"

"Yes. I am sure this was no act of Druids, nor any other local barbarian."

"Why such an elaborate murder?"

"One of the locals commented to me that prior to the girl being killed he saw her with a foreigner, a man who looked like a Roman."

"This man from Rome of whom you speak?"

"No… his son," Gnaeus said.

"Strange. Why would a fellow Roman kill your niece? Family intrigue maybe?"

"Come with me," Gnaeus said fetching a lantern from a nearby table. He marched into the villa and down a hallway. Opening a heavy wooden door, he led the way down a set of stone steps. At the bottom, Thadius saw a workroom with sawhorses, woodworking tools, and craftsman equipment strewn about. Hanging the lantern from a hook in the ceiling, Gnaeus moved towards a set of cabinets where he retrieved some documents and loose papyrus scrolls. He passed them across the table to Thadius. Gnaeus sat down on a stool and lifted his cup in the air.

"To you, old friend. If anyone can get to the bottom of this, you can."

Taking the papers, Thadius began reviewing the information. Several drawings depicted a woman tied to stakes. Lines on the drawing showed where wounds were made. A jumble of notes written in Latin and Greek littered one of the scrolls. Accounts by witnesses with place names and descriptions were neatly written. A scale of value of each testimony was next to each witness, all scrawled in Gnaeus' own hand.

"Have there been any killings since?" Thadius said.

"Not Roman. Not of this nature," Gnaeus stated. "All my letters to the Senate have gone unanswered in recent months. Do you know any news of what is going on in the capital?"

"Not really. I've heard that the plebes grow restless with the Senate over grain shipments and issues of foul water in the Tiber."

"Sounds to me as if there is need of a dictator to calm things," Gnaeus said. Tipping his cup, he drank deeply and set it down on the table. "If I hear nothing from Rome, I will return next year." He picked up the pitcher. "More wine?"

Sliding his cup over for a refill, Thadius continued to look at the documents, reading the information carefully. "It seems to me with wounds as severe as you've marked here, there would have been pools of blood."

"There was not a drop on the ground where the girl was found," Gnaeus said. "But, it had rained the night before."

Thadius moved his finger down the page. "You noted here that there were no weapons found."

"Yes, the assailant probably took them with him."

"And this woman was your niece?"

"Well, really my wife's brother's daughter. They hoped that she would be a Vestal priestess, but she was not accepted, and her family was humiliated."

"Very few get in, as you well know," Thadius said.

"Yes, I do." Gnaeus looked down at his wine. "But nonetheless, they felt it necessary to send her away until the scandal passed. My wife wrote me and begged me to take her for a year. What is a husband to do?"

"So you obliged her?"

"Of course!" He looked at Thadius. "I'm in quite a situation. I fear that my wife's brother may think I had a hand in her death. Or, at the least, be responsible for not having her watched more carefully."

"What of the theft? What was taken?"

Gnaeus shook his head "I'm not sure. A strongbox containing some papers of her father's, I think. Why she was sent with them, I could not tell you."

"Why didn't you have her watched more carefully?"

Gnaeus looked uncomfortable. "Well, you see, she was a young woman, away from home. I let her have the latitude of doing as she pleased. Perhaps I am at fault," Gnaeus said sullenly. "She was truly a sweet and beautiful girl."

"Were you, how shall I say, lovers?"

"Thadius, you see me now. I am no young man."

"Sometimes girls are drawn to power over youth, my friend."

"I assure you that is not the case. But there was a young man who she did spend time with— the son of the man who wrote the official report."

Taking a drink of his wine ,Thadius set down the papers on the table. "Tell me of this young man."

"He was traveling from Rome with his mother and father, Flavius Malco Scapula. You must remember the senator who took your place. It was his son I refer to."

Thadius felt troubled. Even though he never met Flavius Scapula, he did hear about him and his son. Looking up, he noted a look of concern in Gnaeus' face.

"What is it?" Gnaeus' eyes narrowed.

"It is said Flavius Malco Scapula is a wise man, but he has been troubled by his son's health."

"Health?"

"Yes, he suffers from some madness. It was a scandal just a few years ago when Publius stood in the Forum screaming, and then assaulted a woman friendly to Pompey the Great."

"What are you thinking?"

"If he was here, he is the most likely suspect," Thadius said. "But there is not enough evidence to prove it thus far."

"I have waited to inform my wife's brother until we have this resolved. I need to know who did this dreadful thing."

"A wise decision. We don't want to be rash," Thadius said. "I'll want to take a look at the place where she was found."

"Of course. How's first thing in the morning?" Gnaeus poured more wine.

"Fine. What of my traveling companion, Dominus?"

Gnaeus sat back in his chair and smiled broadly. "Do you think me as remiss as to forget my hospitality?" He chuckled. "I have seen to his comfort and yours already. Your room is on the first floor nearest the furnace. Soon Demeter will be returning to the underworld, and the cold will be upon us. You shall be comfortable enough with a warmed floor and walls about you."

"All the comforts of home," Thadius said.

"All the comforts of *Rome*," Gnaeus corected.

CHAPTER 16

Thadius rose in the morning with a slight headache. The terracotta floor tiles warmed his feet as he stood. Putting on his robe and slippers he moved to a wooden table that held an earthen washbasin and washed the sleep from his eyes.

He removed his wool cloak, breaches, and a brown tunic from the armoire. A knock at the door aroused his attention as he was tying up his boots. From under the door a strip of parchment appeared. Picking it up he examined the sloppy Latin scrawled in ink—

I want you, Thadius. Your member is like a great bear's, so I've heard.

Opening the door, he burst forth with a laugh as Dominus' face greeted him. Thrusting a cup of tea and a biscuit into his hand Dominus chuckled. "You know it took me most of the night to come up with that note."

"Clever," Thadius said.

"Drink, my friend. It's willow bark, and the biscuit is picenian. Rather tasty if I say so myself."

"Did you take a surrogate wife last night?"

"A man would be a fool to refuse a woman when she is offered," Dominus said. "So how's the investigation going?"

"We need to ride out to where the body was discovered."

"Will we be back in time for the midday meal?"

"We may. The location is some miles away though."

"Good, because the cook is going to prepare roast boar, egg pie, and sweet potatoes," Dominus said excitedly. "I sure would hate to miss that."

"You've eaten enough recently to fill three feasts," Thadius said. "But we'll try and be back for the meal."

"You're a wise man, Thadius." Dominus grinned.

Thadius nodded. "We've come in search of a murder in the wilderness. We're not wise men."

Loading two saddlebags with some flatbread and cheese from the storehouse, Dominus secured them to their horses. He produced two large wineskins, and filled them from an amphora, then tied them to the horses as well. Thadius approached, all the while he was staring at an unrolled parchment in his hands.

"Concerning that poor girl?" Dominus asked.

"Yes."

"Was she pretty?"

"Do you ever think of anything other than drink, food, and women?" Thadius said.

"There's something else to think of?"

Thadius turned the parchment so Dominus could see the drawing. "A map from Gnaeus. It'll take a few hours to get there. We get two soldiers as escort."

"Do we need them?" Dominus looked worried.

"I hope not, but we are in wilderness, so best to be careful."

"Careful it is then." Dominus took his dagger and secured it to his belt. "Let's be off then."

Thadius motioned forward with his hand. "We'll pick up our escort at the gate."

The gate guard looked up and signaled for them to wait as two Calvary soldiers mounted and made ready.

Dominus took a drink from his wine skin. "We're ready when you are."

"Yes, let's be on our way," Thadius said with a wave of his hand.

One of the cavalrymen took the lead. Casually, he looked back. "I know the way to where you want to go. Our Legatus has commanded me to take you there. Follow me, and do as I say. Remember you're in the land of barbarians, and we have a tenuous foot hold on this island. Try not to irritate the locals." The second cavalryman took up the flank.

"I take it you are the cornicularius?" Thadius said to the lead horseman.

He again looked back. "I am. My name is Fabilius, and I've served five campaigns thus far. The Legatus asked me to take personal care with his two friends."

Thadius took out a piece of dried meat and tore some off. "How far to our destination?"

"About two hours," Fabilius stated. "We'll be pushing north, then west. We'll see some forest, some bogs, and much grazing land."

They rode for some time. The sky cleared and sunlight poked through the tree tops. The road was straight, as if a giant had taken a blade and cut the trees from the land. Paving stones were fresh, laid recently. Thadius observed the many birds and small animals scurrying about.

"By Jupiter, look at that hare!" Dominus said. "So fat that his legs barely touch the ground, yet so fast." The creature darted into the road with one bound, and into the woods with the second.

"Red deer and brown bear dwell in these woods as well," Fabilius said.

The rear guard spoke, "And the gray wolves, they ply these woods with purpose. I'm called Claudius, by the way," he said.

Through the thick green woods they pressed on. The paved road and forest stopped, and the clack of the shod hooves began thumping into the raw dirt. The four men emerged onto wide grasslands. Sheep and cows could be seen roaming in the distance. Coming down the road a man dressed in common Celtic garb led a pony pulling a cart. A heavy wool tunic hung down to his knees, covering breaches made from hemp or wool. On his feet he wore leather boots each tied with a leather strap. A thick black beard hung down to his chest and it looked as if it had never been combed. The pony whinnied and shook his head.

The man raised his hand in greeting. "Greetings and hail to you, Romans," he said with a smile.

Fabilius halted his horse and smiled warmly at the fellow. "Greetings, Corivellius, and how fares your farm?"

"Doing quite well, master Fabilius," Corivellius said. "Perhaps at the end of the week I'll pay you a visit and trade you two cows for some boars and eggs?"

"I shall be there. Come and we'll drink ale, and you and your family will dine with mine."

"Then it will be as you have offered," Corivellius said while moving on down the road with his cart. "Until we meet again," he shouted over his shoulder.

"A noble?" said Thadius.

"He's a local herdsman and farmer. He leads a small clan in these parts," Fabilius replied..

They rode for another hour. The landscape began to change from pastures to farms. After some time the road twisted up and over a hill into a wide valley. A small village with white plumes of smoke rising from rooftops greeted them. They moved along the road through the town until they came to a stone bridge at the far side.

Fabilius signaled a halt and dismounted. "The bridge is a bit rickety." He walked his horse across it, stepping with great care. Turning back, he smiled. "Stay to the left." He waited for the others to cross then removed his wine skin from his saddlebag. He took several long drafts then looked up at Thadius as he approached. The rain began to fall about them. "We'll rest here for a few minutes. Our journey is almost at an end. Up ahead is the town and fortress of Venta Icenorum"

"Have the Iceni given you much trouble?" Dominus asked as he stepped down from his horse and relieved himself by the bridge.

"Not a bit." Fabilius tossed the wine skin to his partner. "Take a drink, Claudius. It was brewed by our friends in Palenorum."

Claudius hoisted the container to his lips. "What a sweet treat, what is it called?"

"Honey wine. The locals call it mead." Fabilius looked at Thadius. "In Rome it would cost a sestertius, but here it's cheap. They don't know yet what it is worth. We'll sell many an amphora in Itium when the next ship sails." He turned back to Claudius. "I'll make you rich, Claudius, along with me of course."

Smiling, Thadius remembered his own gathering of wealth. The wealth came easy, a favor here, a good suggestion there. Men of power love wealth, and with a legion securing lands and trade routes, it came easy.

"Shall we continue?" Fabilius said as he climbed back into the saddle.

They rode on past several farms then passed through a grove of oaks. In the trees ravens chawed and chattered at one another. The sun sliced through the leaves making broken shadows on the road. In the distance the sounds of metal being worked echoed. Voices could be heard in the air and the faint hint of smoke became stronger.

Thadius shifted in his saddle. "It's been sometime since we did any equestrian activities."

Dominus, laughed and steered his horse next to Thadius, "It has been sometime since we did anything but go to the bath and drink in the tavern."

Fabilius looked back. "Thadius?" he said. "Are you the same Thadius that repaired the aqueduct Apia?"

"I raised the funds and engineered the repairs," Thadius said. "But, that was very late in my career."

"Was it hard politicking after so many years in the legion?" Fabilius glanced back.

"It seemed the natural progression," Thadius said.

Fabilius nodded. He turned back to the road. "When we arrived on this accursed Celtic island, there was a man named Mandu Barcius who was experienced dealing with Rome. He was a nobleman of the local king Prasutogus, and was instrumental in brokering peace between Caesar and the king."

"Any daughters?" Dominus asked. "And do they have wine?"

"Both," Fabilius replied. "Prasutogus also has a son named Prasutagus, along with a daughter Milliantua, and a wife Vellacoria. They're the royal family in charge of this principality of the Iceni and are recognized by Rome. The king is eager to meet you both. He loves Roman company."

"I thought we would be going straight to the place where the girl was killed?" Thadius said.

"Protocol, master Thadius. Our existence here is tenuous at best. If it wasn't for the influence of Mandu Barcius we'd probably be back in Itius Portus with our tail tucked."

"Why does he support Rome?" Dominus fished out some dried meat from his saddlebag.

"He likes Roman style," Fabilius said. "And let's face it, Roman style is one great style!"

"And it helps that we keep his coffers full with trade," Claudius added, while he came up alongside Thadius. "His towns are prosperous because we allow his goods in and out of port without taxation. That's why that port back there is crammed with ships most of the time."

"Is the port the original landing site?" Thadius asked.

Fabilius guffawed. "We originally landed at a beach the natives call Deal. Nasty place really. Shortly after Caesar took the other legions back to the mainland, Gnaeus talked with a local tribal chief and we moved to Dubris. A move for the better I might add."

Pulling up on his reins, Fabilius halted his horse and turned to face the others. "Gnaeus has built a strong following here, and if Caesar ever returns he'll have quite a lot of support." Turning again he pointed towards a wide pastureland dominated by a large hill. "Support of this king and his allies." Thadius could see a set of tall earth and timber walls crowned with a palisade. Rising above the walls, multiple two and three story wooden structures could be seen. Towers were placed every two hundred feet, and armed men could be seen on top of the battlements.

"The village is beyond the fortification on the lee side," Claudius said. "Well defended if other barbarians attack – not so good if Romans lay siege. We like them to think they're safe from us though."

"Come along and we'll check in with the king's guardsmen," Fabilius said.

Dominus looked at him. "Perhaps you could suggest paving this road?"

"Here come some riders." Thadius pointed toward the hill fort and ten men on horseback.

The Cavalrymen exited the huge wooden gates, crossed a bridge over a mote, and came to meet them. The lead rider raised his hand halting his soldiers near a modest stone and timber hut.

Fabilius advanced, calling back over his shoulder, "Wait for me to return. They can be a little touchy when it comes to strangers."

Fabilius approached the lead rider. Words were exchanged, and both men laughed with an easiness reserved for friends. Even over the sound of the gentle wind, Thadius heard the guttural tones of the barbarian language filling the air. After several minutes the conversation broke up, and Fabilius returned from the parley.

Fabilius smiled broadly as he rode up. "The king wishes for us to stay the night and partake of his hospitality. We can't refuse."

"When will we go to where the girl was killed?" Thadius asked.

"Now. We'll follow the soldiers to the place where the girl's body was found. Then to the hill-fort for a feast."

They rode up to the soldiers, and then followed them as they moved down the dirt road. Claudius came up alongside them. "Doesn't that just call back the kings?" he asked. "And I was hoping to have supper with my wife... Oh well, no one ever said being a soldier was like a week at the bath."

Laughing loudly, Thadius patted the young man on the shoulder. "You're very right in saying that. Being a soldier is no easy task."

Dominus shook his head. "Call back the kings. I remember when that slang was invented."

"You do not," Thadius chided. "My father used it long before you or I were even a hungry lust in our patris eyes."

Laughing, Dominus waved his hand in the air. "So you say, dear Thadius, so you say. I hope this barbarian king will supply a feast as good as the one we will be missing back at the garrison."

Following the road past the stronghold, they came to a fork. Taking the right path they followed it to the tree line and into the forest. The barbarians chatted contentedly among themselves, and Thadius relaxed a bit.

"I wonder why the large escort."

Leaning in the saddle, Dominus shrugged. "A show of power most likely. Or maybe we're heading for a part of his kingdom that isn't that friendly. Either way, it seems we're coming to a village."

Emerging from the dark green brambles and thick oaks, Thadius saw a village. Few paid much notice to them as they passed. Thadius wondered if it was common for the king's soldiers to lead Romans around.

They traveled on for a short while, then the soldiers stopped and pointed in the direction of several buildings near a hedgerow. "Between those buildings," Fabilius said.

Dominus shivered suddenly as he stared at the structures. "I have a bad feeling regarding this."

"As do I, but we've come this far."

"It's not the distance that compels me," Dominus said. Kicking his heels into his horse's sides, he rode ahead. Coming around the corner of the first building, Dominus halted and dismounted. Turning he saw Thadius do the same.

Thadius paced off the distance from the two buildings and called out to Dominus, "Thirty paces between."

"Should I be writing this down?" Dominus asked.

"Perhaps I should have told you that was the plan."

Dominus retrieved a stylus and wax-pad from his saddlebag and recorded the information. "Thirty paces?" he called back to Thadius.

"Yes." Thadius unrolled a parchment and studied it carefully.

"There," he said walking to a spot and kneeling. "Bring me a stick or something to trace in the ground with." Dominus came over with a long stick and handed it to Thadius.

"Her head was approximately here," Thadius stated. "Her wrists were about here, and her ankles tied to stakes here and there."

"We're out of sight of the road and quite far from the town too," Dominus observed.

"Yes – not too opportunistic a place to kill, wouldn't you say? Anyone could come along the road, or come to these storehouses. They would surely hear the scream of a woman." Thadius looked toward the forest.

Dominus followed his gaze. "What do think?"

"Look at this parchment that Gnaeus gave me." He showed it to Dominus. "He's listed all the cuts, the body, and even the color of her hair."

"So?"

"But what's missing?"

Dominus looked at the ground then the document. "No blood is listed."

"Bravo my friend – you amaze me at times." Thadius walked toward the forest. "Our killer brought her from somewhere, and what better place to perform a killing than the solitude of the forest?" He stopped and looked back. "Are you coming?"

Dominus shrugged and followed.

"The wounds on the girl were too precise to be done by a man possessed by whim," Thadius continued. "So, how would you account for this?" He handed Dominus the parchment.

Dominus looked it over again. "Like a surgeon," he added. "A man...or woman... with no worry of time or interruption."

"Very good. Now remember back to your days in the legion – how did we determine an enemy recently reconnoitered our camp?"

Dominus stopped at the forest fence and examined the foliage and ground. "Broken branches and trampled saplings of course."

"And, what do you see here?"

Several small saplings were crooked on the ground, and ferns were smaller, as if crushed and torn by movement.

"Something was dragged through here," Dominus observed. "The forest does not lie."

"I am impressed." Thadius smiled as he entered the woods.

They pressed on through the dark green foliage. Every few minutes a hare or raven would flee, startled by the two men. Thadius emerged into a clearing where a single tree was surrounded by brush and ferns.

"Here we are," he said.

"She was killed here?"

"I'll bet you a hundred sesterces on it." He moved to the tree. "Here—" he held up a leather strap. "—it has blood on it."

Dominus walked around the tree and knelt down. "I've found several rags with old blood on them."

Thadius examined the rags, and then the ground around the tree. "He knelt and laid out something here... " He pointed to a spot where the sod was dented and the plants stunted. "Our man is careful, and cunning."

"How do you know it was a man?" Dominus asked.

"A feeling."

"Look at this," Dominus said holding up a rusted metal instrument.

"A scalpel? He's in possession of a surgeon's case. That's why he cleared this area here, to lay out his instruments. Not only is our man methodical, but he is knowledgeable too."

"And rich," Dominus added. "Medical tools are not cheap."

"I fear all the clues point to one man thus far."

"Who?"

"Publius," Thadius said.

Dominus blinked. "I don't know who that is."

"A Roman family visited the garrison around the time of the murder, and the son of that family had an interest in our victim."

"What family, and what interest?"

Thadius cleared his throat. "A senator's son interested in a lovely girl."

"If you don't mind me asking, what senator are you speaking of?"

"Didn't I tell you?"

"You seem to be trying not to tell me."

"Flavius Malco Scapula."

"Scapula?" Dominus scowled. "He's a fixture of culture Romanus; a paragon of how to be a proper Roman."

"His son has a reputation also," Thadius stated as they slowly walked back towards the soldiers. "It is said in Rome that he is a brute to the house slaves and cruel to all living things. They say he suffers headaches and hears voices. His father insists that the boy speaks to the gods. But his actions are not divine, but of disharmony and conflict."

Thadius stopped. Dominus stopped as well and glanced up to see Fabilius and Claudius waiting for them.

"Shall we go to the king's fort?" Fabilius asked. "The king has set out a feast of spectacular proportions."

Dominus' eyes widened. "Spectacular proportions? We mustn't be rude," he said as he mounted his horse. "After all, the man's taken the time to honor Rome, we Romans should partake."

Fabilius steered his horse around to the road. "Then let's get out of this wet, cold weather, and enjoy the man's hospitality."

The king's guardsmen led the way up the road. In the distance a cow mooed, as a flock of geese took to the air. They approached the walled fortress by way of the bridge over the moat. The dirty water appeared stagnant. A guard on top of the wall shouted down and the main gate came open. Thadius entered a long hall made of stone that led to the inner courtyard. Men dressed in brown leather and gray tunics strolled about, some carrying arms, and others doing domestic chores. Two youths stood at a chopping block, one hefting a large iron axe, and the other picking up firewood.

Taking in a deep breath, Thadius recognized the acrid odor of urine and manure. They rounded a curve in the road, and a stable came into view. Wooden buildings seemed constructed randomly, and people came and went going about the day's business. A little further on was an imposing structure built of massive timbers. Two large doors were open. On either side were guards carrying pole-arms. Thadius pulled up to the double doors and dismounted along with the others. Handing their reins to some young boys, they turned their attention to the stairs leading to the doors.

Thadius rubbed his lower back. "I had forgotten the feeling of a long ride. I guess I'm no young pup anymore," he said to Dominus.

"You're not young for any animal," Dominus quipped.

"Remind me to give you a mirror for your birthday,".

Fabilius came up next to Thadius. "Follow the captain of the guard to the main hall. I'll be along shortly. Claudius will accompany you and translate when you need it." He turned and walked with one of the horsemen toward a set of shacks.

Claudius pushed on the double doors and they swung inward. A darkness met Thadius as he stepped from the dim light of the overcast day into the king's domicile. They walked a few dozen feet down a corridor that emerged into a wide hall. Smoke surrounded him as his eyes adjusted to the light. In the middle of the hall a circle of stones lay around a blazing fire. The smoke exited through a hole neatly fixed in the center of the roof. Thadius could see many wooden chairs ringing the fire pit. Freestanding sconces littered the stone paved floor providing a warm glow of yellow light. He could see manlike shapes looking at him from the shadows. A man sitting in a wooden chair opposite the fire looked over at them.

Leaning over, Claudius whispered. "That man is the king. We must be announced before we can approach him. Then we can be seated – that is, if we are asked to."

One of the guardsmen approached the king, words echoed in the hall and the guard returned to the group. Speaking in the barbarian tongue to Claudius, the man turned and leaned against a stout-looking wooden beam, pulled out a knife, and began cleaning under his nails.

"The king says we are invited to sit and stay the night. A feast in honor of the king and the honor of Rome will be set out tonight.

Thadius was amazed at the size of the fire. Large tree trunks lay crossed in the middle of the pit and the hungry flames licked and lapped at its bark. It was more than sufficient to warm the inner hall, and Thadius found being close to it uncomfortable.

"Terribly inefficient," he said quietly to Dominus. "Our Roman furnaces are much better."

Motioning for Thadius to take a seat, the king raised a large horn to his lips. Quaffing down the contents he drank deeply for a few seconds then wiped his mouth with his sleeve. Speaking in his rough Celtic language the king imparted the grisly story of how his guards found the girl. Claudius translated.

"There had been no rain, and the spring flowers were in bloom all along the hillsides. The guards were summoned when two boys had gone to the peasant stores and found the girl tied up on the grass. Those boys said they saw a man standing over the body. As they approached, they said the man rushed off into the forest."

"A man? Did they tell you what he looked like?" Thadius asked, and Claudius translated

The king looked uncomfortable and replied. Claudius stated, "Yes, and he told Gnaeus."

Thadius unrolled the scroll. Scanning down, he noted there was no mention of a man next to the girl. "There was a man arrested and executed?"

Turning, Claudius spoke to the king. He turned back. "Yes, and the king had the man seized shortly after."

"*The* man or *a* man?" Thadius pressed.

Claudius swallowed hard and looked uncomfortable before turning and asking the king. "They apprehended a man fitting the boy's description," he said. "After torturing him he confessed, and he was hung that day. There's been no other killing of that type since."

"If I may ask, who was he?" Thadius asked.

Standing, the king moved away from the fire and motioned for them to follow.

Claudius spoke. "He was a tinker who roamed these parts. He wore short blond hair and a dark cloak. He also carried knives, and butchering blades. The guards found him drunk and asleep by his cart."

The king walked to a basket near a low burning wall-sconce and picked up a hand full of coal. Dropping the lumps into the sconce he watched the fire rise, driving back the dark shadows. He spoke again, like a man who had seen too much death. The king called out in his gruff language. From the shadows came a dozen servants carrying wooden trays filled with mutton, beef, deer, wild pig, and fowl. Again the king called out as more servants appeared carrying large pitchers of wine, native beer and cups to drink from.

A tall woman with blond hair approached Thadius with a cup and thrust it into his hand. She tipped a pitcher over the cup and filled the vessel to the top. Just as quickly she was gone.

From the shadows others came gathering around the king, hoisting their cups in the air. Shouts rose in the tongue of the Britons, as a lean fellow with short dark hair spoke. The hall fell silent, and the king looked on with a grim and pensive frown.

"This man is called Trumlutivius, a noble king himself from a kingdom to the southwest. He is an ally of Prasutogus," Claudius whispered. "Trumlutivius is praising Prasutogus for his great works in keeping the peace and having a prosperous kingdom."

Thrusting his cup in the air three times, Trumlutivius shouted something. The crowd also thrust their cups into the air chanting the strange guttural phrase. Thinking it prudent to do likewise, Thadius followed suit.

Prasutogus quieted the crowd, and then drank from his horn-cup.

From the back of the room, a man with a lyre burst forth with song, singing loudly as to overcome murmurs of the group. He wound his way to the king and sat in a chair opposite him. He sang with such melody that Thadius felt transfixed on every note.

"He is singing of the grandfather of Prasutogus who was a renowned chief here a hundred years ago. He founded this settlement and bound the people and the local gods to him with strength of will and battle." Claudius tore a piece of pork from the pig and bit it. "Now the bard is singing the praises of his Great Uncle Trumlutivius, who established a kingdom on the southwestern shores in a land known as Kurnvall. Now he says Prasutogus' kingdom will be remembered as greater than his grandfather's or Trumlutivius', and the gods are pleased."

"Now that was worth the trip," Dominus said, still transfixed on the bard, though he could not hear the man any longer.

"You've gone native," Thadius chuckled.

"What a splendid idea," Dominus said and nodded towards a beautiful woman standing near a passageway along one wall. The light of a sconce lamp made her red hair glisten in the gentle luminance.

Several large men came into the hall, a great twisted and gnarled log upon their shoulders. They tossed it in the fire..

"The king wants to know why you are so interested in the death of the girl they found," Claudius said.

The king was looking directly at him from only a few feet away. "Tell the king that the girl was the daughter of a powerful man in Rome, and it is at his behest that I have come."

Claudius held his face close to the ear of the king. The king's imposing gaze softened, and he nodded. Claudius came back to Thadius. "He says he understands."

Thadius jumped slightly when a hand landed on his shoulder. It was Dominus. "Thadius, old friend," he said over the roar of the fire and the boom of the surging crowd. "I've been invited to tour the garden, or so I think it's a garden." He thought for a moment. "Yes, I'm sure she meant garden. In any event, I'll be out for the eve and will meet you here in the morning."

Having said that, he turned and wove his way through the crowd towards the passageway where the red-haired woman waited.

"The king would like you to sit and meet with him in his private apartment," Claudius said. "Don't worry— I'll be translating for you."

Thadius nodded his head and waited. The king stood and turned to the crowd. Four servants rushed to the king. One picked up his chair, while another grabbed the wooden table that held the king's drinking horn. The third scooped up the sovereign's heavy cape tails and the last rushed ahead, parting the crowd. Quickly, the king and his servants made their way to a stone archway.

Thadius and Claudius followed behind. "Stay close," Claudius said.

"Like a tailored tunic," Thadius replied.

In the hallway, candles sat on brass wall sconces brightly lighting the way. A dark wooden door lay open at the end of the corridor. "Is that a scent of lavender?" Thadius asked.

"While the king is a barbarian, he enjoys some of the luxuries of Rome," Claudius replied.

Rugs lay strewn about, some from the lands of the east, and others made of local animal furs. On the walls ten foot tall tapestries hung, some finely crafted. A fireplace sat at one end, cut from a single piece of stone. Silk pillows, fine wooden tables, chairs, and a raised bed with feather mattresses, also decorated the room. A few oil lamps made to look like elephants stood on either side of the bed providing illumination in a vibrant orange hue.

The king motioned with his hands as if painting in the air and spoke. Claudius said, "The king wishes for you to know that he does not believe his people had anything to do with the girl's death. He punished the tinker for it but was only trying to please the Roman commander and keep this from growing into a concern."

The king spoke again and moved his hands about. Claudius seemed engrossed in the words. Looking gravely at Thadius, the king shook his head sadly.

"The king wishes to impart to you that he does not wish war with Rome over this girl. He is concerned that you might think him or his people responsible."

"Tell the king," Thadius began, "that I don't believe that he, or his people, are in any way responsible for her death. He may put his mind at ease and sleep well this night with no fear of Rome."

Claudius quickly translated. The king spoke again, and Claudius turned toward Thadius. "The king wishes for you to know that the night before the girl was found, one of his subjects came to him and told him they heard in the forest the cries of a woman, but could not make out the language or what she screamed," Claudius said.

The king folded his hands behind his back and stared into his fireplace. Again he spoke, a sullen sound in his voice. Claudius looked even graver as the man talked. "The king's subject thought it a goddess or wood spirit playing a trick on him and feared that there might be mischief about. By the time the man came to the king and told him the story, several days had passed. So he sent his son to investigate the place in the forest."

Thadius suddenly spoke, "And he found a place where blood coated the green-fern, and leather cords of a hunter were in a tree."

Claudius translated, and the king stopped for a moment. His eyes betrayed his shock.

"Yes, the ground was bloodied and leather straps hung from the fat branch of an old oak." Pausing for a moment, Claudius showed some signs of strain. "That poor girl," he said quietly. "To be butchered like game."

The king spoke again.

"What else did he say?" Thadius asked.

Regaining his composure, Claudius continued. "The king's son brought back a tattered woman's dress buried near the oak. The king was worried because he recognized the dress was not one his people would wear. So he knew some terrible fate had befallen one of the invaders."

"Had the king met the girl before?" Thadius asked softly.

Claudius translated the question, and the king stood in silence for quite some time.

"He says that the girl was beautiful, and his son took an interest in her," Claudius finally said. The king believed that a marriage between his kingdom and Rome would do well to secure an alliance. But before he could act, the girl was dead."

"Was there anyone else who the king saw or heard about? Perhaps a foreigner, a stranger to his lands and people?"

"The king says that only one family came to see him during that time. They were Roman. There were three in the family and some slaves."

"Did any stay or visit again?"

"The king says that they stayed the night. The son suffered some ailment – a problem with his head and back. A guard caught the boy speaking with a horse and reported it. The next day they left to tour the countryside."

Quiet settled over the room, and Thadius delved into deep thought. Turning to Claudius he said, "Tell the king we will get to the bottom of this tragedy."

"Thadius," Claudius said, "do you have any more questions?"

The king furrowed his brow and his dark hair was about his face. The king spoke low, so only Claudius could hear, then went to a shelf and took down a copper box. Opening it up, he pulled out a small delicate charm on a thin gold chain and handed it to Claudius.

Claudius walked to Thadius and held up the charm. "The king says it was found on the body. It was inserted in her..." He appeared unsettled with a look of disgust. "—uh, private area."

Examining it closely, Thadius could see it was a silver shaft with a sconce at the tip. "Curious," he said. "This seems a familiar image. May I take it?"

The king remained silent, and then nodded. A knock at the door came, and a beautiful young woman entered wearing a white dress. The king made a motion for Claudius and Thadius to leave.

Two burly guards standing in the hallway looked at the two men as they exited and locked the door behind them.

"What do you make of this?" Claudius asked.

"I've seen this before, the image I mean." Thadius looked deep in thought. "This adorned a Gaul hill fort that I've been too. Why would a charm be made of it?"

"Why would someone insert it in that girl's...?"

"I'm not sure. There is clearly something else afoot here."

The hall was lively and filled with the sounds of lutes and lyres, drums and bells. Thadius noted the massive ring of fire blazing, and the people moved far away from it because of the heat. The stone fire pit looked to Thadius as if the gateway to Tartarus laying wide open and waiting for sinners to fall within.

"If you don't mind sir, I'm going to partake of the food and libations before they are all spoiled?" Claudius said.

"By all means have at it." Thadius found a plate and a cup filled with wine.

For some time he watched rain fall through the hole in the roof. The fire hissed and spit, but the flames gobbled up the water. The hall emptied. His wine cup became heavy as his thoughts became soft and prone to sleep. Staring into his cup he thought of the red liquid that spilled from the girl and was lost to the forest floor. He looked up at the hole in the center of the roof. The rain was gone and so were the clouds. The moon came overhead and shone through.

"What god is that which peers through yon rooftop?" Thadius murmured to himself. He stood and wandered around the hall. Finding an empty leather-clad chair near a passageway he sat down. "Too much drink and food have taken their toll on this old soul."

Some revelers came back into the hall and began talking and drinking. The night blurred into a swirling mist of smoke and noise. Thadius felt a pain in his head from the native beer and wine, yet the soft and comfortable chair lulled him to slumber. The noises of the people faded as darkness overtook him. In his mind's eye he could see a girl dancing in a spring meadow.

She walked to him, stopped a few feet away, and took his hand. She smiled warmly and spoke in Greek. "Thy soul is pure, thy notions well met, in the darkness you sleep, in comfort you're set. Yet lost in your heart, is worrisome thoughts that gnaw at your reason like bristle scarred pots. Take this with you, when wake comes from sleep, mountains are beautiful, a maiden waits for you in the deep."

They danced in the meadow as the warm air caressed his face. She spun about him then began to fade as if made of smoke. "The holy maidens call me, to the snow I must flee, but keep yourself true, passing seasons you'll see. Then turn to the east, a fire burns bright, it will light your way backwards, in the still of the night." She vanished.

Leaping from his chair, Thadius realized he was still in the hall. The fire sent whiffs of white smoke toward the oculus above, illuminated now by the morning sunlight.

Rubbing the sleep from his eyes he heard over his shoulder the familiar voice of Dominus. "Sleep well old friend?"

"Not as well as you, it appears."

"Claudius is ready to go and asked me to find you. I saddled both our horses and refilled our skins."

"Then let's go," Thadius said. "I have much I want to discuss with Gnaeus."

CHAPTER 17

The ride back to the garrison was uneventful and Thadius spent most of the time deep in thought. Dominus maintained a conversation with Claudius and Fabilius about politics and women, while Thadius brooded. The sun blazed out into the open and began to warm the riders as the king's horsemen broke off their escort at the forest. Claudius, Fabilius, Dominus and Thadius rode into the woods.

Claudius halted his horse. "Just a quick stop before we're too deep into the woods." He jumped down and headed off behind some brushes.

Fabilius rested his hand on the hilt of his sword. "Make it quick; I have business to address upon our return."

Removing his cloak, Thadius laid it across his lap and opened the small leather pouch attached to his belt. He cradled the necklace in the palm of his hand, and the small charm reflected the bright sunlight.

"What do you make of this?" he said handing it to Dominus.

"A charm?...I didn't think you cared."

Thadius frowned. "A moment of seriousness is all I ask from you."

Dominus held it close and examined it. "The finish is remarkable. The intricate design on the shaft is amazing, like a succession of ocean waves leading to the sconce. Is it made of silver?"

"I'm not sure," Thadius said.

"It is no mere curio found in a courtyard market. A master artisan made this, and probably to order by someone with enough money for such a charm... and chain."

"Does that image remind you of anything, say forty years ago?" Thadius prodded.

"When we were in Gaul?" Dominus eyed it closely again. "It resembles the freeze that adorned the gatehouse at the Gaul hill fort in Tolosa."

"Why now? Why would we suddenly be reminded of that place here, of all places Britannia?"

"Coincidence?"

"Maybe..." Thadius fell silent. "If only we knew where Scapula was heading..."

Claudius returned from the bushes and climbed onto his horse. "That Senator that was visiting was a royal pain," he said over his shoulder.

"Shut up!" Fabilius chided. "Please forgive my friend... he's speaking out of turn."

Thadius nodded. "That's quite alright. Do you know where he and his family were off to?"

Claudius looked at Fabilius who motioned for him to speak. "He's traveled to the mainland. Going to Rome by way of Lutetia and over the Southern Alps."

"Lutetia? Why Lutetia?" Thadius mused.

"The boy told me that his father has an errand and they planned to travel south from Lutetia. I think they're off to Pisa from there." Claudius stated.

"We must make plans to travel to Lutetia as soon as possible." Thadius looked over at Dominus.

"What? Lutetia is a tiny town on an island. I've heard tell that there is not even a tavern there," Dominus said.

"Publius isn't going there for drinks, I suspect. He's sated his desire to kill for now, but it won't be enough to keep him satisfied, I think. He'll kill again," Thadius said. "It's imperative that we find out the significance of this charm."

Dominus exhaled. "Very well. I'll go to Lutetia with you."

"I don't doubt that, where else would you go?" Thadius smiled.

"Back to the king's fortress, that red haired woman is still there."

"As if she'd have you again."

Dominus chuckled. "You're right. She'd not have me back. Not after what we did and how we did it."

"I'm sure I don't need to know any more," Thadius said. "Nonetheless, as soon as we're back we need to find Eilifr and see if he can take us to the mainland."

*   *   *

The clouds were gathering over the sea again, and the smell of rain was in the air. Thadius and the others arrived at the garrison towards early afternoon, and he went directly to Gnaeus' quarters.

"He is not here," the servant said. "He's gone to the mainland and is not expected back for twelve months or more."

"Why did he leave?" Thadius asked, surprised.

A young officer appeared in the darkened doorway. "He was ordered back to Rome. I'm Hiclius, First Centurion. The commander left orders that you are to have anything you wish and made clear that you are allowed to stay here as long as you desire."

"What I need is the pilot of the Northmen ship, Eilifr, and provisions for a month long journey," Thadius commanded.

"As you wish," Hiclius said. Turning to the servant he issued orders, "Collect some men, find the Northmen and gather provisions." The servant ran off calling for others to come help. "If that is all?"

"For now," Thadius replied.

"Summon me if you need me again." Hiclius turned and disappeared into the villa.

Another servant came by, and Thadius asked him for a cup of wine. The man soon returned with a copper goblet. "Thank you," he said. The servant looked at him strangely then cast his eyes down. "It's alright," Thadius said, noting the man's unease. "Take me to Gnaeus' study. I need a stylus and paper."

The servant led him down a hall and into a long room with a desk at one end. Above the desk was a small square window that allowed sunlight in. The man bowed and waited. "This will do. You are excused." The servant exited.

Thadius drank his wine as he sat at the desk. He found a stylus and ink well. In a tray were several leaves of paper. He took one sheet out and prepared to write some notes when he noticed it had writing on it. "Carvum Carcarium, prepare for my arrival. Soon we will have enough to gain the election. Finally, what has been denied us these many years will be ours. Tell none of my arrival, and both our rewards will be great," he read aloud.

There was no signature, and the paper had not been folded nor sealed with wax. Where the last word was written a blotch of ink stained the paper. Thadius sat there for a long time reading and re-reading the note. A draft, he thought, but whose?

"By Jupiter's grace here you are," Dominus said coming into the room. "I ran into Centurion Hiclius, and he directed me here. This is a big house…I was lucky I found you."

"What do you make of this?" Thadius handed the letter to him.

"It's expensive paper for one, and there is a dab of ink on it."

"Read it."

Dominus was silent for a moment. "It seems some intrigue. Do you think this was a draft of a letter Publius was writing?"

"Perhaps…"

"If it is, the good copy is on its way by messenger most likely," Dominus said.

"Why were you looking for me?" Thadius asked.

"Eilifr is making ready the boat. He wanted me to come find you and bring you to the ship. I suspect he's going to insist that we sleep on that blasted wooden contraption tonight."

Thadius nodded. "Then let's get to the docks. I can do with a good seaside sleep."

*　　　*　　　*

"Wake, Gray Lion," Rolf said. Thadius sat up and rubbed the sleep from his eyes. The sun was not present and the darkness of the water and the sky made it look as if they were suspended in an abyss.

"To the oars…" Rolf motioned with his hands. "We take to the waves now."

They rowed out past the breakers and into the open sea. Thadius strained as he pulled in synch with his barbarian brethren. Eilifr shifted the tiller, and the wind came from the aft. Bojon raised the sail and it filled. The long ship began to cut its way towards the mainland.

"I know this town of which you speak," Eilifr said. "We can go there by way of the river inlet. I have been there many times, and my boat will sail easily up the river during any tide."

The waves were calm as they sailed to within sight of the shore and turned south. By the afternoon the sky began to darken and the sounds of thunder could be heard in the distance. The seas began to pitch and the waves showed their displeasure by forming white caps as they dashed against the ship's side.

"We'll need to take shelter," Eilifr said. "This is no ordinary storm." He steered for a crescent shaped spit of land bringing the boat into a natural harbor. Dropping the sail, he ordered the oars put over and they made for the shore. Ramming the prow into the rocky beach, Yngvi, Bojon, Rolf, and Runolf took up the ropes, leapt overboard, and tied the ship to several trees along the shore.

"Make for the cliffs; there's a cave just up above the rocks," Yngvi said, as the wind picked up. "Take some supplies with you as you go."

They all scrambled up the cliff. Thadius found himself at the mouth of a large cavern. The wind began in earnest blasting the rain into the rocks. Going into the cave the darkness swallowed him. He glanced over his shoulder to see the black clouds and the fierce seas, then turned back to follow the barbarians.

"The gods are angry," Dominus said, as he passed Thadius.

"I've seen it like this many times, it is from the north driven by the One-eyed god," Yngvi said.

"It will pass," Eilifr stated from the cave mouth. He sat down an amphora, placed a funnel in the opening, and exposed it to the storm. Coming inside he grunted, "Tuturk, make some food, Bojon make a fire."

As night came on so did the heart of the storm. Water poured down the cliffs in torrents. From time to time Thadius thought he felt rain hitting his face, though he was more than twenty feet from the cave opening. The fire was burning low, and the wind outside howled with rage and contempt for all things born of the land. In the low light he could see only a few of the sailors, illuminated by the fire. Eilifr lay on his back, the glow betraying a man with few cares as he snored. Closing his eyes, Thadius listened to the wind. Slowly, he slid into the grip of the otherworld... the dream world.

She emerged from a white fog. A goddess? he thought. How can you be here? I know that you have crossed the river... His heart leapt and fear gripped his soul.

"Am I dead?" he asked.

She smiled, and the corner of her eyes crinkled. "Wake, love of my life."
And then she was gone.

The cries of the sea birds woke Thadius. He sat up and rubbed his eyes. The sun cast a long shadow from the rocky overhang. The other men were still sleeping contentedly and he stood and stretched his legs. Glancing down at the ship he sighed with relief that it was still there bobbing gently in the surf. Pulling his blanket around his shoulders he walked out onto the ledge overlooking the small crescent-shaped harbor. In the distance out on the sea he saw sails of many ships in the distance.

Taking in a deep breath, he smelled the pungent odor of seaweed. The cool sea air was crisp and felt good against his face. The deep blue sky was now void of clouds.

"Quite a storm last night," Dominus said, coming out onto the ledge.

"I'm sure that Jupiter had a hand in our salvation," Thadius said.

"If salvation had included a brothel and a hot meal I'd be thanking the old fellow myself, but clearly it doesn't, so…" He turned and went back into the cave. Thadius took in another deep breath then followed.

As they entered, Eilifr climbed to his feet and stretched his arms towards the cave roof as he yawned. He walked to the fire and sat down holding his hands above the flames and rubbing them together. "We shall enter the river's mouth today."

Tuturk and his son removed the wax lids from several large earthen jars. From a cloth sack he also removed loaves of hard-bread made of rye then poured the contents of one jar into a black iron pot. He carried it to the fire and put it in the coals and tossed in sausage and turnips and brought it to a boil. Calling to the men to come and fill their bowls, he spooned out the contents. He ladled out some into Dominus' bowl.

"It's sausage with garum," Tuturk said.

"Fish sauce?" Thadius asked with surprise. "Expensive and unexpected."

"Peppery also," Dominus added as he took a spoonful.

Thadius dipped his bread and tasted it. "Not bad at all. Some very fine flavoring indeed."

"So, today we'll be moving up the river towards the island of Lutetia?" Dominus asked.

Eilifr looked over at him and smiled. "Yes."

"How long will it take?" Thadius asked.

"Two days if the river is up, and this time of year the river is always up." Eilifr took a bite of his bread. "We will sail as soon as the meal is finished."

After the morning meal, each man took his bedroll and belongings and helped carry the leftover supplies back to the ship. After stowing the items onboard, they made ready the oars as Bojon, Wyglad, Thord and Ivar shoved the boat out into the surf. Thadius sat on the bench ready to take up the oar. His muscles now felt up to the task of rowing, and his stamina was markedly increased. Eilifr shouted his command, and Thadius reached down quickly and took up his oar. Looking forward, he waited for the command.

Dominus to his right lifted his eyebrows and then winked at him. "Don't pull a muscle," he calmly said.

"To the water, backward draw," shouted Eilifr, as he held the rudder tilted aloft.

Thadius grunted, and the ship slowly moved out past the breakers and into the sea. The large Northman in front of him flexed his muscles and Thadius wondered if he now looked like that. Lifting the oar he pushed forward, dropped the oar, and drew back. The slap of the sea waves beat out a tempo as the first oarsman began a melodious song. Even though Thadius did not understand the words, he harmonized as he followed the raising and pulling of the oars.

When his muscles felt as though they could no longer do the work, he heard Eilifr say, "Oars up. Rack em and raise the sail!"

Thorir and Melnir moved to the mast and hoisted the sail into position. The wind filled it and the ship moved forward cutting through the blue and white waves.

Feeling the new morning sun, Thadius closed his eyes and turned his face skyward. He thought for a moment of how nice the ocean spray felt as it cascaded over the saxboard and showered him. Looking out over the port side he saw the jagged coastline slowly passing. No fortifications here, just thick trees and vast coastal shrubberies. Birds circled in abundance and the seals lay on the guano encrusted rocks.

Eilifr called down to him. "We head towards a small town called Samara. Then we will navigate toward the Finger. After, we will turn inward and up the river at Sequana." He leaned against the tiller and the ship turned towards the shore for a while, then turned again coming parallel to the broken landscape less than a mile away.

Looking over the side, Thadius saw the reefs passing below the clear water. "This shallow draft boat of yours sure can go places others can't," he said.

Eilifr grinned. "Up rivers, near coral reefs, and even right into Roman baths." He laughed loudly.

Looking to port he could see the sail of a corbita style ship a quarter mile out at sea.

"Not to worry, we are quite safe," Eilifr said. "No pirate who is experienced will follow us this direction."

Dominus came from the bow, staggering left then right as the ship lazily pitched from one side to the other.

"Would you like to steer the ship?" Eilifr said to Dominus.

Looking surprised, Dominus smiled. "Steer the ship? I know little of sea navigations."

"I'll teach you when we get closer to the inlet and the waters grow deeper." Eilifr pointed ahead at the vast numbers of small fishing boats bobbing up and down.

Dominus looked ahead and noted the course of their boat change as they approached a jutting spit of land. Beyond the foliage of the sea cliffs he saw a thin layer of white smoke.

"A town," Dominus said, pointing.

"There are small farms all along the cliffs. But the fishing town is on the other side of the Finger," Eilifr said. "We've cleared the reefs and are into deeper water again. You take the rudder." He changed places with Dominus. "Now take the lever and pull to the left gently."

Dominus felt the ship tilt and shift course speeding out to sea. The ship bucked as it hit a wave then headed straight toward one of the small fishing boats. Some men shouted angrily as the ship shot past them, just missing their net-floats.

"Now lean slightly to the right," Eilifr directed. "Follow the darker water. That will be our path to the river."

They sailed very close to one of the medium sized ships, and the Northman laughed. The fishing ship's crew yelled angry shouts, shaking fists and making rude jesters.

Eilifr laid his hand on the rudder and adjusted the course. "It is easy to control. A ship is like a woman, if you are rough and careless, she will be wicked and brooding, if you are gentle and caring she is as sweet as jasmine tea."

"That juttying land mass there is called the finger." Eilifr pointed. "Sail us around it."

Dominus did so. After some time, Eilifr relieved Dominus and steered the ship toward a broad river inlet.

"That was an experience I would be loath to have missed," Dominus said, as he staggered to where Thadius stood.

"I'm glad you enjoyed the experience." Thadius smiled. "Perhaps you could do some real work now like helping me bait the fishing hooks."

Dominus looked bemused for a moment. "And get bloody fish guts all over myself? I'm now a pilot – I've been promoted."

"Are you the same Dominus who was chased by the local constabulary in the seaside city of Florence? And the same Dominus who hid in the women's dirty laundry at the pleasure house and gambling hall called The Turning Puck? And are you the same Dominus—"

"Handling fish guts isn't as challenging as being forced to remember all that," Dominus said. "So, I'll help you if you stop reminding me about myself."

"Maybe the blessings upon your soul will yield us a tasty fish?" Thadius chuckled.

"Maybe," Dominus said shaking his head. "Neptune willing."

CHAPTER 18

The tide was up, and a strong wind pushed hard against the sail driving the boat up the river. Thadius sat relaxing on an oar-bench; he looked at the string of fish tied along the saxboard. A shout caught his attention, and he realized that there were some brightly painted tribesmen on the far shore watching the boat as it moved up the estuary against the lazy current. The dark green foliage on the shore was thick, choked with trees and bushes. One of the tribesmen drew a circle with his hand in the air and all the men backed up and faded into the undergrowth.

"Tribesman," Thadius called to Eilifr.

"They are nothing to worry about. Most likely they are in want of trade," he said. "You should be worried about the rain though. It comes again."

Thadius saw the gray clouds above. Slowly the rain began to fall as the clouds let loose their bounty. A strong wind swept up the river and the sail frayed slightly as it strained against the mast.

"Drop the sail," Eilifr commanded. "Rig for oars!"

Some men jumped to the mast and took down the sail allowing it to collapse to the bottom of the pole. The wind began to whip up the river around the boat and the dark waters looked as if they were beginning to boil.

Thadius and Dominus quickly took up their oars. One by one, each crewman made ready to row. "All back," Eilifr yelled. In unison the men plunged the oars into the water and drew back hard. Thadius moved in time with his fellow rowers. From the corner of his eye he could see Dominus drawing on his oar, the wind blasting his graying hair back over his shoulders. He could see Eilifr squinting in the driving rain as he steered the boat. The barbarian leaned on the rudder and angled the boat.

He shouted down at Rolf and Bojon to jump to the approaching shore. "Rack oars," he said

Thadius felt the boat strike the muddy bank of the river, sinking softly into it. The bow made a grinding noise as two of the men jumped overboard. Pulling on the thick ropes the men held the ship to the shore. Rolf climbed up the embankment and looped his rope around a stout oak. Bojon moved up the same muddy bank and did likewise. "It will not break free!" Rolf shouted.

"We'll camp in the woods," Eilifr ordered.

The wind battered the boat to the side and drove it against the current and along the dark riverbank. Climbing down, Thadius dropped into the thick river mud. Sloshing his way to the bank he climbed up ten feet of slippery embankment and sat heavily onto the ground between the two ropes. Other men began climbing down too. He could tell by their ill concern that they had probably seen many a storm like this while traveling along this very river.

"Don't be an aung," Wyglad said. He stood next to Thadius. Slung over his shoulder was a bow, and it pressed into his heavy woolen shirt. A quiver of arrows shown on his other shoulder and Thadius could see the feathered shafts peeking over the rim.

"An aung?" Thadius said.

"Yes, the great and slow black oxen that dwell within and without our lands. I am Wyglad. My father was the Lord of Markland and died in battle against the tyrant King Walalglif."

"That is an honorable death," Thadius stated.

Wyglad smiled down at him. "You have proven yourself a brave companion. Come with me and we'll scout for a camp site. And, if the gods are kind, maybe we will find a deer or two to roast over our fire." Her reached down and pulled Thadius to his feet with little effort.

Eilifr looked up from the riverbank. Thadius saw him nod up at them while Wyglad put his hand on Thadius' shoulder. "Let's go find what we need." He found a gap in the thick river brush. "A deer path," he said over the wind.

He followed Wyglad into the undergrowth. The man moved swiftly taking light steps along the muddy path. Weaving his way between the branches of thin saplings and yearling brush he stopped. Rivulets of rain slipped through the leaves as the wind shook the trees. The wind stopped and they stood there hearing only the patter of the rain. They remained still and quiet. Wyglad signaled to move again, then stopped and crouched, holding still like a statue.

A rustling came towards them. Bursting through the brush a large tusked black boar stopped and stared in surprise at the two men. The beast snorted and shook its toothy head in rage. Wyglad leapt into the air and grabbed onto a tree branch lifting his legs high. Locking eyes with the boar, Thadius realized it meant to charge him. He leapt to the side and quickly climbed a young oak as the wild hog shook its tusks back and forth rushing towards him. Squealing with anger the boar slashed at the oak with its tusks tearing fist size chunks of bark away from the base. Stopping, the creature glared up at the two men, snorted several times, then rushed off into the thick of the dark green brush followed closely by a brood of small piglets oinking as they went.

Thadius waited a few minutes in the tree then called to Wyglad, "It's gone now."

Dropping to the ground, Wyglad laughed heartily. "Let the gods test us. We are worthy."

"I hope our next encounter is with a deer or oxen," Thadius said climbing down and glancing around nervously.

Wyglad moved up the path, again taking the lead. Stopping at some thick brambles and brush he peered between the thorns and leaves. Over his shoulder he smiled like a child who found sweet beans on an unattended countertop.

"A clearing," he said. He took his sword and cut a hole, then pushed through the brush.

Wyglad stopped at the other side by the remains of several burnt oak trees covered mostly by moss. The rain slowed, and a strong smell of detritus and wet earth filled his nostrils. Near the middle of the clearing a ring of large mushrooms were contentedly growing.

"Stay out of there, that's a sprite circle," Wyglad said while pointing at the mushrooms. "To go into the circle is to upset the spirits."

The rain fell again, and Wyglad stared into the dark forest. "Much dead wood is about. We can collect some and make camp for the night here in this glade. Go back and tell the others we have found a place to camp and lead them here."

Thadius patted Wyglad on the back then turned and made his way across the grassy expanse. Glancing over his shoulde,r Thadius saw Wyglad pulling several long branches from the forest into the glade.

"Do not let that hog better you," shouted Wyglad, just as Thadius slipped through the brush and back onto the trail.

He moved swiftly following the muddy footprints back down the path to the river. The rain stopped and the air was thick with the cool moisture. Droplets of water slipped from foliage all around him as he came to the thick vegetation that hid the trailhead along the river. Thadius listened at the leafy entrance for a moment, then stepped out. The sounds of the river and the thumping of the boat were loud, even more than the men talking. He could see his fellow sailors sitting on crates and barrels conversing amongst themselves.

Eilifr climbed down from the boat just as another rain fall began. "We've found a clearing at the end of this path," he said and pointed.

"Good," Eilifr said. "We're in need of some respite." He hefted a bundle of canvas to his shoulder and moved up the riverbank to the trailhead. The rest of the crew picked up their stores and gear and followed. Thadius led the way and soon they all emerged into the clearing. Thadius saw Wyglad crouched down making a fire. The wood appeared soggy and covered in places with moss, but somehow Wyglad had the tinder smoking.

"Here, I brought our packs and the folding stools," Dominus said, as he dropped Thadius' bag on the grass. "It'll be good to dry our clothes and get some warm food in us."

"I do long for some warmth," Thadius said while picking up his pack.

"This reminds me of the hunting trips we've taken up on the mountain back home."

Thadius nodded. "I do remember, but we're not so near our homes on this trip."

"Look, if we were to die here it would make no difference, my friend, because we're bound for Tartarus and our sins are great." Dominus chuckled.

"I suppose," Thadius said walking toward where the tent was going up.

Several of the men rolled out the canvas and constructed two tents. They were of simple construction and seemed a bit flimsy at first. But once fully erected the shelters became quite hearty and stable. Braziers were erected and filled with charcoal and placed inside the tents. If nothing else, they would finally be warm.

A mist rose up and the smell of the forest seemed to ride along the currents of the wind. The scent of ferns, moss, bark, and oak leaves were heavy in the air. He watched as white wisps of smoke swirled from the fire and moved across the open grass. The men stopped and watched the whirlwind of smoke travel along the ground to the mushroom ring, where the wisp vanished in a gust.

Eilifr's eyes fixed on the mushrooms. Slowly he moved his gaze from man to man, as if reading their thoughts. Drawing forth his sword he strode to the ring and yelled out while kicking away the mushrooms. In a matter of moments, he scattered the mushrooms about the grass and stood breathing heavily. His sword was tensely held in his large hand.

"You are all fools if you believe that the One-eyed god would be blind to our plight! This fairy ring houses no ancestors, and no evil spirits. See how I shatter it with my strength alone," he chided them. "There is no magic here." Sheathing his sword he went back to the tent as if nothing happened. Slowly, the sailors began to go about their work again, but it was clear there was a heavy sense of foreboding in the air.

Dominus leaned into Thadius. "These barbarians sure are superstitious," he said.

"It's best not to speak of religion when in varied company." Thadius suggested.

"If religion is off limits, then let's discuss the weather. I'll be glad when these gray clouds overhead move on."

Thadius looked up. "The light from the day begins to diminish."

"But we at least have enough wood to keep fires burning through the night." Dominus pointed at the pile of wood.

The sailors began to relax and banter back and forth. Wyglad, Rolf and Raknar formed a hunting party and moved out into the forest. Tuturk began deploying his pots and pans, and prepared some dough for bread. Thadius unfolded his stool and sat down by the fire. Dominus also sat, removed his wine skin, and poured them both a cup of wine.

"This will soothe those tired muscles you old salt," he said.

They sat and talked for a good hour as Tuturk baked flatbread in a pan over the fire. As the darkness swallowed up the small glade, Wyglad, Rolf and Raknar returned. A string of ducks was slung over Rolf's shoulder. Wyglad and Raknar carried a long sapling pole with a deer suspended from it.

"We stumbled across a herd of deer on our way back," Raknar said while lowering the carcass to the grass. An hour later the meat was over the fire.

"I wonder how far it is to Lutetia from here," Dominus mused aloud. Laughing suddenly, he looked over at Thadius. "All those years ago, after we first met, why was it that you pressed so hard for me to be your Tribuni Angusticlavii?"

"I could think of no other better qualified," Thadius said with sincerity.

"I am glad that we're no longer soldiers, though I miss aspects of it," Dominus said.

"My sentiments exactly." Thadius looked into the fire while holding his wine with both hands. He looked solemnly over at Dominus. "Seems a lifetime ago when we were young."

Dominus sipped his wine. "It does."

"We are lucky though to enjoy our retirement," Thadius commented softly.

"We were granted the leave to do so by the gods while many others fell to the side of the *old road*." Picking up a stone Dominus tossed it into the fire. "Do you see that stone as it heats? It may crack or it may not. The rock doesn't choose to crack, the fire will choose for it. The gods are our fire and people are the stones of life."

Thadius sat still, thinking. Finally, he shook his head. "We've seen much of the world, more than most men could hope to see. We've lived longer and done much more than most. But when we meet, after we shed these bags of bones and flesh, I hope you'll still call me friend."

An awkward pause settled in the air, as Dominus finished his wine and refilled his cup. Looking up at Thadius, he shook his head in agreement. "I'll call you friend. Maybe we will avail ourselves of a great orgy of food and drink then too. I'm sure the gods would not deny us such simple pleasures."

"Do you ever worry about the moment your thread is finally cut and Thanatos comes?"

"It's not a worry of mine," Dominus said with a jovial grunt. "I don't get to choose when my thread is cut." He stared at the fire and added softly, "I hope when that time comes I die well."

"I too," Thadius said finishing his wine. "Seems that death is sooner for me than you, my friend."

Dominus chuckled. "There you go again, wearing the sandals of Jupiter." He watched as Thadius put his wine next to his by the embers.

"I hope we can put a stop to this killer," Thadius said.

"It does seem a waste of beautiful women if he continues," Dominus added. "But that, my friend, is also left up to the Fates."

"Time to eat," Tuturk called.

The crew ate quietly, but by the end of the meal they began the loud banter of their barbarian kind. Several jars of wine were finished as the weather grew colder. The darkness was whole and consuming and with the boiling clouds above, no light could be seen from the sky.

"I need to stretch my legs," Thadius said, as he walked around the clearing. He stopped where the mushrooms had been, then moved toward an area where the trees made a long V. He could see the outline of large oaks. "Jupiter, keep my Althea safe in the underworld, until I can meet her again. Watch over my servant Simon, and keep my children and their children safe from harm. Keep Dominus from harm, and see me to my wife when the time comes. In this, your name I pray."

"What are you mumbling over there?" Dominus asked. "Come back to the fire, unless you've found a barbarian maiden to elope with."

He laughed then drank down more wine.

CHAPTER 19

The rain hissed as it hit the fire. Ivar, Jarnskeggi, and Yngvi took first watch. The rest of the crew retired to the tent. Inside the shelter small portable braziers filled with hot coals churned out heat. To feed the portable fire pits, small sacks of charcoal were placed near each brazier. Thadius could see rugs laid out on the ground and rolls of thick cloth placed on top. Folding chairs sat at one end of the tent and near the middle of the tent piled with venison and duck was a thin table made of planks from the ship.

Eilifr insisted that all take their fill of the wine and mead to ward off the coming night's cold. Dice games erupted and men began betting and playing with uncensored abandon. Laughter filled the tent as talk turned to events of their recent trip.

Driving his dagger into the table Eilifr stood and filled his long curved cow horn full of mead. Taking a long draft he wiped his mouth with the back of his hand and set the horn between his legs. Taking the dagger from the wooden table he cut away a large hunk of deer meat, sat back and chewed contentedly.

Dipping his cup into the container of mead Thadius drank some of the sweet wine. He could feel the heat from a nearby brazier and thanked the gods that he was not pulling guard duty. Boisterous laughter echoed in the tent and he turned to see Rolf rolling dice.

"I wonder who got the duty of watching the boat at the river?" Dominus said while placing his hands near the brazier and warming them.

"I'm not sure," Thadius said coming along side. "I hope they're not relieved by us." He stretched, reaching high towards the tent roof. Turning he tore a hunk of deer meat from a darkly roasted hindquarter and stuck the chunk in his mouth. He pulled his cloak around his shoulders and moved toward the door, "Let's sit by the fire. I'm not ready to sleep yet."

Dominus took his cloak and slipped it over his shoulders, pulling the hood over his head. "I'll accompany you my friend," he said while filling his cup.

Thadius opened the tent flap and they stepped outside. Caught by the wind, the flap snapped and flipped wildly until it was re-secured. He moved toward the orange glow of the fire and saw Thorir and Bojon standing just out of the light. The darkness was powerful and consuming. No moonlight escaped below the clouds, and other than the fire of the camp, and the white glow from the tent, no light appeared anywhere else. The wind blew and rain fell sideways against the men in invisible sheets as they made their way to the fire. The rain slowed, and then stopped.

Thadius used the tail of his cloak to wipe off the wet stool. Sitting down he looked into the bright yellow fire. Dominus tossed a limb in. Steam began to rise from the wet section of wood as the hungry flames crackled around it. Sitting down, Dominus poked the fire with a long stick. "We really should try and get some sleep," he stated while staring into the flames.

"The mist feels good on my face," Thadius said. "It reminds me of all those years past when we marched for Rome."

Dominus shook his head, "Thadius you do much wishing for bygone days. So, stop moping about remembering this and that. Live for today and tomorrow, and the drinks you will have, the places yet to see, and most of all, the women you have yet to bed!"

"Yet, that doesn't change the fact that the rain feels good." He poked at the fire. "And, I miss my wife."

"Your wife was a wonderful woman. She is indeed irreplaceable. Yet, you've mourned too many years now and it's time you dwelt with the living and not with the dead."

Thadius shook his head. "I concede you have the clearest sight of all mortals my friend. No more will the melancholy spirits keep me wanting."

Thorir and Bojon emerged from the darkness and stood near the fire. Crouching down next to Thadius, Bojon warmed his hands at the fireside. Turning, he smiled, "You've turned out to be a Northman after all, sitting in the cold and rain. No longer the smart Roman safe and warm in a tent," he laughed.

Thorir laughed heartily too and put a thick piece of wood on the fire. "Tis true that Northman love the cold."

"Why is that?" Thadius said.

"Because it drives women into our beds," Thorir laughed again.

"Bojon stood and walked to the tent, "We'd better eat and take our fill of drink."

"Though there are no women for us in here, I know there are some dice we may cozy up to," Thorir stated. He looked down at Thadius, "Yet, both dice and women will leave you less wealthy in the end, than when you first met," he said. Chuckling, he followed Bojon into the tent. Thadius watched the flames as the smell of smoke, rain, and sod all mingled in his nose.

"Some wine?" Dominus said holding up his wineskin.

"You asked the right question," Thadius stated holding up his cup. The two friends drank in silence for some time as the wind came and went. Thadius held up his cup and Dominus filled it yet again.

"Perhaps we should get some sleep now," Dominus suggested while standing.

"You turn in and get some rest old friend. The ghosts of my past are still not finished with me and I still have much to dwell on."

Dominus chuckled, "When you said old friend, I thought you were talking to yourself, since you are the elder of our company."

Nodding and smiling Thadius looked up. "Is there no respite from your wit?"

"Only my death will separate it from your ears," Dominus quipped. "In this wet and cold, those ghosts will not keep you company for long." Handing Thadius his wine skin he turned and headed for the tent. Over his shoulder he said, "Drink it all before you come to bed. You'll sleep like a farmer if you do."

Sitting alone Thadius listened to sounds of whistles and even laughter coming from the tent. "What is your game Publius, and what curse has you so mad?" Thadius said.

The rain began to fall again and he put another log on the fire. Standing, he shook the rain from his hair and turned toward the tent. Stepping inside he could see several men sleeping already, and the sounds of snoring drifted up from the dark floor. Eilifr still sat at the table, his head hung low and his drinking horn tipped to one side.

Thadius found his pack and changed out of his wet clothes. Lying his wet things near the brazier to dry he found his bedroll and laid out his blankets. Several of the men still played dice and several others were discussing the preparations for the next day's trip. Folding his wool blanket over himself Thadius laid his head on his small travel pillow and drifted off to sleep.

Thadius rolled to the side and looked about. He was sure that he heard a clap of thunder and his wife's voice. Climbing to his feet he noted that the sun was out and the tent was illuminated. He walked to the flap and stepped outside. Warm currents of air mixed with the dampness of the morning. Above him he could see the dark blue of a cloudless sky. A flock of geese honked overhead and he watched them vanish beyond the trees. The smell of boiling cereal filled his nose, and he saw Dominus crouched at the fire pit, heating some wheat porridge in a copper pot. Seasoning it with some salt and sandalwood his friend stirred it vigorously. "Ah," Dominus exclaimed while looking up to see Thadius. "Seems the sinners have been let out of Tartarus."

"You'll be happy to know that this is Tartarus," Thadius commented. He walked over to the fire and warmed his hands. "And, Pluto lets us push the stone up the mountain as much as we like."

"Have some cereal you old war hound," Dominus said handing up a bowl with a spoon sticking out of it.

"Thank you." He sat on his stool. Sitting beside him, Dominus ate the hot cereal out of the copper pot. Lifting a heaping spoonful he stuck the steaming mash into his gaping mouth.

"You could probably have fit a sandal in there too if you wanted," Thadius said while staring.

"A sandal would probably taste as good," Dominus said.

"A sandal would? Or, sandalwood?" Thadius questioned while raising one eyebrow.

"Your cleverness is disturbing dear friend," Dominus stated. "Now just eat so we can get on with this hunt you've dragged me on."

"Dragged you?"

"Well, at least tempted me with," Dominus said.

"To be led by temptation is a sin all of itself, isn't it?"

Dominus smiled. "It's too early for theological discourse. Plus you already established that we are in Tartarus. Perhaps we should just eat our mash and leave paradise and Tartarus to the gods."

Shrugging, Thadius chuckled, "Perhaps you're right."

The Northmen finished the morning meal, and began gathered up their supplies and carrying them back to the boat. Thadius and Dominus took up opposite ends of the tent poles and stacked the canvas on top. Hefting the load up, they made their way through the woods to the river. Breaking through the brush they saw Eilifr standing in the boat.

"Now, we make another step toward Lutetia," Eilifr said. "Let's not waste any more time."

Raknar, Rolf, Sigurd, Orkning and Thord were maneuvering the boat back into the river by hand. They shoved the ship off the shore, the aft caught in the current, and the boat broke free of the land, and moved slowly down stream. Eilifr stood at the rudder. Once his men were on board he called out, "Oars out, prepare to row."

Moving up the river the ship passed several large boats coming down. Thadius watched the strange figures shuffling back and forth along the decks. One ship appeared to be completely manned by Berbers. The dark skinned men handled crates, moved goods around and adjusted the sails.

The second ship was a shallow draft barge piled high with sacks and barrels. A crew of four seemed the only men onboard, and all four men carried long poles that they used to navigate along the curvy river. As it passed, the crew of four watched the longboat go by without any friendly greeting. In fact he detected a hint of some aggression in their posture.

Settling into the routine of rowing Thadius drew and pulled the oars with exact precision. His arms bulged with the effort and his stamina and strength had grown since beginning the trip. Glancing over at Dominus, he watched his old friend performing the same repetitive task with what seemed the same enthusiasm.

From the aft, a breeze began to caress the crew, gentle at first then grew into a sturdy wind. "Prepare the sail," shouted Eilifr. Wyglad and Bojon jumped to the mast and hoisted the sail. "Rack oars!"

The sail filled and the boat picked up speed. Thadius stood and made his way to the aft where he sat in the sun. He retrieved a stylus and ink and recorded the recent events on a sheet of papyrus.

CHAPTER 20

Thadius watched hundreds of gulls circle and chided one another, as the wind pushed the shallow draft ship up the river. He watched as the shoreline drifted by slowly. Along the banks he could see thatched roof huts made of timber and mud. Women stood knee deep in the shallows washing clothes. Children played along the banks, dashing in and out of the bushes, throwing blunted spears at one another or grappling.

Roughly fashioned docks jutted out into the slow moving current. Fishing boats bobbed up and down in the flow of the dark waters. Other watercraft moved along the waterway, and two seafaring boats moved down the river followed by rowboats filled with fishermen. Further along came flat-bottomed barges loaded with goods and being moved by men with long polls keeping to the shallows.

"This serpent is gentle today," Eilifr stated.

"You mean the river?" Thadius said.

Eilifr nodded, "How many seasons have you seen Gray Lion, thirty, fifty, more?"

"I must seem a relic to you," commented Thadius

"In my homeland there are few whose beards grow gray. In Rome I've seen many who wear wreaths of white upon their heads."

Eilifr shifted the rudder and the boat moved out toward the middle of the current.

"I'm sixty three years old," Thadius stated. "The weight of time has been kind to me." He looked ahead, "How many times have you sailed up this river?"

Looking down at him from the rudder Eilifr smiled, "More times than the years you've been alive. I sense that you've been on this river too."

"I crossed the head waters over thirty years ago," Thadius said.

"You've been to the headwaters?" Eilifr looked surprised.

"It was when my heart was lighter," Thadius stated. "There was a beautiful plateau where the springs bubbled from the underworld." Gazing out from the port saxboard he could see in his mind's eye the dark green pastures and forests. "There were dark marshes and large stone circles hidden among the forests and glades. Celtic hill forts were scattered across the countryside built in between the light green trees and flourishing ivy that grew in abundance. I've heard that the area of the headwaters is now called Beaune and the making of wine has become an industry there." He shrugged, "Enough of my past, how far to Lutetia?"

"We will be there in another day. On the island you will be able to find Roman food and even a large bath," Eilifr stated.

"Sounds like Lutetia has become quite cosmopolitan," Thadius commented.

"You said yourself you have not seen these lands for thirty years," Eilifr said. "There is much more that is Roman in that area than Celt anymore."

Dominus approached and wiped his brow with a rag. Pulling the stopper from his wineskin he drank heartily. Handing it to Thadius he looked up at Eilifr. "Ready for me to take the rudder again?"

"We will have to wait on teaching you more. There is some tricky navigation along this part. Sand builds up and hides just below the water waiting to trap unsuspecting travelers. I've seen the wrecks of seagoing ships spit upon sandbars, looted, and rotting in the sun. I'll not have that for my boat." Bojon called back from the bow and

Eilifr adjusted his course again. "At the end of this day we will be docking at a town called Furmorium. There's an estate that's at the far corner of the town. I have business there. You can accompany me if you wish. If not you may stay with the crew in town or stay aboard the ship."

"A mysterious estate entices the senses," Thadius stated. "Count me in."

"I'll go as well, to keep you two out of trouble," Dominus said.

Eilifr lay against the rudder and the ship shifted slightly to accommodate a wide turn. Taking a swig from Dominus' wineskin Thadius looked out at the passing countryside. Handing the wine back to Dominus he made his way to the bow where he climbed up to the prow and looked out. Ahead he could see a ninety-degree bend in the river. Sniffing the air, he could tell they were near some livestock. Over the starboard side he noted a shepherd with a large flock of sheep. The young boy let the rams drink at the river's edge, but kept the young lambs from the dark green waters.

The mid afternoon sun seemed overly warm, and he was thankful that a constant wind instead of their muscles propelled the boat. They passed several small fishing villages and he made note of the change in architecture. Earlier he had noticed the thatched roofs and mud wall construction of the Celtic dwellings, but now timber and stone walled homes appeared, some of which looked like Roman villas. In the river, crates, wood debris, scrap pieces of cloth and broken wicker baskets began to float by.

"We approach Furmorium," Eilifr pointed.

Docks appeared first, then many ships. The shoreline looked a buzz with activity as men loaded and off-loaded cargo working without distraction. Eilifr ordered the sail struck and let the current move the boat up along one of the docks. Several men at the platform tossed ropes to Wyglad who secured them to the ship. The men on the dock quickly pulled the boat in and tied it to some thick iron rings. Extending a plank from the dock to the saxboard the men on the shore said something that Thadius didn't catch. Wyglad stepped onto the plank and stepped down to the dock. "Little Romans," he called. "'Tis time to enjoy the hospitality of Furmorium."

"Yngvi, Thord, you are to stay at the ship until Wyglad and Tuturk return," Eilifr said. Yngvi and Thord moved to the middle of the ship and removed their weapons, retrieved a jar of beer and a dice board.

Securing his dagger to his belt Thadius climbed up to the saxboard, put on his pack and situated his wineskin over his shoulder. He made his way along the marina and up an embankment into the town. The smell of cooking meats and breads mingled with the stench of the river. A man came from a narrow street with a falcon on a leather glove. Two women stood outside a wine bar showing their assets ready to trade for coin.

"Looks like a festival or something going on here," Dominus said while pointing at a man dressed in a colorful costume and juggling several brightly colored leather balls.

Eilifr scoffed, "They are always celebrating something here. They are worse than you Romans at finding a holiday for foolishness."

"Now my dear Eilifr," Dominus began, "you fail to see the beauty of our way of life." Dominus smiled like a money-changer, "If a man is not happy living, how can he be happy dying?"

Eilifr looked confused then shook his head and walked down the street. "Your words are senseless," he said. "A man dies with a sword in his hand in fierce battle against men, or nature. A man who dies with his belly stretched tight and his arms free of scars and his hands missing calluses will find himself shunned by his fathers in the land of the dead."

Thadius smiled wryly at Dominus, "He has a point."

Dominus frowned, "Perhaps Eilifr has never enjoyed the delights of our Roman festivals, such as the Veneralia?"

Eilifr grunted once and led them to a wide avenue where several men in blue linen togas were engaged in an argument. Legionaries patrolled the streets in their finest uniforms, and an expensive chariot passed them with a regal woman dressed in a white toga trimmed in purple and lace. Along the right side of the street a magnificent three story curia stood made of quarried gray stone. Leaded glass windows faced outward to the street and heavy double-hinged brass doors lay open inviting worshipers inside to prostrate and sacrifice.

"This is what you Romans call a Forum. Their Senate conducts town business there," Eilifr pointed to the large edifice. "But, we are off to see the real power in this town."

"A friend of yours?" Dominus said.

Eilifr glanced back. "Yes and trading partner."

"You have quite a few powerful friends," Thadius stated.

"If a man makes his trade making wine, he should have acres of vines to pluck," Eilifr added.

The corners of Dominus' mouth twisted up lightly, "I hope we're not the ones to be plucked."

Thadius passed an inn, two taverns, and a public toilet. Further on he passed a brothel bustling with activity. Several girls waved from an open window on the first floor. "Come in young gentlemen, sample the wares," one said.

Another girl caressed one of her breasts, "I'll be your pony, ride me as you will," she called.

Thadius watched some fellows lighting street lamps that hung from long wooden poles that lined the street. Wagons filled with supplies moved past them with great frequency. In the distance a tall stone wall appeared. Thadius guessed its height at more than twenty feet. Fitted into the wall was a gatehouse made of stone and two large double doors of hardwood bound with steel straps and rivets. Men in armor patrolled the walls. As Thadius, Eilifr and Dominus approached, one of the soldiers called out, "Keep your distance, stay where you are. State your name and business."

"Eilifr Blodriner, of Iron Hill!" He continued advancing as several men with pilums came to the wall. "And, I have business with Master Helvetius."

"Eilifr you say?" The guard looked surprised. "Wait here at the gate." He vanished behind the wall.

"Not very warm are they," Dominus quipped.

"A dangerous land we are in. It is unwise to take chances here," Eilifr stated.

Thadius dusted off his tunic. "I understand what you mean, but we are armed only with daggers and you with a sword, it is clear we are no threat."

Putting his palm on the hilt of his sword Eilifr smiled. "Every man is a threat; politically, financially, personally, and physically, everywhere, even in your beloved Rome. Why would it be different here?"

The gate rattled and began opening. "Is it the stench of the sea that I smell?" came a raspy voice. "Welcome back Eilifr Blodriner, son of Glywal the Black Hand, king in exile."

CHAPTER 21

The man did not come out from behind the wall; instead, he turned on his heels and walked into lavished gardens beyond. Following him were eight sturdy looking warriors armed with swords and pilums.

"Come with me," Eilifr said as he walked through the gate after the soldiers. "Do not stray."

Armed men patrolled along the wall. Thadius could see they wore expensive modern armor and sported military-grade weapons. Each soldier he saw carried a dagger, sword, short bow, and pilum. None wore sandals but instead were wearing on their feet sewn boots made of animal hide laced all the way up to the knee.

They followed along a red gravel path through the middle of the garden. At the center was a plane of light green grass, along the edges purple and red flowers were nestled in brick beds. A great and ancient willow stood to one side hanging over the scene with its branches caressing the ground. Ahead Thadius could see a fountain. The great circular vessel that held the water was rimmed with small marble birds. Around the fountain tiny terracotta deer appeared to be drinking from flowing water. The sun's light reflected off the fountain and made it appear as if it was made of gold. "Remarkable," Thadius said. "The light – the fountain – all by design."

Dominus glanced back over his shoulder, "Would you like a cloth to wipe those tears dear?"

"You truly lack any enchantment by the Muses," Thadius stated. "Perhaps you'd rather the fountain had some prostitutes with legs wide inviting thee in."

"Yes, why didn't the architect do that? Now that would be art." Dominus stated.

"By Jupiter's lance," was all Thadius could muster in response

Stopping at the fountain the soldiers parted and the man who spoke came into view. He appeared gaunt and frail as he stopped at the fountain and sat on the lip. He took up a handful of water and drank it. For a moment he sat there and Thadius could hear his labored breathing. Eilifr stood, feet wide and arms folded across his broad chest, waiting without comment. The guards stood also watching, but it was Dominus, Thadius and Eilifr they watched with some curiosity.

After a few minutes their guide stood and again led them, but this time they traveled through thick bushes covered in berries until coming to a bridge. The man stopped and labored for breath once again. Once sufficiently rested, he led them over the bridge. On the other side, Thadius noted the path changed to yellow gravel as the greenery suddenly cleared. Following the man, they all entered a wide and open space void of vegetation. He could see between the garden and the house swirls of different colored gravel. Taking a mental measurement he judged one swirled circle of blue gravel to be more than twenty feet in diameter. Beside it was a red circle but swirled the opposite way. This theme repeated all along the open space. "What are these patterns?" Thadius said.

Eilifr shook his head, "A shaman has made these. They are to ward off sickness."

"They don't seem to be working." Dominus whispered.

They approached a large three-story villa made from tan limestone blocks. Judging by the size, Thadius figured it covered more than five acres. Stopping at the porch the man sat on the second step gasping. Thadius looked up the stairs to the covered portico. Along the porch, instead of standard columns, strange shapes supported the roof. Some of the odd columns looked to him like twisted and bent human shapes deformed and writhing in pain. "Tartarus," he said under his breath.

"Stranger and stranger," Dominus whispered.

After a few minutes the man stood and made his way slowly up the stairs to the portico. Stopping at the top he pointed to several chairs and a couch then sat down into a padded wooden chair. Next to the chair a small, round, polished wooden table sat, and he reached for a silver bell sitting on top. He froze, his hand hovering over the bell. Wheezing slightly the gaunt fellow again took several minutes to regain his breath. Finally he spoke, "Forgive me for not introducing myself before," he said while gasping slightly in between his words. "But, I find it a waste of breath to discuss such things if I am to walk a distance." Again he stopped and waited. Lifting his hand he waved off his compliment of guards. "You will know when to attend me next."

It appeared to Thadius that his guards were reluctant to leave his side, then the old man again waved his hand, but this time he nodded as he did it. One of the guards wearing a chain mailed coif and brown leather armor cast a wary eye over the visitors, but removed himself down the stairs without comment.

"My captain of the guard is a very cautious fellow," the man gasped. "That is what makes him valuable to me. Now, to my introduction, I am Kaeso Cordius Helvetius," he stated with some effort. "A scout informed me of your coming, thus I awaited you at the gate. Perhaps, you are as I am, parched?"

He reached for the silver bell again. Ringing it loudly he patiently waited. Two servants rushed from the main door down the portico and skidded to a halt. Helvetius mumbled something and made some hand jesters. The oldest looking servant addressed the visitors. "Our lord wishes to know the refreshments you would like. We have wine and beer, cheese, crackers, bread and fowl that we can bring immediately."

Eilifr politely said, "That will be fine, bring it all. It is an honor to have such gracious pleasures from such a gracious host." The two servants turned and quickly disappeared down the hall.

"It is truly an honor to meet with you Kaeso Cordius Helvetius," Thadius said.

"I am thankful that you feel that way. Since you are traveling with my friend, and he has not spoken ill of you, I grant you the privilege of calling me by my cognomen, Helvetius."

"I am Moras Tiberius Thadius and this man here," he gestured at Dominus, "is Peresius Albas Dominus." The servants approached and he paused.

Four of them carried the food and drink. Setting down goblets made of silver next to the seated men they proceeded to distribute small plates with food, and filled each glass with dark red wine. Another servant came from down the hall and set down a wooden table and placed on top a three foot round silver tray. On the tray the servants laid the remainder of the food and several pitchers of wine and beer. Suddenly, Helvetius spoke, "What is your business here in the lands of Celtica?"

"We are in pursuit of a murderer," Thadius said.

Erupting in a coughing fit Helvetius gasped for breath as cough after cough burst forth. Taking a white linen cloth from his coat he held it over his mouth until the coughing waned. He sat still for several minutes. Taking the cloth from his mouth Helvetius leaned to the side and grabbed his goblet. Thadius could see the dark, thick, purple blood on the cloth as the man drank. "Murderer?" Helvetius chuckled. "Take your pick in this wilderness. In these lands murderers are plentiful." He again took a drink and set his cup on the table at his side. "What murder do you refer too?"

"The brutal slaughter of a young Roman girl."

Helvetius, his face twisting with some unseen pain brought the cloth up to his mouth, but did not cough. For a moment he held the cloth there, hovering just in front of his lips then he put it down. "Brutal you say? Was she butchered like a lamb?" he asked, a crooked smile gracing his withered lips.

"Yes," Thadius said surprised. Looking at Helvetius, he tried to determine if the man was merely clever or truly knew something. "Butchered is the accurate term."

Leaning back Helvetius reached out and took up his bell. Ringing it again he calmly waited. A servant came quickly and stood waiting for his order. "Bring me the notes from Lutetia, the ones that arrived just last week."

The young man turned quickly and dashed down the portico and into the main building. A few moments later he returned with a box of pottery shards. Handing the box to Helvetius the young man again waited solemnly.

"You may go now," Helvetius said adding a wave of his hand in dismissal. The young man strolled down the portico and into the building. Picking through the small wooden box he drew forth a fairly large chunk of an earthen jar. Written on one side in white chalk were a date and a message. "Here it is," he stated. "Dated two weeks ago, from a Lutetia city guard named Appius who sends me snippets of news from the island. Concerns a recent happening there." He paused for a moment while gulping in air. "Most shocking, the butchering of a fair haired young maiden and her family. She was butchered like a sheep and her father's throat was cut." Shifting forward he reached for his goblet and drank deeply. He coughed once, wiped his mouth with the bloody cloth, and put the cup back. "There is more written but not of the killing. Does this sound familiar to you?"

"Yes," Dominus said his eyes narrowing slightly.

"Was there a Roman family that passed here on their way to Lutetia a few weeks back?" Thadius took up his own goblet and drank.

"There have been several families to pass this way of late," Helvetius said.

"Any of them traveling with children?" Thadius stated.

"Two of the families had children with them."

"Was there one with a son who is around twenty years of age?"

"Only one."

"How long ago?" Thadius' expression was one of anticipation.

"Three weeks passed. Flavius Malco Scapula and his family were traveling in some haste. In fact…" Helvetius gasped for a lung full of air then exhaled heavily. "They left some items behind and wished me to have them sent to Lutetia by a river barge."

"May we take a look?"

"It is of no concern to me if you do, but do not take anything," he said. "The chests, crates, and sacks are under my care and protection. You'll find them in the west wing of my villa. My head servant Malcolm will take you there when you are ready." Taking up his goblet Helvetius slumped in his chair. Sipping his drink he watched his visitor's reactions with careful concentration.

Thadius noted the man seemed to be in some distress, as his face took on a grave pallor and his eyes closed. A sudden gasp for air made Thadius jump as Helvetius opened his eyes fully and again drank from his goblet.

"They say the magic of the barbarians is strong. It has done nothing for me. They've probably cursed me instead of healed me." A sound like a chuckle broke through his lips. "I will take my rest now," Helvetius croaked. "I will instruct Malcolm to take you to the items when you desire." Reaching over and setting down his goblet he picked up the silver bell and rang it. Quickly his servant came running. "Take me to my chambers," Helvetius ordered. "I wish to take my rest." Turning the young man moved down the hall and returned with four other men and a sedan chair. Helping Helvetius into the chair the four men took him into the house.

"I am Malcolm," the young servant stated. "My master wishes me to attend to your needs while you are here."

Eilifr stood to his full height. "We require a place for the night, food, drink, and a bath."

Thadius looked at the large Northman in surprise and raised his eyebrow. "A bath?" he said his voice filling with some humor.

"Some of your Roman customs I enjoy," Eilifr grinned.

Dominus quickly finished his goblet and picked up a pitcher. "I'll just keep this for now. But, we do require one other thing."

"Yes," Malcolm asked.

"Your master has given us license to look at some items left here by the Malco family."

"He has spoken to me and said as much," stated Malcolm. "Shall I take you there now?"

"It would be best since we may be too drunk to go there later," Dominus said.

"Then if you are ready, follow me," Malcolm stated.

CHAPTER 22

The west wing of the building was a large open hall. Thadius could see the floor reflected by the lantern that Malcolm carried. Dusty intricate mosaic tile work passed under foot as they walked across the dark room. Approaching the opposite side, Malcolm lifted the lantern and held it high illuminating a door. He fumbled with a latch and slid the door open.

"An unusual place," Thadius commented.

"Our master has many unusual things here," Malcolm said.

Thadius looked inside the opening. He judged the room to be no more than twenty feet to one side and twenty feet to the other. Looking around he noted the room was adorned with a rich purplish red paint, ornate carved crown molding, and silver candle sconces. A black chain hung from the roof and he could see at the end of the chain a wrought iron chandelier hovering just a few feet from the floor and fitted with candles.

"What was this room for?" Thadius said while admiring the rich decor.

"Master has forbidden us to tell," Malcolm said. "He wishes it to be forgotten I think."

Malcolm walked over to the candles and fingered the charred wicks making them erect, then removed one and lit it by his lantern.

Igniting each of the candles he then hoisted the iron candle holder back into the air.

In the room a dozen jars, two dozen crates, boxes, and some small sacks became illuminated. "Why are the Malco's items in here," Thadius questioned.

"Because our master ordered it so," Malcolm said.

Dominus raised his eyebrow at Thadius signaling something was strange.

"These are all the items of the Malco's. Do you require my assistance?" Malcolm waited.

"No, I think we'll be fine," Thadius stated. Arranged against one wall several large wooden chests reflected the low light.

"What are we looking for?" Dominus said.

"Anything that might seem suspicious," Thadius replied.

"Anything other than us going through someone else's personal belongings?" Dominus looked annoyed.

"A set of knives, bloodied clothing, a confession maybe," Thadius stated. "Anything that might help us."

Dominus set down his wine and pulled one of the heavy sacks into the middle of the room. Opening it he drew back. "I would think they would have had their dirty laundry done instead of just storing it," he said while wrinkling his nose. Pulling out a women's toga he held it aloft. "Are we looking for something like this?"

Thadius frowned and shook his head, "No."

Again delving into the sack Dominus came away with a darkly printed women's toga adorned with gold lace. "What about this?"

"Keep looking," Thadius said.

Eilifr went to one of the wooden chests and opened it. Pulling out a small leather bag he set it on top of a crate and untied the top. Catching the glint of the candlelight were the steel instruments of a surgeon. "Here are some knives," Eilifr stated.

Thadius turned his attention to the satchel. "Now that is more like what we're looking for," he said. Coming closer he could tell the

146

instruments were of the finest quality. He examined them closely. It seemed that the scalpels and saws had been sharpened only once and he set them back down. Examining the satchel he held it up to the light. Noting no discoloring of the beige material he set them aside. "Seems they're new and have never been used. There's no blood, and the carrying case is clean. I'd say they were spares."

"I've found something," Dominus stated. Holding up a blood stained white cloth, "It's on both sides."

Thadius walked over and called to Malcolm, "Come here with that lantern." Holding the lantern up Thadius examined the stains. "Reddish brown, not dark red. Probably menstrual in nature," he concluded.

Dominus looked at him and back at the cloth with disgust. Dropping it on the pile of clothes he wiped his hands on his tunic. "Well then, I guess I'll just keep looking," he added.

"Here is a set of scrolls," Eilifr said as he pulled four rolled sets of documents from the chest.

Taking one of the scrolls, Thadius untied it and read the pretext. "A medical manual. For treating headaches and…" Thadius stopped.

"And what?" demanded Dominus.

"Parliamentary disease," he said just above a whisper.

Dominus dropped what he was doing and approached. Looking at the document still in Thadius' hands he turned and sat down on a crate. "Parliamentary disease," he echoed. "Of course, it has been known that one afflicted with such could be capable of any horror."

Walking to the door, Eilifr stood looking out into the large hall. Turning he scratched his head, "What is Parliamentary disease?"

"A state of affliction that results in the individual quaking uncontrollably. Second they may have severe headaches and blurred vision, and third they may have fits of madness. It is recorded by Hippocrates that those with this disease have been known to enjoy the torturing of animals and humans, hear the gods telling them to do mischief, and even committed treason based on their feeling that the state is conspired against them."

Eilifr shrugged his large shoulders and walked back to the chest. "If this is in there I wonder what else we will find."

Dominus returned to the sack of clothes and continued to search through them. Thadius directed his attention back to the scrolls. He read the first scroll thoroughly then rolled it up again tying it closed. He took up the next and did the same until he had read them all. "Interesting stuff," he said.

Malcolm stood quietly waiting for them to finish. From the darkness a young boy's voice rang out, "Malcolm, the master needs you."

Addressing Thadius, Dominus and Eilifr, Malcolm spoke quickly, "My master calls. I will return soon." Leaving the lantern on the floor he exited into the darkness.

"A queer fellow," Dominus commented. "Malcolm is as strange a man as is his master," he stated. "And, Helvetius' name is familiar to me."

"Yes, I've heard it also," Thadius commented while looking in one of the crates. "Why does his name seem so clear in my mind?"

"Brewery," Dominus said while looking up.

"Of course," Thadius stated, "the largest breweries in Rome. I think he also has vineyards and several wineries. What is he doing way out here?"

"His health," Eilifr said. "I transported cargo for him ten years ago. He was much healthier then, but still ill. He asked that I find him some land to convalesce on. He'll die here and he knows it."

"I understand that he contracted with the Senate to provide beer and wine to the army, theaters, and gaming arenas, even the Circus," Dominus said. "His family was Greek, weren't they?"

"His mother was I believe. But his father was Equestrian I think," Thadius stated. "Nonetheless, he's moved his estate into the middle of the territories, very strange."

"Not too strange," Eilifr stated while pulling a small box out of a chest. "The springs nearby are said to hold healing qualities, and the shaman of the local tribes have been said to perform miracles. It is a miracle that he needs."

"What is that you have?" Thadius said noting the box in Eilifr's hands. "Dominus, bring that lantern." Dominus held it aloft near the box. Thadius could see no lock and no visible lid. "'Tis a trick box, like the ones sold in the market back home. To open it requires the movement of wooden slides. Let's see…" He quickly found the components and with his thumbs slid them. "See," he said as the lid popped open.

"What are they?" Dominus said.

"Dried mushrooms." Thadius took one out and examined it, "The type that priests and shaman use."

"For communing with the gods?" Eilifr said.

Thadius smiled, "The same."

Setting the lantern on one of the crates Dominus pulled out a box of scrolls. Unrolling one he looked concerned. "Thadius, take a look at this."

Thadius read aloud. "I despise them and their haughty air. If I could, I would cut out their livers and show it to them and feed on it. They don't respect me, and think me weak. Mother says it is a curse, and my head aches all the time now. I can barely keep my hands from shaking. Only blood calms me." He set it down and picked up another and read. "He comes to me in the night, in this land of barbarians. He brought me an elixir that gave me visions, glorious visions of death. He bides me even now to do his work, with reward, to remove this curse and make me immortal. Apollo comes for me tonight, and will lead me to my gift." Thadius sat down on a chest, "The writing is shaky, almost illegible."

"He's truly mad," Dominus said. "Look at this one. Fires of Hade's burns my eyes, but soon it will all be done. He has told me to memorize the names, but in faith I cannot, for my memory is weak. Thus, I have laid them down here. I must discover where the fleece has been hidden. If I don't, Rome will fall and my soul will be lost. Apollo guide my hand to Gladria's secret, to Maxima's deceitful father, to Pollita's wicked uncle, Sulpicia's key, Perenice's eyes, Hedia's map, and Turia's disgraced mother. I will see you Turia in Rome soon after my visit to Germanius to get the jimson weed extract. He knows how to make it, and I will see it given."

Dominus looked up to see Thadius' pale face. "What's wrong?"

"While these names are somewhat common by themselves, when listed like this, they have great meaning."

Dominus held up his hands, "Well, out with it."

"They are the wives and daughters of leading men of Rome, and Perenice was the name of the girl murdered on Britannia. Sulpicia, the daughter of Sulpicius proconsul of Rome was found dead in a vineyard near their estate on the island of Sardinia a year ago. No details, but the gossip was that she was tortured."

"There was the one killed in Lutetia recently," Dominus said.

"We can assume she is Hedia."

Dominus looked deep in thought, "So what of Gladria and Maxima?"

"I assume they were first to be murdered. So, our mad killer is not so deranged after all."

"What do you mean?" Dominus said.

"A mad man picking victims of opportunity does not make a list of them. He's methodical, and focused on these women and their families for some reason," said Thadius.

"Now what?" Eilifr said.

"Stop Publius from his last murder and unravel this mystery." Thadius looked grave.

Finishing their search the three men waited for Malcom to return. It was not long before the servant appeared with a brass oil lantern. "Master has retired for the evening but wishes for you to feast in his absence." Malcom lowered the candles and put each light out, then closed the sliding door. He led the way back to the main building and down a long hallway bordered by Ionic colonnades.

Pointing down a corridor he said, "Down there are your rooms." "You are expected in the feasting hall for supper. I must attend the kitchen now to prepare for your meals." Clapping his hands loudly Malcolm called down the side passage, "Timora!"

150

Thadius watched as a glimmer of light appeared. Slowly the glimmer grew into a bright lantern light swaying to and fro. He could see holding the lantern, was a small girl, maybe no older than ten.

"Timora, take these men to their rooms and see to their needs," Malcolm stated. Then he looked at the three men. "The feast-hall is that direction, you cannot miss it." He pointed into the darkness.

"Follow me to your rooms," Timora said as she flipped her long golden hair from side to side. She took no more than two dozen paces then stopped and opened a finely crafted wooden door. She gestured for Thadius to enter. He looked down into her large round green eyes and felt sadness in his heart; the girl could be his granddaughter, but the reality was she's a toiling servant and would most likely die as such. She, lifted her lantern high, and motioned for Eilifr and Dominus to follow her further down the hall. Thadius watched as she led the two men away to their respective rooms.

He stepped into the room. To his surprise it proved to be an apartment and not just a bed and table. Two couches sat at right angles to one another. On the floor Thadius could see a masterfully woven rug. Small tables made of dark wood and polished to a brilliant shine sat at the end of each couch. Tapestries hung along the walls depicting landscapes and forest creatures. Positioned around the room polished brass lanterns hung from wrought iron stands casting plenty of bright light.

Noticing light coming from under a door he walked over and pushed it open. A lavish bedchamber appeared. Approaching the bed he examined it closely; a raised wooden frame supported a canapé around a soft down mattress, and colorful sheets made of silk with pillows to match. Subtle warmth radiated from the tiles of the floor. It was good to know that even in a land filled with barbarians, the comforts of modern living could be found. Still there was another room off the bedchamber and a light came from there too.

Placing his hand on the brass handle he opened the door. A brass bathtub came into view accompanied by a basin on a raised platform fitted with a faucet. An alcove inside the room included a privy made of marble complete with sponge and cleaning channel next to it. Small lanterns hung from the walls and ceiling giving the chamber a warm glow.

Returning to the bedchamber Thadius saw a writing secretary in the corner and rolls of paper. He admired its masterful craftsmanship and ornately carved legs. Pulling out the chair, he sat down and took one of the rolled papers from a shelf laden with papyrus. Finding a stylus and ink well, he dipped the tip in the dark black ink and began to write a record of his last few days. After filling several papers with writing and illustrations he heard a knock at the door.

Wiping the stylus on a small wet sponge he put the writing instrument back in its holder, carefully sanded the paper and rolled it up securing it with a small length of string. Another knock echoed in the room as he took the document and put it in his pack.

"One moment," he said as he walked across the room to the door. Opening it he found Dominus standing there.

"I have couches too," Dominus stated coming into the room and sitting on a couch.

"Then why aren't you sitting on yours?" Thadius said.

"I like the color of your couches better," Dominus stated. "But, as much as I like your couch, we should probably make our way to get some food."

"Is it that time already?" Thadius said.

"It's been three hours since we parted. The servant Timora came to my door and announced supper is prepared. I of course told her that I would let you and Eilifr know. The Northman has gone ahead already."

"I need to clean up first."

"What have you been doing for these last hours?" Dominus raised one eyebrow. "I shaved, cleaned myself and even used the privy. I have one in my suite you see," he laughed. "I take it you did none of these things?"

"Writing," Thadius said. "Making an account of the last few days…but let me wash myself and change my tunic and I'll be ready."

"As you wish. You can even put your dirty clothes out and they'll be washed and dried by morning. Or, so the girl said," Dominus added as Thadius walked into the other room.

Thadius quickly changed his clothes and did a quick cleaning. He added a few splashes of rosewater under each arm and stepped out of the washroom. "Reborn," he stated loudly.

"And, you are endowed with a better fragrance too. No longer are you a stinky old man, but a heap of sweet flowers." Dominus nodded his head, "It suits you."

Shaking his head Thadius walked to the door. "We all don't have to live like barbarians," he said.

"It's a lot more fun to do so though," Dominus smiled.

"Ridiculous," Thadius dismissed the comment, "You're a Roman through and through. You're just slumming now."

Dominus shrugged, "I can't argue with that." They left the room.

The feasting hall was not large or conventional. It was circular in shape and no more than forty feet in diameter. The roof rose up two stories and was domed. An oculus at the top allowed for viewing of the night sky. A single pane of glass five feet round covered the opening. Looking up Thadius saw clearly the white dots of the stars in the black sky. The low light of the hall seemed to add to the ambiance of the room, and he felt privileged to be there.

In the middle of the room the floor was sunken with a set of steps that led to a circular base. At the bottom, the floor shone with polished white marble. Tables arranged in a half circle followed the arc and next to each, lanterns illuminated the food.

"Reminiscent of an amphitheater," Thadius said.

"Drinks are served," Malcolm stated coming from a door at the side.

"That would be fine. Do we sit down there?" Dominus said.

"Yes," Malcolm added. "The intent is that you sit there to enjoy the room, but you may choose to sit as you please and we will serve you regardless."

Stepping down into the sunken floor, Thadius sat on the last marble stair. Women approached carrying silver goblets of different shapes. Setting down the cups in front of the men the women retreated and Malcolm came down. "My lord wished you to sample his libations," he gestured to the cups. "This is wine made of berries grown native to this region." Pointing to a short round cup, "and this is a product of distilled grain. And this here," he pointed at a tall tankard, "is daisy beer made most recently." Stepping up, Malcolm looked at each man, "Your appetizers will be out momentarily." Turning he disappeared through the kitchen doorway.

"Distilled?" Dominus said surprised while looking at the squatty cup. "An expensive process."

"Have you ever had any?"

"Far too expensive for me," Dominus stated.

"Me too," Thadius commented. "What about you Eilifr?"

"I have had this drink several times," he said pointing at the short cup, "but nowhere other than here."

Taking up the wine Thadius took a taste and was shocked by how sweet it was. "Like licking a hand full of sugar," he said.

"They say it is made from the nearly withered grape picked late in summer and mixed with the moodle berry," Eilifr stated.

Thadius set down his goblet and turned his attention back to the room. Pastel colors adorned all sides. Subdued by the lamplight he could just make out abstract shapes painted on all the walls.

"A wonder isn't it," Malcolm said.

Turning Thadius shook his head. "Your master is a genius."

"You're right. Everything that is here has its roots in his vision. There is more, much, much more that you do not know about." Malcom motioned with his hands all around. "I am blessed to be a witness to all this."

Several servants appeared and set out plates of small finger foods. Malcolm stepped down into the circle and pointed to the items on the plates. "These are for your enjoyment. Here we have grilled yellow squash, basted in honey, pine nuts from the Alps, spices from India, and topped with goat cheese. Here is a baked wheat cracker topped with salmon eggs, garnished with seaweed, olive oil, and vinegar. And here you'll find toasted bread basted in ox butter, salted and spiced with garlic and garum. Now, if you will excuse me," he again left and went back to the kitchen.

The men finished their wine and hors d'oeuvres and took up speaking of their trip. They chuckled about the pitfalls of their travels then turned their attention to the next leg of the journey. Laughing, Eilifr raised his cup to them. "You are stubborn Romans. Though this trip is wearing and hard, you stand to the front by taking up oars and rowing with my men. May the gods give you both spectacular deaths in battle at the end of your lives."

Dominus raised his cup, "And, let's hope that's a long way off."

Lifting his cup Thadius said nothing, but took a long draft then reclined in his seat. Setting his cup down on the table, he took a cracker and put it in his mouth. He chewed and savored the wonderful flavors of the salmon eggs and vinegar. "How far now to Lutetia?"

"Another day's travel up the river," Eilifr said.

"The barbarians seem cultured in these parts." Dominus hoisted his cup and drank some wine.

"Barbarians?" Eilifr wrinkled his nose and narrowed his gaze at him. "Rome has influence here in these parts, and the local tribes benefit from that influence. They are becoming less barbarian and more members of the Pax Romanus."

"No offense meant," Dominus added.

"I and my men are friends of Rome, but not promoters of it," he smiled. "No offense meant," he added.

"None taken," Dominus stated. "If I wasn't a citizen, I'd probably not be so keen on Rome's expansion either. But, I do appreciate the luxuries, the commercial granaries, steel mills, fresh water aqueducts and plumbing, the girls, breweries, wineries, olive presses, cement…" He took another drink. "You get the picture."

"All pushed along by the Roman coin," Eilifr added.

"Not just pushed, but often times shoved," Dominus commented.

Thadius put down his cup. "The use of coins has made a difference in the way Rome has flourished, but you of all people who benefit from commerce must know that Roman coin can make amazing things happen."

"Indeed I do," Eilifr chuckled then commenced to eating the last of the hors d'oeuvres.

As the plates were emptied, the main entrée arrived and Thadius delved into the fish and greens with much anticipation. More fresh baked bread arrived and the men ate heartily. Finally the dessert came, and he marveled at the amazing sugar covered berries, puddings, and pies.

Malcolm demonstrated that they were to dip the berries in the squat cup and then eat them. The white crystals of sugar that coated the berries melted away in the liquid. "The tradition is for the drink to be consumed only when the berries are all gone," Malcolm stated.

The taste was unlike anything Thadius had ever tasted. It burned slightly, but after a few sips, became quite smooth. He continued to talk and dip berries late into the night. Finally, with the berries gone each man took up his cup and sipped the liquor until their glass was empty. "I will be saddened to leave this place," Dominus said while standing and walking along the walls examining the images painted there.

Thadius sat back picking at his teeth with his fingernail. "I don't believe I could consume another bite. And this liquor is fantastic. I feel quite relaxed.

Dominus ordered more of the distilled spirits and reclined on the steps resting on one arm. Eilifr stood and walked about the room to stretch his legs. Thadius set down his short cup and walked up the stairs. "I think I will retire. Good evening my friends," he stated.

He made his way to the bedroom hallway as he swayed slightly. Finding his room he entered and undressed. Entering the washroom Thadius looked down at the brass bathtub. He turned the faucets and soon the steam filled the air. He touched his finger to the water. It was hot. After a short time the water level was half full and he turned off the faucets. Slowly, he climbed into the tub. His skin tingled from the hot water. Settling in he closed his eyes and listened to the creaking sounds of the house as a sense of calm fell over him.

CHAPTER 23

Coming awake he grasped at the sides of the bathtub. Sitting upright he looked about the dimly lit room. The lanterns were still lit, but the incense had gone out. He'd been in the water for hours. Taking a towel from a golden towel rod, he climbed out. A knocking sound echoed from the other room and he walked out to see Dominus opening the door. "It's daylight and Eilifr wants to get back on the river as soon as we can."

"I fell asleep in the bath," Thadius said.

"I take it you almost drowned then?"

"I'm lucky you came to check on me."

"We're all quite glad you didn't die. Now, you'd better get dressed. There are some loaves of fresh bread in the feasting hall and you can get a cup of hot broth to go with it," Dominus stated.

"Give me a moment," Thadius said. "Where's Eilifr?"

"Eilifr has already gone to the boat to prepare for the departure."

Thadius quickly dressed and gathered his things. He moved down the hall and toward the feasting room. A small table in the center of the sunken floor was filled with fruit, bread, and a steaming teapot. Malcolm came from the kitchen and motioned for Thadius to take a seat.

"I'm afraid that we're in a hurry. I'll just take some bread and broth," Thadius said.

"By your command," Malcolm stated signaling for another servant to bring a mug. Wrapping some bread in a cloth Malcolm handed the bundle to Thadius, then poured some broth into a large mug and handed it to him.

"Tell your master that his hospitality reflects a noble soul, Thadius said while blowing on the hot broth.

"The master will like that. He is not feeling well this day and has elected to remain in his bedchamber. He wanted me to give you this, but said for you to open it once on the ship." Malcolm handed a folded piece of paper sealed with wax to Thadius, then turned and removed himself to the kitchen.

"Let's hurry to the ship and get up the river. It's time we got to Lutetia."

"As you wish, oh great commander," Dominus grinned as they both left the villa.

Thadius commented as they passed a line of carts filled with produce, "A costly affair to own so many people, to keep them fed and clothed just to continue to serve one's needs."

"Servants are costly my friend, first to buy, then to keep. Be thankful you only have a few dozen," Dominus said.

"A few dozen at my home, but at least five hundred if you count my mining, farms, and mills," Thadius stated as they approached the town limit.

Dominus slowed to a fast walk. Thadius did the same. Passing the main government hall they turned and headed towards the marina. Citizens and servants passed them in the street. A woman with an infant swaddled on her back carried a basket of bread to a vendor's stall. A tall man in a gray tunic stoked a fire under a black cauldron. The smell of baking bread and river mud mingled in the air.

Emerging onto the docks Thadius could see Eilifr standing on the boat by the rudder pointing and issuing orders. He looked up,

"Ah the little Romans have arrived. If you will get onboard we will be off to the island."

"How far," Thadius asked.

"The better part of the day," Eilifr said as he signaled for the ship to be untied. The current pushed the boat from the dock and began taking it down river. "We have a good strong breeze today blowing up the river. We shall make good time."

Laying against the rudder the boat turned into the current and he gave the order to raise the sail. The wind filled it and the boat began to move slowly against the current. Even in the early morning other ships and boats moved down the river from Lutetia.

CHAPTER 24

The water was smooth like glass. Ahead boats of varying configurations came. Some were barges, and other's rowing boats, some were Corbitas, and even a few rafts floated by. Thadius sat by the port saxboard looking at the passing countryside.

"Now here is a poser for you. What is that letter tucked in your belt about?" Dominus said while pointing at the papyrus with a red wax seal.

"Oh, I nearly forgot. The servant gave it to me," Thadius said taking the letter from his belt and breaking the seal. "It says that Eilifr is to deliver these goods to a man named Darius at a place called Lodgers House. If we want more information regarding the Malco family we will need to talk to him," Thadius said.

"So, what do you think of all this," Dominus asked.

"First, Gnaeus summons me to help him, why? He says he's worried to tell his brother-in-law about the death of the disgraced girl. Second, the killing happened a month before, so the evidence is lost, save for Gnaeus' hand written notes. Last, the information is spotty, yet the killer is obvious."

"Yes, almost like we are being directed to conclude that Malco's son is the killer."

"My thoughts exactly. But, by who and why?" Thadius stated. "I guess we'll find more clues in Lutetia," he added. "Quod erat demonstrandum."

"Yes, you're very smart Thadius. But, what happens when his father has us killed and then no one is the smarter? Or worse; he involves his personal lawyer?"

Realizing the truth in Dominus' words he sat down. "You're right. It seems we'll need the local legion commander's help to issue a warrant and send troops."

"All Publius has to do is say he wants to be tried in Rome," Dominus added.

"Yes, and he's entitled to that by his rights as a citizen," Thadius stated, "but, we don't quite have him in our snare yet."

"We don't even know if he is still in Lutetia. And, since there are many unknowns here, I believe I'll take a nap." Dominus laid back on the rudder deck and folded his arms over his chest. "Wake me when we're tied up to the docks."

Thadius fetched some wine and bread and sat on a rower's bench to think. Looking out he could see the thick green trees lining the river bank. In the distance he could see wisps of white smoke rising into the blue sky. Eating his meal he wondered if the Malco family had moved on already. *Could they be there waiting? Is it just coincidence, or are the Malco's fleeing?* Thadius thought. He reflected on what Helvetius had said; that the killer struck in Lutetia butchering a girl and her family. *But, were the Malco's responsible? After all, barbarians are quite capable of murder. Or, had the Malcos taken flight and moved south, towards the mountains, towards the Tuscan hills and Rome beyond?*

Drinking the red wine, Thadius lay back and stared up at the sky. No clouds were visible and he thought of all the blue skies he had seen in his many years of living. It seemed not so long ago he was a boy studying in Greece, staring up at the same blue sky.

Listening to the flapping sound of the sail, he closed his eyes. The sloshing of the water and the soft warm breeze caressed his flesh. Drifting to sleep his mind began to wander. Was he still in the boat? Was he still on the river?

The sound of Tuturk and his son moving pots and pans woke Thadius. He looked up and saw the sun directly overhead. Taking his wineskin he drank deeply. Wiping his mouth he moved to the bow and looked out over the prow. Green dirty water passed by. Looking out to the shore he could see some women collecting earthen pots of water and carrying them into the green underbrush.

"Not too far now," Eilifr said.

High up on the banks Thadius could see mud-brick huts. Men and women moved about along the river tending to daily chores. Small, round, fishing boats tied to trees or sturdy posts strained against their tethers as the current tried to sweep them down river. Looking forward he could see debris and garbage swirling and rippling in the water. Old crates bobbed up and down, discarded clothes wrapped around branches that floated past, and produce and refuse clogged the waters. He glanced back and saw Eilifr, the man's expressionless face gave him the air of a marble statue. The acrid smell of sewage filled Thadius' nose one moment then the pungent odor of a slaughterhouse and tanneries overpowered him the next as they approached an outcropping of land.

As they came around a bend in the river he could see the waters forking around the end of an island. Though the river narrowed here, the wide right branch seemed to flow more swiftly. Further up along the island's bank, he made out rows of wooden buildings. Clay pipes jutted out from the rocky shore, leaking sewage and other nasty fluids into the river. A group of ten men stood along the edge of the river tossing in garbage from large-wheeled carts. They seemed to take little notice of the boat as it passed them.

On the mainland he could see the irregular natural limestone walls of the river's bank. Above the bank were tufts of green grass and sheep milling about. Several hay carts moved along the rim, pulled by slaves. One of the slaves looked down, and then turned his cart inland. "Well old friend, we're near Lutetia," Dominus said coming up and slapping Thadius on the back.

Eilifr shouted and Wyglad and Rolf rushed up to the bow and grabbed the ropes. Thadius could see along the shore a wide two-story building. The building sat atop a high mound and children were rushing in and out of the doorway. Its construction was a simple rectangular shape, and appeared to be made almost entirely of stone blocks. The shore of the island curved inward and as the ship cleared the apex a gathering of men came into view. Rushing up the men began shouting in what seemed Latin, but the accents were heavy.

"Take up river cheap! Two Aureus," shouted a stout man with a wide black mustache. A lanky blond haired man jabbed his elbow into the stocky man's chest and leaned out over the channel. "I take you up river. One gold Aureus," he yelled.

An older man stood back up the river and waved a yellow wad of cloth at the crew. "I have five donkeys, take you up river cheap! You pay two silver."

The boat slowed as the current began to outmatch the wind. Wyglad waited. Eilifr watched intently as several fistfights broke out among the men on shore, then he nodded to Wyglad who then held up several silver coins. The man with the yellow cloth called to him and Wyglad spoke back to the man, then tossed a rope to the old fellow and put his foot up on the prow. Rolf did the same. The old man took the ropes and secured them to a large iron rod sticking up from the limestone shore. He waved at a young boy up the bank who came down the road and brought a pack of five donkeys all harnessed together with wooden yokes. The old man untied the ropes from the iron rod, carried them to the donkeys, and looped the ropes through a set of iron rings and turned back to Wyglad. "He is ready for us to drop the sail," Wyglad said to Eilifr.

"Drop sail," Eilifr called out.

Once the sail dropped the old man moved to the front of the donkeys and took the lead animal by a rope. Slowly he led the animals along the road. The old man made no attempt to look back, but lumbered forward as the donkeys dragged the boat up river.

Eilifr stayed at the rudder and watched the murky waters for any obstacles. Wyglad watched over the bow and shouted back commands to his captain when rocks or debris appeared. Within what seemed an hour, the ship came around a bend, the river widened, and many other ships moored at a marina came into view. Workmen and slaves alike hefted produce in shoulder baskets, carried crates, and moved merchandise from the ships. A strong, sour smell filled the air. "Seems every port-of-call has a stench about it," Thadius said.

Dominus laughed, "I was wondering if that smell was coming from us?"

"We'll get a good bath tomorrow," Thadius stated.

The old man with the donkeys brought the ship to several burly looking men and untied the ropes. Wading into the mucky waters he waited for Wyglad to drop him his money. Handing down the expected two silver coins, Wyglad added an extra coin to the man's treasure. The old man looked up with a toothless grin, turned and waded back to shore, all the while saying words of praise to the men on the ship.

The burly fellows who held the ropes pulled the boat to a mooring by a long wooden dock and tied it off. One of them extended a long plank to the ship's saxboard, while two workmen stood at the ready. Climbing down from the rudder platform, Eilifr made his way to the bow. "You little Romans have come as far as I can take you," he said with a frown. "From here on out I think you will be on a horse or cart."

"You've been an excellent host my friend," Thadius said. "I have learned much about myself, sailing, and being a barbarian on this trip."

Dominus looked dismayed. He shrugged his shoulders, as he looked the large Northman in the face. "It saddens me that we may not see you again."

Laughing loudly Eilifr grabbed Dominus by his shoulders and held him firmly. "You little Romans are all alike, so sentimental. There is a good chance that we will see each other again. In a few months I will take my boat back toward your home village. Perhaps we will even winter in your town. Then we can feast and drink much of your wine." Stopping Eilifr motioned for Wyglad to come over. "These I want you to have on your journey." Wyglad set down two large bundles and stepped back. "Take them my friends and when I see you again, I will have more gifts to impart."

Thadius looked at the items with surprise. He reached down and hefted the bundle closest to him. "Heavy," he commented.

"Yes, it's a chain mail coif and vest. Wear this while you are here and on your travels. I have included two steel daggers and a leather belt to carry them by. And, you have warm, fur lined clothes for the last of your journey south and over the mountains to your home."

"May the gods always bless you, your men, and your ship," Thadius said.

"As well, I will pray for you, and I'll give offerings at the temple for you and the crew," Dominus added.

"Be wary, and be safe." Eilifr looked about then pointed at an over plump, large man with a black beard, standing just up from the riverbank watching the commotion on the docks. "That man is to take the Malco's items." Having said that, Eilifr called some commands to his men and climbed out of the ship and onto the dock.

Putting on his pack Thadius grabbed his gift. He climbed onto the dock, and carried his bundle up onto the shore. Dominus followed him closely and the two men stood dockside looking up into a swirling crowd of pedestrians. Thadius found a group of men with carts. "What about one of those fellows with the cart?" he said to Dominus.

"As well as any I guess."

Thadius hired the man and his cart. Waiting, he watched the Malco servant load the family's goods onto a cart a few yards away. Thadius directed his cart driver to follow the Malco's. Resting his hand on his dagger he watched the crowd. Throngs of people moved about. Roman roads seemed to run in all directions. In the distance he could see the main fortification. A wall was under construction, and large, limestone blocks were being fitted into place by Roman legionnaires.

The road led them into a town bursting with natives and Roman soldiers. Structures appeared to him shanty at first, but he noted their marked improvement as they moved further along toward the middle of the island. As they turned down the main boulevard, shops and five story apartments appeared. Pots of soups and stews bubbled at a nearby thermopolia, while men crowded around waiting for their respective meals. Cloth of every description was displayed in windows, and pottery, plants, kitchenware, and artwork, all were being peddled in the market.

"That fellow you want, he went into there," the donkey cart driver said as he halted and pointed.

Thadius looked at the name-stone and read it aloud, "Lodging House."

"I can read you know," Dominus said. "We better watch our moves here. Once we ask some questions there might be some who find profit in killing us."

"Then we must be wise about what we ask," Thadius added.

"Indeed," Dominus smiled.

Thadius arranged for the owner of the donkey cart to wait and watch their items, while he made his way to the entrance of the Lodging House. Standing a fair foot and a half taller than he, the innkeeper acknowledged him. Smiling back at the man, Thadius took measure of him. His face was scarred from scalp to cheek, and his left eye was missing. Dark hair fell to shoulder length, and the innkeeper's mouth formed a permanent scowl due to the scarring. The innkeeper regarded Thadius with his one eye then he said something in the local tongue. Seeing no recognition the man spoke in Latin. "Do you need a place to stay?" His gruff voice projected loudly from behind the broad dark oak desk.

"Yes, my companion and I are seeking a place until we can take a caravan south and over the mountain," Thadius stated.

"I have but one room left, you will have to share it," said the man.

"That will be fine," Thadius commented.

"Any servants, slaves, or cargo?" The man asked.

"Just personal items, enough for the back of two oxen, or donkey."

"You will pay one quinarius per night if you intend to stay."

"Do you know when the next caravan is leaving for Pisae?"

"It left three days ago. But there is one leaving for Narbo by way of Tolosa tomorrow. You can get a ship at Narbo to take you to Pisae," the man said.

"Tolosa?"

"Yes. I can have my son fetch the caravan master if you like?"

"Yes. That would be fine. By the way, I have a friend who might be traveling this way too. I would like to leave a letter for him and his family. May I leave it here, in the likelihood he arrives soon?" The innkeeper nodded his consent. "He will be traveling with his family, a son, and wife, plus some servants. He's been purchasing items on his trip for his home in Rome."

"What is this man's name?" The innkeeper asked.

"Flavius Malco Scapula," Thadius stated.

"You have missed them. They left with the last caravan, traveling for Segusio then over the alpis to Pisae."

"Ah, then it would be of no use to leave a letter," Thadius said while reaching into his pouch at his belt and pulling out a quinarius and setting it on the desk.

"One night I see," the innkeeper said. "If you wish to have a message delivered to Flavius Malco Scapula, I suggest you give it to his servant who has remained behind waiting for some of his goods."

"And what name shall I call this man?"

"He has but one name he goes by, Darius, and he is taking the caravan tomorrow to Narbo."

"I don't know this servant, but, perhaps he can help us book a passage to Narbo too. Where might I find him?"

"He will be present for the evening meal. Tonight will be fair weather, so we will have dinner served in the garden rotunda at nine of the clock," he said pointing at a small water clock sitting against the wall. "The clock is a gift from our benefactor," the innkeeper said. "I will have my son show you to your room for the night. You may inquire with the man Darius as to booking passage, for I think he knows the caravan driver personally."

Pulling on a gold braided rope, the sound of many bells rang out. The innkeeper fostered a wry smile as a small boy no older than ten dashed in. Thin and wiry the boy appeared a miniature of his father, minus the scars and missing eye. The man motioned for the boy to go fetch Thadius' luggage.

"Next time I take a vacation with you we really need to plan better. Stay a while in one place maybe?"

"This is no vacation as you know," Thadius reminded him.

The boy brought in the items from the cart. Taking them to the room, the boy waited smiling. Thadius reached into his leather satchel and produced a copper coin. He handed it to the child and watched the boy dash off happily.

"Now what?" Dominus said.

"A bath," stated Thadius. They went down stairs. Stopping at the innkeeper he asked for directions to the local public bath.

"It is by the garrison, built over a wonderful healing spring. Go through the courtyard and out the side gate," the man said then pointed out a doorway. "Follow the road toward the olive orchard and you can't miss it. Enjoy."

Walking through the courtyard he noticed the wonderful garden in the middle. Narrow paths crisscrossed and small platforms of cement held marble tables and benches. Several fountains spit water into the air. A woman and her two children moved about the garden. She pointed at plants and her children appeared excited by the lesson. An older couple sitting at a table sipped wine and looked about anxiously.

Thadius and Dominus exited out into the alley and followed the cobblestone street to an orchard of olive trees. The heavy scent of the bitter olives filled the air as did the smell of incense from a nearby brothel and wood smoke from a bakery. In the distance a dog was barking, and as they turned out into the Forum, the smell of cooking food wafted over Thadius like a wave.

CHAPTER 25

Gaul, Burbur, Roman, Greek, Egyptian, and many others were represented in the Forum. Thadius and Dominus moved through unnoticed and came to a cross street. "Legonis XXX, Ulpia Victrix," Dominus said aloud.

Thadius nodded, "They're a busy Legion."

"On the building is an arrow," Dominus pointed out. "It says, Lutetia Bath, that way."

"I can't wait."

They moved down the cobblestone street toward the bath. Dominus glanced over to see the worried expression on Thadius' face. "What's wrong?" he said.

"I feel strange, like we're being followed." Thadius glanced about casually surveying the surrounding crowd. Many wore cloaks and capes to ward off the chill in the air. It was difficult to identify any one person since most of the cloaks were gray or brown. He looked back at Dominus who fostered a cagy smile, "What is it?"

"I've been keeping an eye on a person in a gray cowl and cape some twenty paces behind us. He's been following us since we left the inn. I'm wondering if he wants our money, or something else?"

Pointing at a street vendor selling tubers, turnips, and rhubarb, Thadius spoke just loud enough for Dominus to hear clearly, "Do you recognize our pursuer?"

"No."

"If he means us harm we're not without weapons nor alone," Thadius stated.

"True," Dominus said. "And, we also don't know what he wants."

In the distance the bathhouse complex appeared. The main building sprawled over roughly two acres of land with red terracotta tiles covering the gabled roof. Out front it looked like a market square. Food vendors all around sold roasted nuts, red meat and pork on skewers. Some vendors sold sandals and towels, while others sold salts, soap, oils and powders.

To the side of the colorful building Thadius could see the wide and long grassy playing field. A sign was posted, *Harpastum game today. Garrison Satyrs against the City Slaughterhouse. From noon until dusk. Betting courtesy Filmulius and Associates.* Turning to Dominus Thadius commented, "How I use to love harpastum. I wonder how our city team is doing."

"I heard they won the region and were going to play down south and maybe even in Greece," Dominus stated.

Stopping at the arched entrance of the bath, Dominus turned to speak to Thadius. This gave him an unobstructed view of the throng behind them. The crowd split, some passing towards the large field and some moving toward the bath. Speaking to Thadius of food, and entertainment, Dominus kept his eye on the gray hooded figure. The man passed by going to the field. Dominus leaned against the frame of the doorway, "Perhaps we're worried for nothing?"

"I wonder," Thadius said.

Entering the bathhouse was a chore. The wide entry was crowded, and between the vendors and the patrons, space was at a premium. A man in a baby-blue toga directed them to the men's changing hall. Finding a couple of unused cubbies to store their change of clothes Thadius and Dominus dawned their cotton towels and sandals, and took their bathing instruments. They moved into the anti-chamber of the steam room. Thadius could see steam leaking out from under the broad yellow wooden door. Opening the door he stepped in. Thick white steam obscured his visibility, but he found his way to a row of benches. Sitting down, as the heavy steam pulled open his pores and allow the filth to be drawn out. The sounds of several languages echoed in the confines of the room, and he tried to identify where each group sat. Feeling the moist heat caressing his body, he scraped away the dirty sweat. "By god, this feels good," Thadius said.

"Almost better than a good meal," Dominus laughed.

Thadius took meticulous care scraping all the areas of his body. Taking a small glass bottle from his bathing satchel, he applied a handful of dark green olive oil to his skin. Soon he was feeling revived, invigorated, and relaxed.

"I'm going to wash my hair," Dominus stated. "Though I don't expect the gray to vanish with the dirt. I hope they have a downpour here."

"I'm sure there is one," Thadius added.

"Do I hear the words of a fellow countryman?" A gruff voice erupted as the sound of a door closing could be heard. "Who are you and from where do you call home?"

"I am Moras Tiberius Thadius and this man here is Peresius Albas Dominus."

"Moras Tiberius Thadius?" the man said as if in thought. "I served in the Third Legion Tiberius under such a man. Are you he?"

"I am," Thadius stated, "and, who are you comrade?"

"Suetonius Tradgen Ulanius is my name." The man came through the steam.

Thadius rubbed his eyes. Examining the man he could see he was in his late forties. Grabbing the man by the shoulders he pulled him in and embraced him. "By the gods I see that young soldier in your face."

"That soldier is all gone now," Ulanius stated. "But, I can never forget my Uncle whom I love. What brings you here to this city on the frontier?"

"Seems less a frontier town and more a Roman city," Dominus quipped. "Seems quite a popular place to spend silver and gold coins too."

"I remember you well," Ulanius stated while looking at Dominus. "How has life been for you Dominus?"

"Well and good," he smiled. "And I'm surprised that you remember me."

"We are here on an errand, a grim bit of business it is. But, this is not the place to discuss it," said Thadius.

"Then when you two have finished here, come to my villa and we shall feast. We will drink my family's wine and you will say to yourself, 'Gods ambrosia, elixir of Olympus!'" Ulanius boasted.

"We accept," Dominus quickly said.

"Where is it you're staying?"

"Lodging House," Thadius stated.

"Ah, yes, a fine establishment," Ulanius laughed. "The owner is very strict, and his servants are above reproach."

Sitting down Thadius again scraped his skin removing even more dirty oil. Ulanius crouched down. "I fear I must be off. When you're ready, take the east road out of town. You will see my vineyards and fields and you'll find my home at the end of the road. I will leave word with the guards to let you two come in." Placing his hand on Thadius' shoulder Ulanius smiled, "Good to see that the gods have been kind to you, both." Turning, he disappeared into the steam. The sound of a door opening and closing could be heard.

Thadius turned to Dominus, "Most unusual; I had no idea he was living here."

"Seems he's doing well though," Dominus stated.

"Shall we find the downpour?" Thadius said.

"We should. My hair is caked with grime."

They exited from the steam room and made their way down a hall to a room with a large square sunken bath. Water ran from a miniature aqueduct and poured into the bathtub. Thadius gauged the tub to be roughly ten feet to each side, and nearly five feet deep. High windows allowed the late afternoon sun to fill the room with pale light. In the corner of the room was a pipe fitted with two lion heads that spit water out onto a concaved floor with a drain fitted in the middle.

Setting his bathing tools on a granite bench Thadius removed his olive oil soap and moved to the downspout. He stood under the cool water and took the harsh soap rubbing it between his hands. Slowly it began to form a foamy lather. Wetting his hair he quickly washed his head and rinsed, taking particular care to make sure all the soap was washed out. He stepped out of the downpour, moved to the bench, and put his soap in its cheesecloth wrap. Taking out his bottle of olive oil he put a sparing amount in the palm of his hand and massaged it into his hair and scalp as he waited for Dominus to finish his soapy task and dry off.

"Do you feel like soaking in the hot bath?" Dominus said.

"No, I think perhaps we should get some food and return to the inn. We'll need to meet this Darius fellow."

Dominus packed his sundries while Thadius moved to the door leading into the hot bath and scanned the room. Hundreds of men stood about or relaxed in the steaming hot water. A few children darted about unattended. Turning he shook his head. "Doesn't seem such a bad place to live."

CHAPTER 26

Stopping near the doorway, Dominus stared out into the darkening sky. The crowd watching the harpastum game echoed with both cheers and boos. Dominus stayed in the shadow of the door. "That hooded fellow, he's near the hedges by the filed. There's one way to put this to rest; I suggest that the slowest of us might stand out and let the faster stand ready to intercept him."

"You don't mean that I'll be the hen clucking about waiting for the fox do you?" Thadius said, a frown growing across his lips.

"I'll stay back just enough to keep an eye on you, and a watchful eye out for our stranger," Dominus stated.

"Very well, but I'd hate to think of you being delayed because of some perfumed beauty."

"You wound me," Dominus said. "Don't you worry, if there's trouble, you'll not feel the point of a knife while I still live."

"Don't stray too far," Thadius stated while stepping out into the street and walking towards the main town boulevard.

Dominus watched from the doorway as Thadius reached the harpastum sign. The crowd was thin, and only those fetching food and drink wandered about. From near the hedge the hooded man took up the pursuit. Dominus fell in behind. A strong smell of lavender wafted into his nose. He moved into the long evening shadows. Ahead, the hooded figure stopped and watched Thadius intently. Thadius turned to walk down the street towards the inn. Halfway down the street Thadius stopped at a street vendor and ordered some food. The hooded man merged into the crowd and moved towards Thadius. Dominus stopped at a vegetable cart down from the man and watched him. The fellow's cloak bulged around the middle and Dominus surmised he carried a short sword. Passing Dominus, a young boy with a torch was lighting the sconces mounted on roadway posts.

The haunting yellow light flickered in the gentle breeze that bathed the festive street. A group of jugglers passed, their batons held at their sides. *No doubt,* Dominus thought, *they were going home in the failing light.* Looking over, he could see that the pedestrians were putting on hoods. Focusing on the man in the gray cloak, Dominus made his way towards him.

He side stepped a young boy and came within ten feet of the man. The lavender was strong in the air. Edging his way past a pregnant woman carrying a basket with groceries, Dominus came closer. He glanced across at Thadius and could see he had his back to the stalker. Looking back at the cloaked fellow he saw the man turn to the side into the classic attack position. A man in a dull yellow toga suddenly blocked his view.

Drawing his dagger, Dominus shoved aside the man. He moved quickly reaching the attacker and grabbing the man's weapons arm. "Hold it there," Dominus shouted.

Moving with incredible agility and speed, the man turned abruptly immobilizing Dominus' weapon hand, then stepped into him to throw Dominus to the ground. Countering the stalker's attack Dominus crouched low and shoved his hip into the man's stomach to throw him. The stalker countered, straddling Dominus' hip and placed his hand in the small of his back. Pulling Dominus around the attacker raised his fist to strike, but Dominus dodged to the side and blocked. Jumping slightly the man slipped around Dominus. Placing his hand in Dominus' back, he then looped his other arm around his neck and pulled Dominus to the ground.

The cloaked man dashed into the crowd, and the darkness. Thadius poised himself to pursue the man, but Dominus reached up and seized his leg. "Don't bother," he stated. "Help me up." Taking Dominus by the hand Thadius helped his friend to his feet.

"Have you been robbed?" A legionnaire said coming through the gathering crowd. In his hand was a gladius, and his posture dictated that he was ready to fight.

"No, just a mistake," Dominus stated. "I thought the man was going to attack my friend."

"We've lots of cut-purses here in the market lately. Are you all right? The man didn't stab you did he?" the legionnaire stated.

"I'm only wounded in my pride," Dominus said.

Pulling up his dagger, he made ready to put it back at his belt. Holding it up to the yellow torchlight he stared at the knife. Blood fell from the blade. Quickly checking himself Dominus looked confused. "I clearly didn't stab myself, so I must have wounded the man during our struggle," he stated.

The legionnaire looked Dominus up and down for a wound. "You're alright. Must have nicked the robber. We'll keep an eye out for someone with a fresh wound," he said. "If you don't mind, what are your names so I can fill out my report?"

It took only a few moments to provide the information to the legionnaire. The man was gracious when he recognized Thadius' name, and even suggested some loggings. After gathering the information, the soldier wished them good journey, and left down the street.

"That flatbread looks good," Dominus said while sheathing his dagger.

"Get yourself one and let's get back to the inn before Darius leaves."

Walking over to the vendor Dominus ordered a flatbread with goat meat and vegetables. The man across the counter removed some meat and set it on the flatbread, then ladled out some vegetables. Seasoning the top with spices he rolled the bread and placed it in what looked to Dominus to be a cone shaped sheet of papyrus. Handing it to Dominus the man grinned, "Thieves are a-plenty here in the market. It is good you put that fellow in his place."

Taking the food Dominus paid the man. "I sure hope our encounter with this Darius isn't as exasperating as with the evasive fellow in the gray cloak," Dominus said between bites.

"Me also my friend," Thadius added as they walked back towards the inn.

CHAPTER 27

Keeping an eye out for trouble, he and Dominus made their way back to the inn. Discussing the event, Dominus postulated that the man in the gray cloak was a military man.

"Why do you think that?" Thadius said.

"His manner, calmness, quickness and the fact that I used a couple of grappling techniques on him, and he used the classic counters to them," Dominus stated.

"Still doesn't tell us much," Thadius said as they approached the inn.

"True enough," Dominus began, "but, he also smelled like lavender. I think he was perfumed, and it was not cheap."

"Expensive? Why would a common thief wear expensive perfume?" Thadius thought out loud.

"Perhaps he was not so common," Dominus quipped.

They went up the stairs and entered the inn. Thadius walked up to the innkeeper. The gaunt man turned and looked at him, "Yes, and how can I assist you?"

"The man called Darius, is he still in?"

"He is dining in the courtyard with the other guests," the innkeeper stated. "And, for your information I will be closing the doors and barring them after eleven of the evening." He pointed at a water clock against the wall.

"Very well," Thadius acknowledged.

Walking through the main hall and into the courtyard portico, Thadius moved towards the garden. Hanging lanterns were abundant and the patrons of the inn lounged about talking and eating. He could see the same two young children from the afternoon politely reclining in Roman fashion with their mother and father. An old man was talking with two other men, each holding a copper cup which the elder refilled from an earthen pitcher. Across the garden Thadius could see Darius. The man sat in the back, nearest to the rooms. He sat upright on a limestone bench and stuffed slices of a meat-pie into his mouth with a scoop. A dark mat of coarse hair grew from his plump face, but little grew atop his head. Grease hung thickly, suspended in the man's beard as he looked up to see Thadius and Dominus approach. "Yes," he said.

"The innkeeper suggested that we talk with you. My companion and I are traveling to Narbo and we wanted to know what caravan you have contracted with?" Thadius stated.

"Companion, eh?" Darius said, his bulging eyes scanning up and down the two men as if they too were part of his meal. "Do you have many slaves?"

"No, just my companion, our luggage, rations, and nothing else."

"To Narbo, and, further maybe?" Darius probed.

"Just to Narbo. I have business there," Thadius stated. "But, we might decide to travel on to Pisae. My friend here has an estate there."

"Tuscan?" Darius said. "The man you want is Shymor Beirmont. He and his men are Gaul's, but of good repute. They'll provide escort, provisions, and accommodations to Narbo." Taking a mouth full of food Darius watched them as he chewed. "I could introduce you, but it is short notice, we leave tomorrow at first light. I hope you've brought some gold coin with you. He will probably be persuaded, only with gold," he stated just before shoving more greasy meat between his lips.

"Come morning we will be ready. We need little but accommodations and meals. Perhaps you could speak with him and hopefully he will grant us passage," Thadius added.

"Very well, I'll go see him tonight. I'll come by your room and let you know what his answer is. If you are not ready by morning though, he will leave without you," Darius stated between gulps of dark red wine.

"Of course. But, we will be ready," Thadius stated.

"Good," Darius said as he wiped his hands on a linen napkin.

Turning, he and Dominus walked back to the front desk. Thadius waited for the innkeeper to acknowledge them. "Yes?" the man said.

"Could you send a servant to wake us at –," he turned and examined the water clock, "four of the morning?"

The innkeeper looked annoyed, "That is rather early, no?" he said.

Thadius put down a silver coin. The innkeeper briefly smiled, "I'll see that you are woken at the proper time."

"Now, could you suggest the best way to Ulanius' villa?"

"Ulanius the Roman merchant and vintner?" The innkeeper put his finger to his chin. "Yes, he is at the end of the eastern road. Follow the Demas Boulevard, until it runs into the Caesar concourse. Follow the street until it forks. Take the right fork and follow it until you come to Ulanius' home."

"Should we be concerned about bandits," Thadius asked.

"Not many here on the island. The penalty for robbery here is death. Most thieves and robbers do their highway work on the mainland instead of the island."

"We'll stay vigilant nonetheless," Dominus said while patting his dagger.

"You have a fine inn here," Thadius stated to the innkeeper.

"I thank you for your patronage," the innkeeper said his sneer turning slightly upward at the corners.

Going to their room Thadius and Dominus gathered up their warm cloaks and again headed out. While passing the innkeeper the man called across the room. "Remember, that I bar the doors at eleven. If you return after, pull the red cord near the door and I will be alerted by the bell."

Lamplight filled the street with its pale orange glow. Evenly spaced wooden posts rose to roughly ten feet. A cross bar fitted to the top allowed a wrought iron chain to hang down. Attached to the chain was an iron pan that held a thick wick that blazed with light. In the gentle cool evening breeze the pans shifted to and fro causing shadows to appear as animated. Crowds mingled, some entering taverns, and others sitting or standing at wine bars. Gaming houses churned out loud voices and laughter, and food carts and prostitutes moved among them all.

Looking down, Thadius could see recently placed cobblestones fitted tightly together and grouted into place. Not much wear showed on the face of the stones, and they still appeared to have the original application of lacquer on them. The smell of baking bread carried in the air as did the nearby scent of grilled pork, goat, and beef, churned out by the many thermopolium.

"You know if all the citizens of the Republic ate this good there would be no need for wars," Dominus mused.

"True, but the Republic is hard to manage and starvation keeps those ill minded rebels at bay," Thadius said while adjusting his belt and dagger. "Here, in the frontier, smaller is better I think; maybe less amenities, but a better distributed harvest, more reasonable prices for goods, and enough soldiers to keep the peace."

Coming to the end of the main boulevard, they turned onto a street marked by a white marble plaque, *Caesar Concourse*. Following the street to the fork, they turned right and traveled on. Walking slowly down the wide road, they moved deeper into the rural part of the island. Sounds of running irrigation water filled the air, and Thadius squinted into the darkness trying to discern the ditches that crisscrossed the vast fields. In the distance somewhere beyond the hills, a bright white light became more intense.

"We'll have a full moon soon to see by," Dominus said in a hushed voice.

"We probably should have brought a lantern," Thadius added somewhat irritated that he did not think of it before.

In the distance he could see the simmering flames of the large wall torches that marked Ulanius' villa. And, in the shadows cast by the light there were unnatural shapes of the farm buildings. Several small homes had been built off the road. Barns and sheds were erected also, and the detail of each became more apparent as the moon crept up over the hills.

A growling sound erupted behind the two men. Turning Dominus stepped to the side with his dagger drawn. Thadius instinctively stepped opposite, nearly falling off the road and into a ditch. Pulling free his dagger he quickly surveyed the area around them. Standing on the road facing them was a large wolf. It bared its teeth which reflected the light of the moon. Appearing unearthly in the darkness, the creature's reflective eyes peered back at them. It looked from Dominus to Thadius and back again as it gnashed its teeth. The stench of wet dog washed over them and Thadius raised his empty hand to his nose. "Son of Jupiter, he stinks!" The creature's hackles stood vertical.

As Thadius made ready his dagger he noticed several other dark shapes closing in from the fields. "He's brought a host of wolves with him."

"We've got a challenging situation here," Dominus said calmly. "We have a good chance of being devoured by hungry wolves, but not before I defecate in my breeches."

"We're too far from Ulanius' to call for help, and if we run we're done for," Thadius stated.

"I agree," Dominus added.

Snorting and growling filled the air all around them. Thadius turned in a slow circle, while removing his second dagger.

"Perhaps their determination is unwarranted," Dominus continued.

"Your point?" Thadius said while turning as to keep an eye on the pack.

"Maybe we should show them that we are not so easy a meal?"

"Ah, yes. Go on the offensive to give the enemy the pause to consider less aggressive prey," Thadius said making ready to attack.

"Exactly."

Inching forward, the lead wolf crept towards them. As the wolf moved, the others of the pack became agitated and rushed around snarling. Passing close to Thadius a dark black wolf snapped its teeth at him. Passing near his legs another did the same. He crouched low and struck at the beasts, but his blade cut only air. The furry blurs came from the sides of the road and passed between him and Dominus.

Releasing a tremendous howl, the master wolf leapt at Dominus gnashing its teeth wildly. The creature's claws scratched at his weapon-hand. Dominus struck the animal a glancing blow sending it to the side and into another attacking wolf.

Thadius moved with graceful steps as if he was a young man again. His agility and power surprised him. Easily knocking away an eighty pound wolf, he side stepped another and struck with his dagger. The creature yelped with pain and fell away into the darkness. Stepping forward, he did a forward kick, striking another attacker and driving it back.

Dominus quickly dodged to the side. Striking with his fist, he blocked using his arm, and attacked with the dagger fatally wounding one of the monstrous animals. "Do you hear that?" Dominus shouted.

Thadius could hear what sounded like wheels and horses approaching. The whistle sound of arrows passed by. Howls of pain, cries and whimpers rose from the pack of attacking wolves. Lucky survivors dashed into the fields and the night. The unlucky dogs fell around Thadius and Dominus.

A chariot moved quickly past the two men. Coming to a halt, the horse's hooves skidded over the cobblestones. The charioteer jumped down, his sword flashing brightly in the moonlight. Two other chariots came to a halt around the two men and several archers jumped from their cars.

"Blasted creatures," Ulanius shouted into the fields. Turning he looked down at the fallen dogs. Walking over to each, he pointed his sword down at the animal and kicked it. Blood was thick on the ground around them. "They're dead," he stated. Walking around the edge of the road, Ulanius counted the carcasses with arrows in them. "Good shot lads. A large pack this time from the other side of the river," he said. Turning to Thadius and Dominus he stated, "Are you both alright?"

Dominus sheathed his dagger. He felt blood, cold and wet on his legs. Looking down he could see several bloody scratches along his forearm and on his legs.

Thadius checked his arms and legs, stepped forward and declared, "I seem to be untouched."

"Isn't that like the great Thadius," Dominus said.

"Yes," Ulanius laughed. Turning to his charioteers Ulanius pointed at the dead wolves. "Bring them, and have them skinned and tanned. I think our friends here would like them as a reminder of their visit." Shaking his head Ulanius said, "You're both lucky and unlucky this night."

"What do you mean?" Dominus wiped his wounds with a handkerchief.

"Well, you're unlucky in that you were attacked by a pack of wolves. People being attacked by wolves hasn't happened in a few years here. You're lucky in that I was coming to fetch you since you had not arrived yet." Ulanius laughed, "Now, maybe you two would like to ride to my abode in some comfort?" He climbed aboard his chariot and nodded to the empty part of the car.

"It would be most gracious," Thadius said, climbing up.

"I think I need some beer for these wounds," Dominus stated.

"You're going to pour beer on your wounds?" Ulanius looked confused.

"Don't be crazy," Dominus stated, "The beer is to be poured in me, not on me."

Laughing loudly Ulanius turned his rig around and snapped the reins. Moving at a trot, the chariot glided quietly down the road. Expecting the jarring that typically accompanied a military chariot, Thadius stood up and looked out at the road. "Not too bumpy," he commented.

"I installed bump reducers. An invention of Helvetius," Ulanius stated.

"We stayed with him only a night ago. His estate is truly amazing," Thadius commented.

"You don't know the half of it," Ulanius smiled. "Wait until you see my home," he said.

CHAPTER 28

No sooner did the gates of the main wall close behind them, when Thadius froze in amazement. "What is this?" Stepping down from the chariot he took a minute and looked all around. He could see a wide, level field of dark green grass extending in all directions and he was captivated. Neat rows of no more than fifty mature fruit trees made a small orchard to one side nearest the main wall. Several small hedges formed a diamond pattern around a modest fountain. Other than the few trees and hedges only the stark green of the grass accented the garden. The cobblestone road leading from the gate ended in a wide circle. From the circle a chariot path led to the stalls and chariot-house. All was visible by a multitude of strange lights.

A bright greenish glow was all around and the grounds were bathed in its luminance. White columns of granite stood along a path leading to the house, and spaced every twenty feet a large glass ball emitted a bright green light.

Ulanius spoke, "Out there is the building that houses our machine for making the gas that causes this illumination. From the machine it is brought into the house and around the grounds by soldered copper pipes."

"Swamp gas?" Dominus said.

"No, but like it," Ulanius stated, obviously delighted that the two men were awestruck. "But, that's just a small sample of the modern way," he laughed. Turning, Ulanius pointed at the guard towers and gatehouse. "There's another bit of amazement. It takes only one man to open and close my gates, and they weigh more than five tons a piece."

"Only one man?" Thadius said surprised. "How is that so?"

"Water my friend. Forced into cylinders and pumped into and out of another cylinder. I'm not sure that I understand it completely, but it works very well. No one will batter down that main gate," Ulanius laughed while brushing the dust from his tunic.

"Helvetius' ideas?" Dominus stated.

"Nearly all that I have here is. Between him and me, we could afford the construction of these things. But, you can bet your last copper asses that the apartments of Rome will not have such luxuries."

"The garrison?" Thadius said.

"Why don't they have such things?" Ulanius finished Thadius' thought. "They can't afford it of course." Extending his arm in the direction of the atrium, he led his guests to the main entrance of the house. "Shall we? Our evening meal is nearly ready."

"I feel as though I've fallen into Elysian Fields," Dominus stated.

"Just the affect I wanted," Ulanius laughed loudly as they walked under the bright glass balls.

"This is the strangest light," Thadius said. "How is it made?"

"Lime my friend, just lime." Ulanius looked back. "I suppose he did not show you, but Helvetius has one of the most complete works on inventions. It is said he had the copies made in Alexandria and brought here for his library."

Entering through an archway into the atrium, Thadius noted the ceiling open to the sky. Centered in the middle of the room, sat a large white marble fountain. Clear water shot from several pipes in the top. Projecting from the wall were decorative brass castings of serpents. From the serpent's mouths were flickering yellow flames. Polished brass mirrors reflected the light around the room. Intricate mosaic tiles coated the floor depicting a scene of Perseus slaying Medusa. From the floor to nearly five feet high, rich cream-colored marble bordered the room. The upper portion of the walls seemed to

Thadius, coated in dark blue plaster and finished to a smooth surface.

Traveling through the atrium and a lavishly decorated hallway, they exited out into the paristylum. Thadius found himself on a second floor portico that surrounded an opulent pool. Two-tone marble pillars held up the rooftop, white on the top and blood red at the bottoms. Down below children rushed around the cement pool. One child dove in causing a splash of water to land on several ladies sitting in recliners along the side.

"Brucetus," shouted a woman with raven black hair. "If you want to continue swimming you'd better behave." The woman looked up and saw the men. "They're here. Out of the pool children and prepare for evening supper." The children moved in an orderly fashion to a small building on the other side. The oldest boy looked back at the pool then vanished into the structure.

A few moments later the woman from the pool appeared in the doorway.

"Thadius, this is my wife Aconia Paulina. When last we met I wasn't married, but the fates have a way of changing even the most sullen of souls. A finer marriage the gods could not have granted."

"Do not mock the gods," chided Paulina.

Thadius could see her beauty. Her face held strong features, a prominent nose, narrow chin, and full lips. Her black hair was long, and hung down around her shoulders in a casual fashion. She wore a simple robe that tied in the middle, yet her breasts were clearly visible from underneath. She walked with purpose and her long slender legs gave the illusion of her gliding across the ground rather than walking. She bowed slightly in greeting and extended her hand for Thadius to take.

"My husband has told me much of you my dear Thadius," she began in the familiar. "He is a great husband, and a loyal servant of Rome." Turning to Ulanius she smiled warmly. Turning back to Thadius she fluttered her eyelashes. Gently releasing her grip she turned her attention to Dominus. Dominus smiled waiting for her to extend her hand. "And, you must be Dominus. You are a handsome fellow indeed."

"Be wary Dominus, or she will devour you," Ulanius laughed. "My wife has an appetite for good looking men. I am the evidence to prove it."

"Come, both of you, we shall feast and talk of friends and adventure," Paulina stated as she turned and walked into the dining room.

The room appeared simple to Thadius, white walls painted with frescos, a circular table in the middle of the room, and marble benches topped with colorful pillows. Heat radiated from the mosaic floor keeping the room at a comfortable temperature. White porcelain plates rimmed in gold were placed around the table. Trident forks and meat knives lay beside the plates. Brass candelabras provided some of the light as their yellow wax candles blazed. Along the wall he saw the flame fixtures giving off extra and ample amounts of light.

Entering the room, the three children appeared, dressed in fine white linen togas. The two boys wore their togas short, at the mid-thigh, the traditional male fashion in Rome. One boy wore a red leather belt, to the side of which hung a small dagger, its hilt encrusted with red and blue gems. The other boy had a brown belt, and to one side he had a pouch. The girl, the youngest of the three children, wore her toga long, to her ankles. Trimmed with blue lace the garment lay about her shoulders, as did the small satin cloak fixed with an ivory broach.

Thadius could see that both boys' hair was cut short and styled simply. The little girl caught his attention with a shy smile. Dark hair fell to the young girl's cloak, and each strand had been meticulously curled causing it to bounce as she walked over to her parents.

"This is Valeria Messalina," Ulanius said pointing down at his daughter. "And these two fine young men are my sons, Suetonius Camillus Atticus and Suetonius Paulinus Brucetus." Crouching down to the children's level Ulanius pointed at Thadius. "This is the man whom I've told you about. He is your great uncle who was a General for Rome. Your father fought beside him in may a battle."

Atticus, the oldest boy, nodded his head. His father patted him softly on his dark black hair, "That's a good boy indeed." Ulanius beamed with pride as he said these words. "Maybe if you are not too tired, he will tell you of the time we fought the Helvetii in the mountain forests of Cisalpine Gaul." The boy made no sound, just stared, his large brown eyes fixed on Thadius and Dominus. "Uncle Thadius' friend is called Dominus. Can you say Dominus," Ulanius asked the boy who smiled and darted behind his mother's robe.

"I must go dress for supper," Paulina stated. "I will leave you in the capable hands of my husband." Leaving the room she looked back at the gathered group and coyly smiled.

"Prepare for the feast," Ulanius called to his waiting servants.

Food began to arrive. The first platter contained pork ribs baked in honey, covered in pine nuts. Cheese came next, sliced thinly, along with platters of toasted bread. Roasted pheasant, pigeon and goose, were piled high on platters. Turnips, onions, and mushrooms dripped with thick gravy and lay on every plate. Pitcher after pitcher of wine was brought; red wine, white wine, berry wine and apple wine flowed.

Pauline entered the room and sat down. After much conversation and eating she turned to Thadius, "How is the meal?"

"The presentation is fantastic," Thadius stated.

Smiling shyly Paulina dished out some more fowl and tubers to her children and took particular care in cutting up the meats and vegetables into small pieces.

"So Uncle, what was it you said to me in the bath? You have come here on grim business?" Ulanius said. "Do tell us all about it?"

CHAPTER 29

"Since when have you performed bounty work?" Ulanius asked a bemused expression on his face.

"It's new to me," Thadius commented. "I understand, here in Lutetia, there was a murder of a Roman and his family?"

"True," Ulanius stated while wiping the mouth of his youngest child. "While we are no strangers to murder way out here in the frontier, this one in particular was most gruesome."

"It happened a little more than a week ago I am to understand," Thadius said.

"In fact, I believe it was two weeks ago that it occurred," Ulanius stated. "Caused quite an uproar. The woman who was killed was a Roman named Hedia. Her father was a man you might have actually known, Titus Maximus."

Thadius set down his cup. "I did indeed. He was in charge of the Century that went looking for the lost shipment of the Tolosa gold."

"The Tolosa gold," Ulanius laughed. "That gold Servilius Caepio stole? Clearly he kept the gold for himself. At least that's what the gossip has been for the last thirty years." He took a drink of wine, "Didn't you serve under him at that time?"

"I did, and traveled with Titus Maximus to find the vanished gold shipment."

Paulina lying on her side shifted onto her elbow. Her light blue toga hung loosely around her neckline. "What did you find?"

"Few clues, and many dead Centurions. We thought the Celts had done it. Strange that we didn't even find any wagon tracks from the convoy to follow. It was as if the gods had swept the whole shipment away," said Thadius. "What of the girl and her family who were murdered here?"

"A scandal if I am not mistaken," Paulina said as she plucked a grape from her plate and gently bit it in half. "She was secretly seeing some local whose father commands the river trade. Can you believe it, a common Celtic tradesman?" A hint of disdain was in her voice.

"My wife is telling gossip she has heard from her hair dresser. I don't truly know what happened," Ulanius said.

"Isn't it obvious," Paulina stated, "she was murdered by those savages who don't want Roman blood to be mixed with their Celt blood." She shook her head. "I can't blame them."

"Who investigated the killing, and was there anything recovered from the body?" stated Dominus.

Ulanius took a slab of pork and tore off a chunk of fatty flesh with his teeth. Chewing quietly he seemed in thought. "Come to think of it, I heard while at the Forum, the woman's family was tortured, as if the killer was looking for something. I believe a strongbox was stolen. The Regent assigned a tribunal to investigate. They concluded it was most likely a robbery and done by a local tribe of Celts who have been up to no good. "

"Ulanius, stop, you'll give the children nightmares," Paulina stated.

"Don't be silly," Ulanius said. "Now where was I? Ah, yes, the wife was left in a very bad way, and only a small trinket was found, a small, jeweled necklace hanging between her legs. She must have tried to hide it before being assaulted. Strange that the murderer didn't find it."

"Do you remember who found the body?" Thadius said while dipping some bread into his wine and eating it.

"A man named Draco, or Malco. Yes, I believe it was Malco. He and his son discovered the body. They had some business with the family. It so disturbed the boy that he was very ill for several days. So much so that the father made arrangements to leave and take him to a doctor in Rome. They left a few days ago I believe."

"Any arrests?" Dominus said.

"No. In fact there is a reward of ten denarius offered by their family in Rome."

"Truly a horrible thing," Paulina stated while taking an entire pork rib into her mouth and removing the clean white bone. "I only hope to Jupiter that they find that fiend and boil him rightly, or burn him at a stake proper."

"My wife finds value in the barbarian traditions," Ulanius stated, "What she means to say is that the villain should be flogged and crucified for all to see."

"I do not." Paulina protested, but was silenced quickly by a darting look from her husband. She frowned, then smiled again, "My husband is right," she conceded in a whisper. "But I believe the local way is better."

Rolling his eyes so only Thadius and Dominus could see, Ulanius stood and fetched a pitcher of red wine. Pouring himself some in a small earthen bowl, he dipped some toasted bread in it. "How long are you here for?" he said.

"I fear we must leave in the morning," Thadius stated. "Dominus and I are traveling with a caravan to Narbo."

"You are here for only one day?" Ulanius said. Looking up, his eyes filled with sudden understanding, and he nodded his head in agreement. "I see." His gaze narrowed, "You are close to the murderer then?"

"I believe we are," said Thadius.

"A little too close," Dominus added.

Having finished their meal, Thadius and Dominus followed Ulanius into the aula quies, where the men could relax and talk. The black and yellow painted walls and fine furniture reminded Thadius of his own study. In the middle of the room was a finely crafted wooden secretary. Brass serpents hung on the wall exhaling the flaming gas that illuminated the room. "We must leave soon," Thadius stated as he sat down and drank the remainder of his wine.

"I'll have one of my charioteers take you. That way you'll avoid any four legged interruptions along your way." Shifting in his seat, Ulanius set his wine down on the secretary. "I really wanted to show you the workings of my estate. I particularly wanted to show you the hydraulic systems, the gas producing process, and the silver and gold laminating pools that Helvetius and I developed." Ulanius frowned. "But, I understand your haste."

Thadius stood. "We must go now. No time for sad good byes. Let us part company happy and filled with drink and food." He nodded to Dominus who also stood.

"I'll call Gladrius, my best charioteer," Ulanius said while standing and going to the wall. On the wall was a wooden plaque with two rivets, the rounded brass heads of which were visible. In the middle was a thin golden rod with a small wooden handle at the top. Ulanius, rotating it to the side and in the distance the sound of a bell rang out. Looking at Thadius with a grin Ulanius added, "We have bottled Jupiter's thunderbolts too." Walking over to the device Thadius examined it closely. "I wish I had time to explain," Ulanius said patting him on the back, "but alas there is not."

"Write me in Herculaneum, detail everything. I am most interested," Thadius stated.

"I shall," Ulanius said. "For who else could understand better the marvels of Helvetius, but the master engineer of the Republic, my uncle."

Appearing in the doorway, Gladrius bowed slightly. "My lord."

"Take these men to the Lodging House," Ulanius said. "May the gods be by your side for the remainder of your trip."

"Please tell your wife we're sorry to leave in such a hurry. Jupiter permitting, perhaps we will see each other again. You have a beautiful family and a great life here Ulanius. Your father would have been most proud of you, as I am."

"Fare you well Uncle," Ulanius said. Turning to Dominus he gripped him by his wrist, "To you old salt, may the gods be kind and gentle. May you travel in good company and reasonable comfort."

Dominus and Thadius followed the charioteer outside. Waiting at the turn-about was the chariot. Gladrius climbed up and took up the reins. He motioned for his passengers to climb aboard.

"Why the sour crabapple face," Dominus asked Thadius as they made their way to the car.

"It is too bad we are in a hurry," Thadius stated. "I would have truly liked to have visited a little longer."

"Indeed," said Dominus as he glanced back at the villa to see Paulina standing under the roof of the portico. "A little longer would have served us all better."

Thadius felt the crisp sting of the night air on his face, and watched the countryside speed by. Passing the fields he could see in the late moonlight that the harvest was full, and Ulanius would soon be adding to his riches. The chariot raced along the nearly deserted streets. Pulling up to the inn, Gladrius watched in silence as the two men disembarked. Standing in the doorway, Thadius looked on as the charioteer turned the chariot around in the street and pulled up next to them. "Be watchful on your journey. For the waxing moon tells all of the division between friend and foe." He snapped the reins and the chariot raced away down the street and into the night.

"What do you suppose that was about?" Dominus said as he yawned.

"A chilling account of the unthinkable," Thadius commented. "Or, the poetic verse of a soldier bard," he chuckled.

"Either way, we shall keep to our guard from here on out," Dominus said.

"I think that would be wise old friend."

Pulling on the cord hanging down from the entryway, Thadius heard a set of bells ring. A few moments later a sleepy looking innkeeper opened the door and let them in. Saying nothing, the innkeeper re-bolted the door, turned and walked back to his room somewhere beyond the main hall. Thadius led the way back to their room. Opening the door he looked down and noted a folded piece of papyrus. Opening it he read it aloud. "Caravan leader agreed to take you on the trip to Narbo. Cost is viginti sestertii and all comforts included. Bring your items to be shipped to the bridge. Someone will come for you. Be ready early morning prior to dawn. Valcadii Opidius Darius."

Thadius looked up at Dominus, a weary expression on his face. "We have a few hours. Let's get some sleep and finish our packing in the morning."

"Agreed," Dominus said as he fell heavily into his bed. "How will we know what time it is?"

"I asked to have the innkeepers son wake us at four," Thadius said as he lay down. His eyes fell closed as his head hit the pillow. Darkness enveloped him and soon the colors of green trees and fields met his sleeping gaze. His father appeared in the distance and he so very much wanted to talk with the noble man.

CHAPTER 30

Thadius slowly opened his eyes. Sitting up in bed he could hear the rapping of something against the door. Alert to possible danger he grabbed his dagger from its sheath and jumped to the floor.

Dominus sat on the edge of his bed staring at him. "Sometimes you scare me," he said.

Thadius looked around the room, "The door," he awkwardly began. "The knocking woke me."

"It woke me too, but you don't see me leaping about with a gladius in my hand do you?"

"Sir," called a young voice from the other side of the door. Sliding the wooden bolt Thadius opened the door wide. In the hallway the innkeepers son stood in his sleeping shirt and slippers, his hair all mussed. "Sir, the hour is four of the morning. I have come to wake you as instructed."

"Very good young master," Thadius said as he retrieved his leather pouch and gave the boy a copper coin. "If you keep this and add it to others you receive, one day you will be rich," he smiled.

The boy looked at his sudden treasure then up at Thadius, "Thank you kind sir." Turning, he ran down the hallway and into an intersecting hall, disappearing from sight.

"I'll be glad when all this business is over and we can relax on the beach at home," Dominus groaned.

"Soon enough my friend," Thadius said while picking up his pack. "We need to take our possessions to the main entry."

By the time the clock marked five of the morning, they had all their items stacked neatly at the front door and ready for shipping. Sliding the bar from the door, Thadius looked out into the misty cold morning. Shop owners moved about and produce shippers were hauling carts filled with turnips, carrots, lettuce, and other vegetables destine for market. Listening he could hear horses in the distance. "I'll get us a cart," he stated as he stepped out the door.

Turning toward the docks he spotted a few men getting their morning meal at a thermopolia. He approached the men and their carts. One man with a wide black beard looked over. Thadius waited for him to finish his meal then spoke simply, "I need a cart and driver to take my belongings to the other side of the island." The man nodded and soon had his rig and donkey moving toward the Lodging House Inn.

They helped the man load the cart, and Dominus and Thadius walked behind the load keeping a wary eye out for any suspicious characters. Coming down the boulevard, Thadius saw the bridge. He realized it wasn't finished. Half the bridge was still made of wooden supports. The stone masonry had not been added. He noted great stacks of limestone blocks piled up along the river's bank. The streets paving stones stopped at the bridgehead, and he could see wooden planks that made up the bridge's surface. Even at this early hour, people were crossing making the wooden planks clank and undulate as the carts and pedestrians moved across it.

"Is this the place?" the cart man said.

"Yes, this will do," Thadius stated.

Removing their items and stacking them on the side of the road, the cart driver stretched his back once and then waited for his payment. Thadius reached into his pouch and plopped down a silver coin into the man's palm. "For your service," he said.

"I wonder where the caravan is," Dominus commented.

In the new morning twilight, Thadius looked across the river. A much larger city appeared to be sprouting up. From his vantage, he could see Roman-like villas dotting the other bank, vast fields of wheat, barley, and rye, and to the North, a large reservoir.

"You two," a voice from behind them said. "Are you waiting to caravan to Narbo?" Turning Thadius saw a dark skinned Nubian, a long steel sword at his side. "Come now, I haven't got all day to wait," he stated.

"Yes, we've booked a late passage to Narbo," Dominus commented.

"And you are acquaintances of the man called Darius?"

"Yes," Thadius said.

Raising his hand and bidding someone to come from behind him, the Nubian brought up a cart pulled by a horse. "Load these goods," he told a young man with the cart. "Most of the caravan is assembled. We are just awaiting your arrival. There are two horses on the other side ready for you. If you will follow me."

"Yes of course," Thadius said. Following the man across he could see the wooden planks of the unfinished bridge extending twenty feet onto the bank. Stakes anchored each board to the dark soil. Looking over he saw cement pilings poured for the platforms that would support the archways, and scrawled in the cement a name could be seen. At the other side he noticed a signpost topped with a wooden sign marking the beginning of another city. "Civitas Parisiorum?" he said. "It appears the island was too small and the settlement burst its boundaries."

"Surprising to say the least," Dominus added as they came to a caravan preparing to depart. More than two hundred people, luggage, and items for transport filled the streets. Ponies, donkeys, oxen, cattle, goats, sheep, and dogs, were in one way or another attached to the train. Some of the wagons were covered and others open. Carts and single riders on horseback were being addressed by dark skinned men in armor and arms. All appeared anxious. A rather large Nubian on horseback came up and grinned showing several missing teeth. "You will maintain your position with this group of carts at the rear and don't worry about raiders, we will protect you well." He turned his mount and rode toward the front of the train.

Emerging from the crowd a barbaric man made an appearance. His thick brown curly hair was unkempt, and he wore a tangle of hair for a beard. Shaggy eyebrows covered brooding eyes, and the man sneered with indifference as he looked upon Thadius and Dominus. He wore a heavy leather tunic, and over that a hammered brass breastplate secured with leather straps. A cloak made of animal hide hung down, and a hood made from the head of a wolf draped loosely off the back.

His saddle appeared strange to Thadius and it was only a matter of moments before he knew why. Leather straps hung down from the saddle with iron rings attached to the ends, and the man had his boots in the rings. He stood up in his saddle and called out in Latin to the assembled people. "I'm Shymor Beirmont and you are about to embark on a perilous trip. Even though it is warm here the weather is unpredictable and can change at a moment's notice. You must obey the commands given by me, or any of my men no matter what you think of them. If you do this, you will reach Narbo alive. If you do not you will die; there is no in between!" He slowly rode down the train. "If you have a problem you may ask any one of my men for help. They will help you. If we see you have a problem we will help you. We travel as one and no man moves faster than the slowest of us." Pulling on the reins the horse came to a stop near Thadius and Dominus. "Rely on your companions, for if one fails we all will fail." Turning his horse he galloped back to the head of the train. "Mount up and prepare to depart," he shouted.

A young warrior brought two horses down the road. Thadius could see a Roman saddle was secured to each. Stopping, the young man nodded his head and handed a pair of reins, one to Thadius, and one to Dominus. "Take good care of them," he said.

Dominus climbed into the saddle and settled in for the long ride. Thadius did the same. Gripping the reins tightly he looked over at Dominus. "From sitting at oars, to sitting in the saddle, I don't know how my backside can take any more," he laughed.

"Sore asses are the least of our worries," Dominus chuckled.

Thadius took inventory of his saddle. A length of rope was secured to a brass hanger, as was a set of leather bags. By the bags hung a scabbard with sword and a pair of large wine skins within easy reach. Bundled to the rear of the saddle were several wool blankets with broach pins to secure them as cloaks.

"Well my dear friend," Dominus said. "Here we go again." A call from the head of the caravan echoed down the train. "Forward!"

CHAPTER 31

As they moved in the darkness through the newly constructed city they dominated the cobblestone road. The dawn illuminated the sky and the once black irregular shapes came into focus as buildings, some under construction, and others completed. Thadius could see workmen performing duties of every description. Masons, carpenters, plumbers, surveyors, and engineers all were working at full speed. Bricks, stones, and piles of mortar were at every street corner. They passed by city blocks containing five story apartments, three story homes, two story inns and shops. Construction crews moved about the streets, some cursing the passing caravan for slowing their work, others praising it for the opportunity for a break from the work.

To Thadius it seemed that when Lutetia burst its banks, it expanded like a funnel, shooting out into the surrounding countryside. As they moved along the road, infrastructure construction began to appear. Sewers, water pipes, streets and lampposts were all being installed or erected. Building frames and footings were laid out in grid formation. After traveling a dozen blocks the caravan made a turn and took a wide side road leading out of the town. On one side of the road, workmen were erecting a barrier to keep unsuspecting souls from falling into a deep trench. In the trench men were constructing the forms that would be used to set the stonework of a sewer. Looking up the men collectively frowned at the passing caravan as dirt and debris fell into their trench.

The train made its way to the outskirts of the city, then took a right at a crossroad onto a long highway stretching past fields and newly constructed private villas. In the distance, not more than half a mile, scaffolding and stonemasons worked on a local amphitheater. As they passed, he could see great stacks of limestone, granite, and marble sitting in ordered and numbered piles near the construction.

Ahead were vast fields of yellow wheat, and tan rye stretching in every direction. Small farms, their round stone houses with thatched roofs, appeared like large mushrooms dotting the valley. Smoke trailed from the smoke holes in the middle of these homes, and Thadius wondered what the inhabitants thought of the modernization happening around them.

Following the highway for some time, the caravan came to another crossroads. The train made a turn. As he and Dominus reached the fork, he could see a stone signpost with a milestone next to it; Tolosa. "Who would have thought we'd be going there again?" Thadius said.

"Funny how the Fates play us such fools. We had to sail halfway around the world just to go next door," Dominus chuckled.

The highway was long, straight and boring. Miles of farmland stretched on. Little of the forests remained, and cattle grazed in large numbers. Every few miles they would come to a town or village. Upon arriving the caravan would stop and the travelers would stretch their legs, buy goods, and slack their thirst, then mount their modes of transportation and be off again. It became quite clear that the towns and villages along the way made a trade off the caravans, for hawkers and hucksters of every description would appear selling food, drink, sex, and hygiene sudries. Then, when the travelers had spent all they were willing to part with, the caravan would leave and vanish in a cloud of dust.

Mostly the roads were well maintained, and a Roman outpost lay every ten miles. Even the old Celtic forts were now supervised by the Roman authority, and were a welcome sight. They passed other travelers; many carts and pilgrims, drifters, and settlers, heading north along the highway, heading toward the city of Civitas Parisiorum and Lutetia.

"I think that one day Lutetia and Parisiorum will be as large as Rome," said Thadius.

Dominus chuckled, "Really, as large as a million people? I think not." He reached back and took up his wine skin. "This dust in the back of my throat is as thick as a Syrian mud brick." He opened the skin and took a long drink.

Looking out through the dust, Thadius could see the gentle rolling hills of Southern Gaul. Vineyards and farms dotted the landscape as well as groves of woodlands. Small tributaries crisscrossed and the caravan plodded through them leaving a muddy trail in its wake.

"Have a drink my friend and wash some of this Gaulish dust from your throat," Dominus said while handing his wineskin to Thadius.

Taking the skin, he drank a sparing amount of the tart wine. Rinsing his mouth he gargled once and then swallowed the liquid. "Seems we're making good time. Perhaps in a week we'll see Tolosa." Thadius handed the skin back to Dominus.

Dominus took another drink and put his wine skin back on the saddle, "I do look forward to seeing the old place though it was just a raised and burnt Celtic fortress when we last saw it."

"Indeed," Thadius stated with a crooked smile. "But, I'll not be surprised if it has blossomed into a bustling center of trade like Lutetia." Listening to the barking of a dog somewhere up the caravan, Thadius looked ahead. "Something's happening up there."

Dominus cleared his throat, "You know the Tolosa gold might still be there."

"Where?" Thadius said.

"In Tolosa."

"I'm sure it isn't. I supervised the loading of the shipment. It did leave the city, and it did get ambushed later."

"You lied to Ulanius. You said you had nothing to do with the gold," Dominus smiled.

"I didn't want to be questioned about it. Anyway, you know how that goes. All Caepio had to do was promise a percent of the gold to one of his generals and they'd steal from Rome," Thadius said. "No my friend, there is no Caepio gold left, if ever it was hidden." Shifting slightly in the saddle he flexed his back, stretching left and then right. From far up the caravan a voice called back, "Halt caravan, dismount and make camp."

As the dust settled, Thadius could see a wood building near an outcropping of large stones. A long concrete structure with an iron grill lay below the eaves of the roof. Several of Shymor's men began to place piles of coal inside and ignite them. Large jars and wooden barrels were brought out of the building, and from these containers the guards produced dried meat, flour, apples, and long links of pickled sausage. Another soldier unloaded jars of wine and began ladling out a serving to each person.

The sky filled with a fire-red hue that slowly turned to a pastel pink. Darkness followed as did a sumptuous feast. Dominus ate heartily and consumed his wine sparingly; Thadius followed suit. As night came on the soldiers segregated them, five tents for men, five tents for women, and a set of smaller tents for families. Directing each person to their respective tent Shymor's men followed a strict adherence to a formal process. In the distance Thadius could hear the cries of some wolves. Their lonely howls made his heart ache for his home, and his lost wife. Looking over, he saw Dominus unfold a wool blanket and wrap himself in the thick cover. "You'll surely keep warm in the cool night," he said to his friend. In the distance he could hear some guards talking as they passed, but what they said was only fragments and mumbles. Laying his head down he drifted off to sleep.

For nearly a week they traveled throughout the day and camped at night. Thadius noted the change in the landscape. Ahead the road began a gentle rise. As the day waned they slowly began climbing up a set of hills. The farmland gave way to oak forests. Looking back he could see a curving river winding its way along the valley floor.

Dotting the river's path were the small villages and towns they had passed.

As the sun began to set they came to a wide turnout where several springs flowed into cement troughs and down an estuary toward the valley. They halted and he climbed down from his saddle. A clear inscription stood out on the trough. It bore the mark of the seventeenth legion of Caesar. "Make camp," Shymor called as he rode down the length of the caravan.

The escort began making camp as the travelers mingled and stretched their legs. The soldiers unloaded the wide and complex tents and the large free standing braziers. Barrels of wine were brought out from the wagons, and cook fires were lit. Men moved about removing beef, pork, and fowl stored in boxes of salt, and vegetables from the pickling jars. They uncrated tubers, onions, and turnips and began cutting, boiling, and cooking the food. The Nubian moved about letting the travelers know that the shelters were set up and they could put their items in the tents.

Taking his pack and supplies, Thadius made his way to the men's tent. He opened the flap and entered. Looking up he noted that the vents had been tied open to allow air to circulate freely, a practice done when the braziers were hot. Dropping his pack and bedroll, he turned around and went back outside.

By the time of the evening meal the rain fell. A slight breeze stirred the tents, but quieted as the night wore on. After supper Thadius and Dominus moved to the water trough and cleaned their faces, bodies and teeth. Returning to the tent Thadius made his bed and lay down. The past few days had been hard traveling, and he felt a bit of fatigue. Looking around the tent he noted the other travelers, passing the time reading or playing various board games or dice. Glancing up at the roof he realized it had once been painted. In the fabric he could see the pattern of white clouds with a powder blue background, now faded. Dominus lay down and put his arm over his eyes. After a few minutes he snored then rolled over and was quiet. The sound of the fire in the braziers lulled Thadius to sleep. He welcomed it with open arms as he entered the darkness of the dream world. A voice spoke to him, "trust in the gods, for friends will betray you." He saw a ray of golden light as the dream commenced.

A loud clanging echoed throughout the camp. Men shouted loudly for all to wake and make ready to leave. Thadius got to his feet, grabbed his grooming items, and made his way out of the tent. He waited in line for the water. After doing a quick whore's bath, he bundled up his items and retrieved his horse. As the carts and other modes of transportation became hitched and saddled, Thadius surveyed the landscape. Ahead the hills continued to rise as the forest grew thicker. Oaks, spruce, and ivy dominated, and within the forest, tangles of saplings, briars, and shrubs grew in abundance. The road zigzagged through the growth and darkness, for little light pierced through the tree's high canopy.

For ten miles they traveled until the forest gave way to a clearing. In the middle stood a small garrison with a village around it. Villagers awaited them, and vendors lined the highway on either side. As the train entered the town the men and women who did a mercantile service shouted and dangled items out for sale.

Some of the travelers exchanged money in return for wears, or food, and some for cups of stout beer or local wine. By the time the caravan reached the other side of the town, the vendors grew less frequent and eventually all but vanished. Looking back he saw those merchants moving their carts away from the roadside; surely, only until the next caravan arrived.

For the next few days the sky brooded gray and at times drizzled, but didn't unleash any significant rain. The highway was free of puddles and Thadius thanked the gods that the heavy moisture suppressed the dust. Dominus looked uncomfortable, but remained quiet most of the day. Toward afternoon the sky's dour disposition relented and rays of sunlight bathed them. The evening came and went and again they found themselves lurching upward. They reached the top of the mountain and Thadius could see a wide plane with a broad river flowing through it. As they started down, the blue sky bathed them in warm sunshine.

"The Garonne River," Dominus said, "my soul just aged thirty years."

Thadius gazed out toward the walled city. "They put up one fierce struggle last we were here."

"Looks quiet enough now," said Dominus.

They descended toward the valley floor. At the bottom a broad clearing appeared, and a garrison. It looked as if a cohort were stationed there, and legionnaires watched as the travelers passed by. Like a long snake the caravan wound its way past and toward the woods. Eventually Thadius and Dominus, and all those at the rear were devoured by the dark forest. Oncoming travelers passed infrequently, and from time-to-time had to yield to the never slowing caravan. The road was well maintained and the traffic moved along it with little delay. Two hours passed until they reached the Tolosa city gates guarded by Roman Legionnaires. There was no halt as the caravan moved steadily into the city. Thadius passed the soldiers, who slapped at the dust in the air.

"I hope your stay will be a good one," sarcastically shouted one of the soldiers and they all broke into laughter.

Going through the city reminded Thadius of Lutetia in its layout. Merchants lined the streets and hocked their wares while the caravan passed. After a few minutes they came to a bridge that crossed over the river. The air seemed fresh and unspoiled he thought. Unlike the green waters of the Serpent River that flowed around Lutetia, the Garonne waters were dark and fast moving. Thadius sensed there was great power behind that black water.

Traffic yielded to the behemoth that was the train. Once over the bridge Shymor Beirmont ordered a halt. Thadius and Dominus watered their horses and tied them to the back of the cart. Stretching their legs, the two men moved about the market purchasing dried meat, roasted almonds, and filling their wineskins with local vintage.

"Look at this," Dominus pointed up.

Thadius came over and looked up at an archway leading into an alley. "It's the old main gate with the torch symbol carved on it."

"The Celt's treasury was somewhere over there," Dominus pointed toward a set of red brick buildings.

"They had much gold here." Thadius peered into the alley. "Along with silver and brass." He turned and looked into the street. Many people moved about, but not enough to warrant calling it a crowd. "Look here."

Dominus came and looked on in amazement. The charm found at two of the murder scenes was there hanging from an awning. "Who makes these?"

An old man came out of the shadows, "I see you like good craftsmanship."

Thadius held up the one he carried, "Did you make this?"

"I did," the old man said.

"A man bought seven of these. Perhaps you remember what he looked like?" Thadius stated.

The man took the bauble and smiled, "Yes, I remember. He asked me to infuse ruby and amber powder onto the flame. I thought the number of charms was strange too, but who am I to question when gold is paid." He looked at Dominus and Thadius then sat down on a stool under the awning. "He was about your age, balding with a ferret face. He barked orders to me like a Roman, and so I believe he was."

"Did he say where he was going," Dominus asked.

"Some place north, I don't recall exactly."

"North?" Thadius said. "It must have been Malco. He must have sailed to Narbo, taken this path up to Lutetia, and then down the river to Britannia."

"So, we're following their ingress path? Why didn't they come back this way?" Dominus said.

"Remember the boy's journal, how he mentioned needing some jimson weed extract? He must know of a source towards the Alpis Cottia."

Dominus looked skeptical, "He's been calculating so far. What else lies along that path that we might have missed?"

Thadius popped a few almonds into his mouth. "Lugudunum, the Alpes Cottia Pass, and Italy."

"Why not sail by sea. It would be faster?"

"Publius mentioned in his journal of meeting someone named Germanius, remember? Perhaps he lives along that route?" Thadius said.

"We'll be in Rome before they reach the via Appia." Dominus stated.

"If only we knew more," Thadius said.

"Would you like to buy some of my other charms?" The old man held up several silver Celtic knots and god effigies.

"No thank you," Thadius said.

"I have one last question," Dominus stated. "Did the man who bought the charms travel alone?"

"He was alone when he bought the charms," the old man said.

"Curious." Thadius turned to see some of his fellow travelers heading back toward the caravan. "We'd better go."

They got back to their horses as the town water clock chimed three of the afternoon. Shymor Beirmont rode down the caravan making sure that all the travelers were back to their transports. Finding all in order, he called to his men to start moving the train out the southern gate and down the river valley road.

"I really wish we could have stayed the night here," Dominus piped as he goaded his horse forward.

"I'm sure the good town's people would have liked that too," Thadius said as he looked about at the mix of Roman and Gaul faces around them.

Moving past the Forum and out through the gate Thadius made note of the fine looking public buildings. To his right he could see a temple to Jupiter, formed from granite stones with columns crafted of fine marble. The temple to Apollo looked to Thadius to be made from red brick with stone columns shaped in the Corinthian style. He could see the Senate building fashioned of cut yellow limestone and topped with a roof of black terracotta squares. Passing the arched gateway he read aloud the carved sign over the arch. "Via Narbo. At least we've replenished our wine reserves," Thadius said with a knowing wink.

"I hope our fortunes are better found at Narbo," Dominus added, "since we didn't find any of the lost gold here in Tolosa."

As they left the city Thadius spoke, "The silver shipment went first, and made it to the port at Narbo. The next day the gold left Tolosa along this very road and was lost; it never reached Narbo for shipment."

"I didn't even learn it was lost until I reached Rome. Caepio was then indicted for the loss of the army at Arausio and stripped of all his citizenship privileges and was banished. That's when I came to work for you and the Third," Dominus reminisced.

"Don't fool yourself," Thadius said. "Caepio lived like a king in exile. Where his wealth came from none could tell since his properties were seized."

"So you think he stole it?" Dominus said.

"Hard to tell, but someone did."

"Well, I think those Celtic bastards did something with the gold...buried it most likely so Rome could never get it." Dominus took up his wine skin and drank. "Narbo is two days from here. I for one will be glad to get on a ship and sail home."

"The convoy was ambushed a day's ride form here." Thadius stated. "When I arrived on the scene, three quarters of the Century were dead, and the others missing. No wagons, no gold, and no tracks."

"Do let me know if you see a sign that reads, *Caepio's gold this way*, will you?" Dominus said.

Two more days elapsed as the train maneuvered up the hills and down. Rain fell on both days and Shymore made camp outside towns that catered to the travelers. In camp the cooking fires were made and the foods prepared. Braziers were set out and as the night came on the passengers sat huddled wrapped in blankets around the firelight. Not far off was a lake and Thadius took his wooden stool and a small pot of hot wine over to it. Following, Dominus brought his cup and a loaf of bread. No stars could be seen, and the heavy clouds shifted overhead. In the distance Dominus could just make out the dark clump of trees at the lake's far edge.

"What do you make of the clues we have?" Thadius said.

"I don't like it at all," Dominus stated, while pouring himself a cup of hot wine. "Publius is up to something more than just murder I think."

"My observation also," Thadius added while sipping his wine, the steam mixing with his own breath. "But, what and why?"

"Also, it would seem he's selected these families based on some criteria. It smacks of a political intrigue," Dominus said.

"Political? Who would it serve?" Thadius stated. "No, I think it has something to do with-."

"Romans," a gruff voice said from behind them.

Thadius looked up at the caravan leader. The man wore his wolf hood and from where Thadius sat looked every bit the part of a barbarian. He wondered how many trains he'd driven along this road.

"Once I fought against you and your kind. I was young, and stupid," Shymor said coming up to the water's edge. "Change came anyway, and with it gold coin and trade." He stood there for a moment. "The goddess of the lake is there, and listening to us. I can feel her presence."

The hairs on the back of Dominus' neck stood on end. A tingling covered his body as the barbarian spoke. "She knows your heart."

"Goddess?" Dominus said.

"Yes," stated Shymor, a distant loneliness in his voice. "She watches over all who travel these roads, even Romans. But you probably have no use for our goddess for you both have your Roman gods to watch your steps." He chuckled in a sardonic way. "I am boring you with tales of my people. Do you need anything? More blankets perhaps?"

"We're fine," Thadius stated.

Turning, Shymor walked between Thadius and Dominus, his foot falls crunching the pebbles as he moved. Stepping up onto a flat granite slab he looked back, staring into the darkness again. "She comes tonight I think," he said then turned and walked back to camp.

They sat there for a while listening to the wind and the rain. High above lightning illuminated the sky followed by distant thunder. Turning, Thadius saw a flash of white light near the opposite bank. From across the lake a shimmering globe appeared. The reflection in the water pulsed as it came closer. A blue fog surrounded the object. Dominus shot to his feet. He learned in the army the dangers of lightning. The glowing ball came closer. Thadius took a step back. Dominus' hand was on his shoulder as he stared at the glowing orb.

"Get back," Dominus shouted. A blinding flash and a crack of thunder echoed in the valley. Both Thadius and Dominus were knocked to the ground as if hit by an invisible hammer. Scrambling to his feet Dominus dragged Thadius up. Other travelers came running and stopped at the granite slab. They stared down at Thadius and Dominus. Thadius wrinkled his nose at the acrid smelling smoke in the air. "You got a little singed old salt," Dominus said. Thadius patted the smoky areas of his clothes.

Dominus did the same as he climbed up the granite rock and turned to stare out at the lake. "I've had enough of goddesses for one night," he said. "Let's get back to camp."

The walk was brisk and in the sky lightning flashed, but thunder was absent. Once back at the fire Thadius sat down. Shymore came and warmed his hands. "The goddess would like you to know that she is watching you," he said with a grin. "She will not hurt you. She is warning you to be wary and heed her power."

"Jupiter's thunder bolt; I remember hearing tales of it rolling across the ground and leaping from armored man to armored man," Thadius said under his breath.

"I remember the warnings," Dominus began. "From when I was up near Agust, all those years back. Thunderbolts killed eleven men one night in a storm."

Shymore stood and walked into the darkness, "Sleep well Romans."

"My heart is still racing," Dominus stated.

"Mine too. Perhaps we should turn in before a gorgon comes along or some other such thing," Thadius said.

Dominus chuckled, then stood up, "A splendid idea," he said. "I'm not one for superstition, but that took the wind from my bellows." He made his way back to the tent, followed by Thadius. Opening the flap he stepped inside. Some of the other travelers were settled into their beds as the low murmur of conversation died out. Lying down on his bed, Dominus wrapped his two wool blankets about himself. Looking over he could see the glowing coals in the brazier keeping the tent warm. "I fear my dreams will be less exciting now that reality seems more like a dream," he commented.

"You're right. It's not every night a man is molested by a Celtic goddess," Thadius said while drawing his blankets about himself. "When we get home, we'll look back on this while drinking a large flagon of fine wine and have a good laugh," he chuckled uneasily, then lay his head down. He lay there for hours, until finally drifting off to sleep.

CHAPTER 32

The morning was uneventful, and the train was moving before dawn. Slowly the caravan made its way along the road toward the coast. Thadius reflected on the trip wondering what Publius was really up to. *Why would he steal a strongbox, but leave other valuables behind in Lutitia?*

Ahead he could see the small settlements with garrisons grow more numerous. Roadside stops started to become more civilized the further toward the coast they went. The common rural goods were replaced with the manufactured items of the Republic.

Villages and small towns were as plentiful as the flowers that grew beside the road. As the caravan approached, villagers mobbed them, selling fruit, produce, prepared food, and many other items. Some travelers bought, some didn't. Thadius felt tired deep down in his bones; a weariness that taxed more than his strength, but also his spirit.

Dominus pointed at a set of hills in the distance. "The coast is just ahead," he said.

Thadius nodded then reached for his half empty wine skin. Taking a drink he stared out over the farmland and the miles of waving wheat stalks. The sky was blue and all the rainy clouds far behind the caravan. For hours they traveled as the sun rose to the noon position. In front, the hills looked like large mounds covered in dark green foliage; the very hills that surrounded the city of Narbo.

The weary caravan approached the city. Thadius could see its walled battlements showing brightly in the afternoon sun, and the tan colored stones making up the well maintained wall. The road led to a fork, one way going to the gatehouse of the town, the other heading east toward Italy.

Arriving at the main gate Thadius noted the legionnaire's polished armor and finery. The Legionnaire-optio shouted up in greeting at Shymor as the train entered the city. Guiding the caravan into Narbo they passed through the town square, made a wide turn and halted.

"This is as far as I take you," Shymor said. "Good journey to all who are going on from here."

The caravan travelers began unloading their goods. Men, women, slaves, and servants all made haste in securing transportation, or lodgings for the night. Signaling a man with an empty donkey cart, Thadius asked him where they could find a place to lay their heads.

"My sister runs a house not far from here. She will feed you and give you lodgings for only a quinarius," he grinned.

Shymor rode up and looked down at them. Thadius pulled out some coins and handed them to the man. "This is for your care in guiding us without incident," Thadius said.

Smiling from under his wolf-hood, Shymor nodded. "You are a lucky man. The goddess blesses you and your friend. Fear not, she will see you to your home and hearth." He laughed while putting the money into a leather pouch. Turning his attention to another traveler he rode into the mob. Thadius turned to Dominus and shrugged his shoulders. "Barbarians," he said, "who can understand them?"

The man with the donkey cart patiently waited, then when Dominus and Thadius were ready, he led them to a three-story inn. Steps allowed access up to the entry and patrons entered and exited as they approached.

Entering the dwelling, Thadius noted the fine examples of pottery and decorations as well as the smooth plastered walls and richly tiled floor. A plump woman approached them and she spoke with great glee as she addressed them. "My brother tells me you are seeking lodging for the night. Or will it be longer?" She smiled.

"One night. We are in need of transportation for tomorrow also," Dominus added.

"My brother will take care of that. I will see that you get a room for the night," she said. "I must ask," she paused, "for a quinarius."

Dominus this time removed his leather pouch and produced the silver quinarius and handed the coin to the woman. Taking the coin she motioned for the two men to follow her. They climbed up two flights of stairs to a landing. Beyond, was a dark hallway with a small window at the far end. Shining through the leaded glass was the last of the afternoon sun.

"Here is your room," she said to Thadius while opening up a bright blue door. "And here is your room my lord." She took Dominus down the hall to another blue door.

Entering, Thadius took in the small confines. A raised bed made of wood and crosshatched horsehair rope, and a rolled up straw mattress at the foot of the bed. Above the bed was a small window of glass fitted into the stucco. A table stood near the door and on it was a pitcher and basin. The whole room couldn't have been more than seven feet wide by ten feet long.

"Burburus, my brother will bring up your things and store them in your room," the woman said. "You may call me Fabia. If you need anything else don't hesitate to let me know. Supper is at nine strikes of the town clock bell." Turning she walked down the hallway. Coming up the stairs was her brother lugging two heavy bundles of clothing and supplies. As the two met in the hallway they became trapped for a moment in what seemed to Thadius an amusing dance of frustration. Fabia hit her brother in the head with her hand and called the man a 'ninny' before disappearing down the stairwell. Dragging the bundles down the hallway the man set them down at Thadius' door. Wiping his brow with the back of his hairy hand he exhaled loudly. "Since she lost her husband last year to sickness, she's been a little flummoxed. Please don't mind her," he said apologetically.

"We took no offense," Thadius said, a bemused expression growing across his face. Burburus removed a yellow handkerchief from his belt dabbed his sweaty head, then replaced the rag back into his belt. "Good, good," he said looking relieved. Turning he walked to the stairwell, but stopped and faced the two men. "Tonight she is cooking goat stew with dumplings. She's a very good cook, and may even make a lucky fellow a good wife," he said this with what seemed to Thadius a hint of desperation. "It will be a good meal none the less." He turned and moved down the stairs.

Pulling his bundle into the room Thadius found it a challenging quandary to find a place to stow his items. There was no room on the floor, he couldn't put it on the bed, and it wouldn't fit under the table. Finally he found a place and propped it at an angle at the foot of the bed.

Unrolling the mattress he set his travel pack down. Looking about for sheets or blankets he quickly realized there were none. He took out his soap and moved to the basin. Pouring out some water from the pitcher into the bowl he proceeded to wash his face. After drying, he changed his clothes, put on a burgundy colored toga and his good sandals, opened the door and stepped out into the hall.

Hearing a knock at the door Dominus moved slowly to open it. Thadius stood there dressed in a fine toga. Dominus grinned, "I didn't ask for an escort."

"I can see if Burburus will fetch his sister for you?" Thadius goaded.

"Never mind. The matron Fabia would make an ill wife for the likes of me," he chuckled. "Never the less, I shall dawn my own garment of fashion." He opened his pack and removed a white silk toga with gilding along the edges. Pulling out his sandals he quickly stripped and redressed in his fashionable clothes, splashed himself with perfume and ran a comb through his hair. "Now I am ready," he declared.

"I don't think Narbo is ready," Thadius quipped.

Moving down the stairs and into the main street, Thadius looked up at the name of their boarding house, The Black Bear Inn. The sign was made of wood and hung by a set of wrought iron chains dangling from a crossbeam. He moved into the street and strolled along the side of the road.

"Where are we heading?" Dominus said.

"I have some questions for the physician here."

They walked down the cobblestone road. Thadius stopped and asked a passer-by where the doctor was located. The man pointed down the street and indicated they should make the next corner. They were soon in front of the doctor's shingle. Thadius went in and walked around the small room. He took a look at the pharmaceutical items along one wall. Evenly spaced clear glass jars and jugs sat on shelves made of fine dark wood. Against another wall, rows of herbs in tiny brightly painted earthen pots sat. Strong scents filled the air and he wondered how the physician could get use to the smell. "Can I help you two?" came the soft voice of a simply dressed woman.

"We would like to see the physician," Thadius stated making note of the woman's exceptional beauty. She bore long golden locks of hair that draped down to her waist. Her milky white skin, freshly oiled smelled of lavender. She wore no sandals but stood barefoot on the clean, red, marble tiled floor.

"I am the physician here. I practice Hipporcrates and Theophrastus medicine," she said. "Are you in need of medical service?"

"No," Thadius stated, "but, I have some questions to ask about parliamentary disease."

She looked amused by the question. "Parliamentary disease?" she said while walking over to a large bundle of papyrus and leafing through them.

"Yes," Thadius added.

"I have the document here." She read down the paper, "Skin pale, suffering body tremors, and erratic behaviors. The subject complains of painful headaches, and body aches. The patient is known to speak in tongues or to invisible spirits, and is prone to violence. Here it says he can be prone to suggestion or manipulation. It says also to use poppy extract and willow bark extract, either in a potion or pill form. Here it says that heliot dream-mushrooms can be used and seem to have some curative affects."

"You had that document pretty handy," Dominus said.

"Two months ago a man came here and asked if I had any information on treating the disease. I made a copy of this for him." She rolled up the paper.

"Was he traveling with a wife and son?" Dominus pressed.

"Not that I remember. A military man from Rome I think, though he was dressed in a common toga." She fostered a slight smile, showing white teeth. "Is there anything else I can do for you? Maybe some sessile or parsnip?"

"What did he look like?" Thadius said.

"About your age, pointy nose, balding."

"What is jimson weed extract good for?" Thadius asked.

She looked thoughtful, "Used by legion surgeons to sedate the patient when performing surgery. It's used with poppy resin, and other medicines. Not common."

"Thank you for your time." Thadius turned to leave.

"Oh," she said, "when applied in low doses, it makes the person inclined to say what's on their mind."

"Again, thank you." Thadius reached for the door and stepped outside.

"Does the description of the man sound familiar?" Dominus stated as they both walked out.

"I've seen Scapula; it could be the old man. But, if not him, then who?"

Dominus stepped into the dark street, "Maybe a servant?"

"She would have noticed his collar. No, a freeman of some sort I would think." Thadius began moving back toward the inn. "Evening is coming and the streets here have no sconces."

"Probably not the safest place to be then," Dominus said eyeing several unsavory fellows lurking in the shadows.

They made their way back to the inn. The streets were mostly dark, save for the few lamps lit on the main avenue. Once at the inn Thadius went straight to his room, opened the door and a note fell to the floor. Picking it up he opened it; *the truth is known. Your part well met. I've been watching you and your friend. In Rome I will do my last bit of work, and you will not stop me. The fires of Tartarus blaze and the Golden Fleece is at hand. Rome will not fall, and you will have no salvation from what you did."* The hand writing was steady. He carefully checked behind the door. The room was empty. Entering, he closed the door and sat down and realized the bed was made. A shadow at the base of the door caught his attention. Someone was outside. "Come in Dominus." The shadow vanished. Thadius squeezed past some of his luggage and opened the door. The hallway was empty. Dominus emerged from his room. Noticing Thadius standing half in and out, he came down.

"Were you just outside my door?" Thadius said.

"No. I was busy in my room thinking of how hungry I am and why we haven't had anything to eat yet."

"Strange," Thadius said. "When we got back there was this in my door." He handed the note to Dominus. "Then, someone stood outside my door for a moment."

Dominus took the note and went to the stairs and looked down. He returned and unfolded the note. In the lamplight of the hallway he read it. "Golden Fleece? What you did?" He handed the note back. "What did you do?"

Thadius took the paper and shrugged. "It doesn't make any sense. The Malco's are probably half way over the Alpis Cottati Pass by now moving toward Rome. Who left this note? And, why indicate that I'm culpable in something? Did you get a note?"

Dominus went back to his door and looked all about. "No."

"Could it be Darius who wrote this? Is it possible that Publius or his father has followed us?"

Dominus came back down the hall, "Unlikely."

"Whoever it is knows we're on this path. Who else but Darius knows?"

"Darius doesn't know why we traveled here; he probably doesn't even know what his masters are doing. That leaves no one," Dominus said.

"No," Thadius closed his door. "There is someone else involved, but who and why I cannot say. You mentioned a political intrigue before. I'm not so ready to dismiss that now."

"Shall we go down and mingle with the other guests?" Dominus smiled.

Thadius nodded a weary yes, "Be on our guard though."

"I'm learning to do that more often," Dominus said.

They found the parlor and mingled with the other guest until supper. The other guests numbered only thirteen composed of two families of four, one newly married couple, a group of five business men and two lone travelers.

"We are at full capacity," Burburus said.

Fabia came in and directed some servants to place the platters filled with food. "We can actually hold twenty here with comfort."

"Is there anyone staying who is not here now?" Dominus asked.

"No, everyone staying here is here," Fabia stated. "Try some of our local wine. It's rather good." She poured Dominus a full cup.

"Thank you," he replied.

Thadius approached, "I overheard one of the business men say he was sailing to Rome tomorrow. I believe we can book passage on the same ship. He said it's quite an experience traveling on this ship."

"Which person?"

Thadius pointed at a short blond haired man in a greenish toga. "That man calls himself Aeitus and he can help us. He says he typically travels with his business partner, but the man is not here; away on some errand I believe. He assures me that the ship he's sailing on to Ostia can take a few more passengers."

"Galley or strictly sail?" Dominus took a drink from his cup.

"It's a galley with two sails."

Dominus smiled, "Should be fast. I sure hope we're not rowing this time."

CHAPTER 33

The trireme sat low in the water. No crates or sacks remained on the docks. The captain was standing at the gangplank with a scroll and was reading when Thadius and Dominus arrived. "Are we late?" Dominus said.

The captain looked up, "Late?" He rolled up his scroll. "No, if you were late, you would find the birth empty. But, I did want to meet you and welcome you onboard personally. When Aeitus told me you were coming, I was quite excited. I'm Captain Renalius Sesius," he offered his hand. "It's not often that I get a hero of the Republic as a passenger such as Moras Thadius." He motioned for a sailor to come down. "Take these men on board and show them to cabins four and five. You'll find our accommodations worth the price."

"How often do you make this trip?" Thadius said.

"Up to five times a month. This ship was built with the comfort of passengers in mind. Though we also take cargo, we have some luxuries that few others can offer."

"Like what?" Dominus looked intrigued.

"A bath, a wine and beer bar, superb dining, and a brothel. We shuttle men of nobility and commerce on every trip."

Dominus' smile grew into a grin, "Tavern, and brothel?"

The captain chuckled, "You'll be as comfortable as a prince in a palace."

"How many days to Rome?" Thadius said.

"Three days to Ostia Antica."

"How many passengers?" Dominus stated.

"Twenty four." The captain turned and began walking up the gangplank, "If you'll just follow my men they will take you to your quarters."

They boarded the ship. Quite a few people in togas were on deck, goblets in hand looking out to sea. A sailor smiled and motioned for Thadius and Dominus to follow him down one deck, where he stopped at rooms four and five. Thadius entered his room and was amazed to find a bed with a down mattress, a table for writing, and a privy. He put down his pack and came back out. Dominus was nearly to his door. "Did you see the privy?" he said.

"I've never seen such a ship before."

The sailor stood in the hallway. "We're about to depart. If you would like to view the departure, you can, and if you would like, I can take you around the ship to show you the amenities for passengers?"

"Please show us the ship," Thadius said.

The sailor smiled. "I'm Titus and I'm in charge of the servants who look after the passengers. If you will follow me," he led the way along the passage. A few other passengers passed them. "Down one more level are the rowers. You don't have to worry; you'll not be bothered by them." He turned a corner and opened a door into a room with two pools of water. Two older men sitting in the steaming pool turned to look at them. "This is the ship's baths. And, through that door is the steam room." He turned and exited, found a set of stairs and went up onto deck. A dozen passengers lined the railing.

Titus motioned toward a wide room fitted with windows at the aft. He entered the room. "Here is the dining room. Meals are served at eight, three, and seven, and ten. You'll hear the bells." The room was resplendent. Finely crafted furniture were fixed to the floor, wide glass windows looked out over the deck and the sea, and rows of goblets and glassware were stacked in hardwood cabinets faced with frosted glass. "Servants will clean your rooms daily and any servant will get you whatever you need. Now, if you'll follow me, I'll show you the tavern and brothel." He led the way toward the front of the ship where another set of structures were built.

"Amazing," Dominus stated. "Who would have thought?"

Thadius chuckled, "I'm not surprised by anything now."

Titus led them through the bar and brothel, though small both were exotic and finely crafted. Finally, he led them onto the deck and to the railing. They were at sea already, and the land was fading behind them. Three rows of oars were rhythmically moving, and the ship was picking up speed. "If there is anything you need, don't hesitate to ask." Titus turned and vanished below deck.

"How big do you think this ship is?" Dominus said.

Thadius looked back, then side to side, "Two hundred feet long and forty feet wide at least."

"It's one big ship."

"Indeed it is," the captain said coming beside them. "It's actually two hundred and twenty feet stem to stern, and fifty two feet across the beam. No expense was spared in making her or outfitting her." He looked out toward the distant coast. "We're building four more just like her. There's quite a trade growing in fast passenger transport. I'll check back with you tomorrow to see how you are enjoying the voyage." He turned and walked over to several sailors.

Thadius shrugged, "I think I'll enjoy this voyage."

The first day a quarter of the passengers were sea sick. The other two thirds drank in the tavern, partook of the brothel, and steamed in the bath. Fresh water was offered in a silver pitcher, and plates of olives, figs, dates, and bread were set out in the dining room. Wine flowed from amphora specially made with ball-cock spigots, and beer was served from large jars. Courtesans roamed among the men, and political banter reverberated late into the day. The dinner was cured ham, sausage, sea urchins stuffed with pine nuts, crab, and lamprey, roast chicken and pidgeon, and more wine. By the time the dining room cleared, Dominus swayed with wine and rubbed his swollen belly. He staggered out onto deck and back to his room.

Thadius had been less enthusiastic and drank only modestly. The hour was late and he followed Dominus to make sure the man didn't slip overboard. Once back at his room he put on his night shirt and climbed into bed. Sleep came slowly, as the ship rocked to and fro.

The second day came with a clear sky and empty seas. Thadius woke early and took a steam at the bath. Once groomed, he headed up on deck to take in some fresh sea air. Sailors tended the sails and a strong breeze pushed the ship along at a rapid pace.

"How are you enjoying your voyage?" The captain said coming up to Thadius.

"Quite well. I must say that this ship is remarkable. I've never traveled in such luxury before."

"It is a vision, a new way of doing things, a Roman way of doing things," the captain chuckled.

"You said that you transport cargo and passengers from Ostia to Narbo five times a month?"

The captain looked out over the railing. "Yes. Our rowers are the best, all skilled and well paid too."

"By chance do you remember taking a passenger a few months ago who was about my age, balding with a narrow face?"

"Look around you," the captain said. "Most of my passengers fit that description."

"Please, try and remember. His name may have been Malco, or he was related to the Malco family. Anyone strange you can remember?"

The captain thought for a moment. "There is a man who travels to and from Rome once a month. A strange fellow. Stays in his room most of the voyages and has his meals there. He explained to me once that he's an officer in the Legio septima Claudia Pia Fidelis."

"Are you sure?"

"Like I said, when he was onboard he kept pretty much to himself, but when he wanted to talk, he wouldn't shut up," the captain laughed.

"Did he say what his business was?" Thadius said.

"Something to do with medicine I think."

"Why do you say that?"

"He asked about the physician in Narbo," the captain said. "I'm sorry I can't help you more."

"You've helped more than you know," Thadius stated. "Now, if you'll excuse me, I'm going to have a cup of wine in the tavern." The captain nodded and approached a group of men standing near the forward mast. Thadius went to the bar and sat down. "I'll have a cup of wine, and leave the pitcher," he said.

CHAPTER 34

At the end of the second day the lookout called down from the rigging, "Ostia Antica!" Within the hour the galley maneuvered into an open birth. Sailors tied the ship into port and the gangplank was extended. Passengers began filing off. Though there were still several hours of sunlight left, torches burned brightly around the marina. Thadius knew the marina area would be busy well into the night. "Come on," Thadius said to Dominus, "we need to find a couple of horses."

It took them only a few minutes to find the livery. Thadius used a gold coin and purchased both horses and tack. Leading the way he maneuvered his horse through the streets towards the city of Rome. The Via Ostiensis was crammed with people even at the late afternoon hour. The strong smells of animal feces and human sewage washed over him like a wave and filled him with disgust. "Yet again the gods see fit to remind me why I left this awful city," Thadius said.

Looking amused, Dominus shook his head solemnly, "The same reasons I never lived in the city," he stated.

The road paralleled the river Tiber and Thadius slowly made his way towards the Porta Raudusculanae, the traveler's gates to the city. As they approached, the traffic slowed to a crawl. A long line of merchants with carts, pedestrians, and people on horseback waited to gain entry.

The sun was vanishing in the west and a brilliant pastel-red sunset illuminated the sky. A brawny smartly dressed centurion wearing a freshly laundered red battle cape waved them forward. With a wax tablet in his hand the guard finished scrawling something then looked up at Thadius, his stylus poised and ready to write. "State your name," he more demanded than requested.

"Moras Tiberius Thadius, from Herculaneum. Visiting the great city."

"Moras Tiberius Thadius?" the centurion said. "Not the Senator of twenty years ago?"

"I was once a Senator of Rome," Thadius stated.

"I am honored," the soldier stated. Writing the name in his tablet he smiled up at Thadius. "You may pass," he called out.

Thadius pulled ahead, stopped, and waited for Dominus. Pulling up to the centurion, Dominus stopped and pointed at the waiting Thadius. "Peresius Albas Dominus, I'm from Herculaneum also, and I am traveling with the *great* Thadius," he said his voice choked with sarcasm.

"Oh, by the way, would you know where we might find the Senator Septimus Turinius Catulus?" Thadius casually said.

The guard put his hand on his chin, "Well, one place is the Senate. The other is at a place called The Two Calves, a wine and beer tavern, near the Senate. He also has an estate outside Rome. In fact you may have passed it; that is if you came from the harbor?"

"You are an honorable soldier," Thadius said.

Dominus pulled up alongside, "Why did you ask for Senator Catulus?"

"While you were sleeping on the ship I had a conversation with the captain. Something struck me as odd. Then it hit me, Turia's disgraced mother; Catulus' wife is Turia, daughter of Servilius Caepio whose wife was Drusa Caepio Lucretia. She was disgraced along with Servilius and later divorced him."

"So?"

"Don't you see? Each of the victims is in some way connected to Caepio. I'll bet Gladria, was the daughter of Opidius Gladrius Vanitius; Maxima's father is probably Antonius Maximus Fabricus; Pollitas, I'll wager is the grandniece of Sutonius Pollinius Nero; Sulpicia, killed in Sardinia was the daughter of Pomponius Sulpicius Varinius a proconsul." He took a breath, "Hedia, is the wife of Titus Januarius Decimius."

"Decimius? The Legatus in charge of the Tenth Legion at Aquae Sextiae?"

Thadius nodded, "The same. That name was the keystone to my revelation."

"Now where to?" Dominus said.

"We'll be heading to the Via Sacra, then to the Senate, and see if we can speak to Senator Septimus Turinius Catulus, the young centurion who commanded the Tenth as Primus Pilus. I suspect we have two days before Flavius Malco and his son arrive, and two days to keep Publius from completing his list."

"What if Catulus is part of the plot?"

"Then he'd probably have us killed," Thadius said. "I'm fairly certain that he is ignorant of all this. But, I'm beginning to suspect a rat is loose in the grain," Thadius offered up.

"So you do not believe that Publius is alone in this?"

"I believe he believes he is alone in these acts, but someone has been influencing him. But, it is more than cold blooded murder, and political intrigue. It has something to do with the gold."

"The Tolosa gold?"

"Precisely. I can't tell you at this moment why I suspect this. Suffice to say, all the dead, in all of this, rightly expect atonement."

"From Publius?"

"Though he is the instrument, he is not the villain. It is the puppeteer that I seek. And, if my guess is correct, we've met him before."

"Really? Where? How did you come up with this thought?" Dominus pressed.

"It's the puzzle pieces. Publius suffers from parliament disease; he is killing families associated with the Tolosa gold... high ranking Roman families. But, they're high ranking because of their wealth garnered from conquest serving under Servilius. All these families had someone present at the battle of Aquae Sextiae, and the sacking of Tolosa. All of them I knew, and some of them you knew. So..." He looked off then looked at Dominus.

"Don't look at me like that. What would I gain from being dragged all over the Republic and the wilderness with you?" Dominus looked indignant.

Thadius smiled, "Not you old salt." He kicked his heels into his horse and the beast began moving. Dominus followed. "Keep an eye out. I suspect we're being followed."

Dominus looked about, "By who?"

"The fellow who left me that note in Narbo."

Slowly they made their way around the hordes of pedestrians and carts. Down the street they went until they passed through the Subura. This part of town was shabby, and poor. Lining the streets were apartment complexes, shops, gambling dens and brothels. The small street was barely wide enough for a chariot. Dark corners and shady characters moved about. Strange and unpleasant smells abounded. This part of the city Thadius knew well, since he spent a large amount of his time in the Senate trying to have it torn down, and new streets and buildings constructed in their places.

"Be on your guard, it can get very dangerous in this part of town," Thadius shouted over the clopping sounds of horse's hooves, the slapping of sandals, and the clack of chariot wheels. Adding to the noise were the shouts of men and women, as they purchased goods, or procured services. Dominus checked his dagger to make sure it would come free at a moment's notice. Finding it ready for use he gave a look around. It was impossible to discern any one person from the crowd.

Turning onto the Via Sacra, Thadius led the way into the main street through the center of Rome. Passing the sacred Vesta Temple, and the Villa de Vesta that was along its side, Thadius pointed, "There's the hearth of Rome my friend."

"An impressive sight indeed," Dominus said.

Further up the road they came to the Senate building. Here the great representatives of Rome plied their trade and made decisions best for the city, and themselves. Men came and went from the columned building, their gaudy togas trimmed in gold, purple or red, all worn short.

"Who are we here to see?" asked Dominus.

"Sextus Dexius Atticus," Thadius said.

"And who is that?"

"The Lictor for Flavius Malco of course."

Dominus halted his horse near the Senate. The sky grew dark and the men who set fire to the public torches were out. Shopkeepers brought out lamps and set them out in front of their buildings to show they were still doing business, as the street vendors continued calling to passing pedestrians.

Thadius climbed down from his horse and moved up the stairs towards the Curia of Pompey. Looking up he noted the ornate carvings depicting scenes from Roman history. He knew the Senate often made use of the building, and it didn't hurt that it was part of the larger theater complex of the Campus Martius where the senators went for entertainment. He came up the stairs to the colonnaded portico, and entered through the dark red, double doors. A man stood at the entrance, wearing a smartly fitting uniform of the Senate Guards. Seeing Thadius and Dominus approach he stood stiffly, and rested his hand on his gladius. "Do you have business with the senate?" he said.

"I am looking to deliver a message to Sextus Dexius Atticus."

"Yes, he is waiting and has instructed me to take the messenger to him immediately. But, he did not say there would be two messengers," the guard said eyeing Dominus suspiciously.

"None the less we are here," Thadius stated.

"Very well." The guard waved another guard over from the shadows. "Take these two men-". He stopped in mid-sentence and looked at the arms hanging from Thadius and Dominus' belts. "Your weapons must be surrendered before you enter," he said.

"Of course," Thadius stated calmly.

Removing their daggers they handed them to the door guard. Taking the weapons he placed them in a wide chest to the side of the door. Handing Thadius and Dominus each a pottery shard with a number on it he shrugged his shoulders. "I'm sure we won't be getting any more visitors this late, but you'd better take these retrieval numbers just in case we do. If I'm not here when you return give the shards to the guard on duty and he'll retrieve your side arms."

Entering the Curia, Thadius and Dominus followed the guard to a stairwell leading to a second floor causeway. The main hall was lit with hanging brass oil lamps, and their thick wicks burned brightly. At the base of the stairs a lamp allowed one to see the first set of steps without falling. At the top of the stairs another lamp allowed one to see the top steps and landing. Even in the lamplight Thadius could see the famous dark marble floor with white streaks running through it. A strong smell of sandalwood incense filled the air and he could see hanging brass spheres, smoke pouring from the slots. Walking down the aisle he noticed a man selling bread and slabs of cured ham. Several Senators purchasing wine, bread and meat looked at them as they passed. Thadius figured the men were going to be spending long hours in some negotiation.

Leading Thadius and Dominus to a closed door, the guard stepped away and smiled. "Here's the office of Sextus Dexius Atticus, personal assistant to Senator Flavius Malco. I'm sure you can find your way out when you're done." Turning on his heels the guard promptly walked down the hall. "A cup of wine and a porcarus panis if you please." The guard's voice echoed from down the hallway where the vendor stood.

Thadius knocked on Atticus' door. "The messenger," a voice exclaimed from behind the door. The door swung wide and hit the wall with a loud clang. Startled by his own exuberance the man jumped and then frowned. "Do you have a message for me from the Senator?"

"First off," Thadius began. "Are you Sextus Dexius Atticus?"

"Yes," the man said impatiently. "Now tell me the message. Where's the senator? Should I go to him or is he coming here?"

"He is not far now," Thadius began. "But, Publius…" He let the sentence fade as if he worried about the content.

"Oh yes, come into the office. We can talk there," Atticus stated while stepping away from the door.

Entering the modest office it was apparent the room had been hastily arranged. Looking around Thadius noted another office connected via a short hall and a door.

"Publius," Atticus asked. "Has he done something again?"

"Yes," Thadius stated.

"By god, not another murder?" Atticus looked grave.

"Yes," Thadius repeated.

"Since the last message? I was fearing he might. Is his health better or worse?" Atticus' face betrayed a true concern for the family.

"Worse," Thadius stated.

"Worse?" Atticus turned a bit pale.

"Perhaps, we should discuss Flavius' return," Dominus goaded.

"Yes. Does he want me to meet him at the city gates still?"

Thinking for a moment Thadius shook his head. "Let the last message serve," he said.

"The last message," Atticus asked. "All the note said was to have the Malco personal guards ready to take Publius into custody and remove him to the Malco estate in Lucania."

"Nothing has changed," Thadius stated.

Atticus sat down and poured some wine into a goblet. He drank it down and steadied his hand. "Should I bring him?"

"Who?" Dominus said.

"The surgeon, as I said in my last note. I asked if the Senator wanted me to bring his personal surgeon." Suddenly eyeing Thadius and Dominus, Atticus appeared to be formulating a question, "From where did Flavius send you?"

A knock at the door made Atticus jump. Cautiously he moved around Thadius and Dominus and opened the door. A gangly young man stood wearing a sweat-stained tunic tied with a thin brown leather belt. "I was sent here to deliver this," he said a bit out of breath as if he just ran up the stairs.

Taking the folded papyrus note Atticus broke the red wax seal and unfolded it. Growing paler, he swayed and nearly fell. Thadius caught him by the arm and led him to the chair again. "He's murdered the Senator and his wife and run away," Atticus said softly as if his thoughts were far away. Looking back at the messenger he spoke, "I have read the note and will do what I can."

The young man turned and dashed back into the hallway. Atticus reached for the pitcher of wine and his cup, then just put the pitcher to his lips and drank. Wiping his mouth with the back of his hand he noticed Thadius and Dominus again. "I – uh, where was it Flavius sent you from?" he stammered out.

"From Pisa, but I see newer information has arrived," Thadius said. "We will trouble you no more." He turned to go.

"What were your names?" Atticus pressed with concern.

Reaching the doorway Thadius and Dominus exited into the hall. "Our names are of no matter," Dominus stated.

"But, wait," Atticus shouted down the hall. "What are your names?"

They moved swiftly past the food vendor. The young guard eyed them. The Senators looked on with what appeared to Thadius bemused expressions. Down the stairs they went and stopped at the door. Handing the door guard his shard, Thadius retrieved his dagger and put it back on his belt. Dominus did the same and they both walked down the steps to their waiting horses. "Now what?" Dominus said. "Do we shadow Atticus? Or, watch Catulus' wife?"

"Good question," Thadius stated. "If the boy has run off, he is surely heading this way. I would say if he rode through the night, he could make it here by dawn, but his condition would require him to rest. I would say that at the earliest we can expect him here by morning."

"How do we know he's going to come here?"

"Simple," Thadius stated. "He has to complete his list."

"But, what do we do in the meantime?"

Thadius mounted his horse. "Have you ever eaten at the Pillars of Hercules?"

Dominus raised an eyebrow, "Brothel or termopolia?"

"Thermopolia and it's just down the street."

"Well, I sure hope it serves the best," Dominus said.

"After all these years, I hope it does too," Thadius stated.

CHAPTER 35

After eating, Thadius went to the storehouse where the cart-man had delivered their goods. He hired another man with a cart to carry their items to an inn. "We'd better get some sleep. By morning we'll need to be fresh for what fate awaits us," he said to Dominus. They stopped at a building with a shingle that showed a bed on it. "This inn will do for the night," he said.

Opening the door he entered a small reception room. An overly plump man stood at a dais burning some olive branches in a ceremonial brass caldron. Seeing Thadius and Dominus enter, the man turned and shyly smiled, "Forgive me, tis time for sacrifice."

"May your home be blessed by Vesta," Thadius said.

The man smiled warmly as if he was greeting friends, "You must be weary from your travel. May I offer you a room and board?"

"We are weary, and yes we will take two rooms," Thadius stated.

Appearing even happier the man inhaled making his large belly expand, then exhaled with a laugh. Clapping his hands together he moved towards the door. "Any slaves, servants, items or baggage you have that need to come inside?"

"It is not much and we'll get it," Dominus stated. Going back outside, Thadius and Dominus moved to the cart and their belongings. Dominus, picking up his bundle turned to Thadius,

"Pulling those oars all those weeks did me some good. This bundle seems lighter now."

Paying the cart driver, Thadius hoisted his bundle and carried it inside behind Dominus. "We've been eating provisions making them lighter too."

Dominus frowned, "I feel stronger anyway." They entered the inn again.

"One room is a quinarius per night. How many nights would you like?" the innkeeper said.

Dominus pulled out two coins. "One night will do," he stated. "And remember, we'll have our own rooms."

The man regarded the coins, then moved to a shelf against the wall and took down a roll of papyrus. Also, taking down an inkwell and stylus he unrolled the paper.

"Please sign here, and don't forget to put where you are from and how many nights you are staying. Supper will be in a few hours, and I lock the door at eleven. Please, if you can, be in before eleven," he stated. "The Forum is beautiful at night, but can also be rough. There have been roving bands of politicos running about causing mayhem. Be on your guard."

"Where are the rooms?" Dominus said.

"On the third floor, just up the stairs. Follow me." He led the men up the stairs panting all the while. At one point at the second floor he stopped and put his hands on his knees. "Let's wait here for a moment, I'm a bit winded," he said. A moment later they were moving again as he led the way up to the third floor. Along this stretch of stair, the wood creaked loudly under the weight of the three men, and for a moment Thadius worried they would all end up on the second floor, broken and in need of a surgeon.

The innkeeper pointed down the dark hallway and said, "Your rooms are down there." Taking on a befuddled look he shook his head disappointedly. "Usually the lights are lit up here. I must apologize." The innkeeper turned and yelled down the stairwell, "Herot, bring up a lamp."

The sound of someone scurrying up the stairs echoed. A flickering yellow light appeared. Coming around the corner approached a small boy carrying a lamp. "Here master," he called up as he handed the innkeeper the lamp.

Thadius watched the large man's face change from a grin to anger. Striking the boy softly on the head he chided him, "How many times must I tell you, keep the third floor lights lit." Grinning again, the innkeeper waved his hand dismissing the boy, then turned down the hallway. "At this age slaves are hard to train," he said as he came to a darkly stained wooden door. Pushing it open he stepped inside. "A better room you will not find at any inn in Rome."

Glancing about, Thadius noted the room was typical of all the inns in which they stayed; a bed, a mattress and pillow, and a stack of blankets. To the other side was a small table, dresser, wash table with basin, and mirror. "This will do," he said.

Looking quite pleased, the large man helped him with his bundle. He then escorted Dominus to his room. Helping carry his bundle into the room the plump man said goodnight and moved down the hallway and down the stairs.

"Why is it that we get placed on the top floor of these flea traps every time we go somewhere?" Dominus stated.

"Perhaps they know what sort of fleas we like," Thadius chuckled. "But, I must say that at least we have a room to sleep in, we could have been sleeping in the stables with the horses."

Thadius unpacked his belongings and made his bed. Chimes rang from the city's water clock signaling ten of the night and he thought of his wife. His heart ached for her company. His muscles ached too and he was truly bone-weary. Sleep came quickly as the darkness came to his eyes, and he dreamt of his home in Herculaneum.

Thadius' eyes flew open. Sitting up he looked about the room. The darkness was unsettling. Getting to his feet, he moved to the washbasin and poured some water into it. Washing his face he wondered what his dream meant. A knocking on the door made him turn. Dominus opened it and looked in.

"Well old salt? Shall we get some food?"

"Yes, let's get some food, then we need to see Catulus and find out where his wife is going to be over the next few days."

Dressing quickly in his beige tunic and white toga, Thadius looked down at the gifts Eilifr had given him. He held up a finely crafted coif and vest of chain mail. Also, two steel daggers, one quite small, almost like a fruit knife, and the other as long as a normal combat blade. For a moment he studied the items. A strange feeling was in his gut. He knew it well. It served him many times in the past, but now there was also the haunting fear of a friend's betrayal. "I'll be down in a moment," he told Dominus.

"Suit yourself," Dominus said and headed down the stairs.

Thadius sat on the bed. "Into Tartarus, those convicted of crimes of life shall be cast. No paradise, no pleasures, no satisfaction, and no redemption," he said quietly. "Then let it be so."

He met Dominus in the dining room. The morning meal was already on the long table. Other patrons were seated and eating. Fresh baked bread, fish cakes, robin's eggs and dormice were on the menu. Dominus seemed to have no interruption of appetite, but Thadius was loath to eat. Yet, he forced down some bread dipped in olive oil. Afterward he drank a cup of wine and waited for Dominus.

Once outside they retrieved their horses and moved toward the Curia of Pompey. Thadius spoke, "I wouldn't expect Publius to try and come through the Porta Raudusculanae."

"I guess not," Dominus offered with a frown. "He'll probably come through at the Porticus Aemilia where all the river merchants come through. It would be the last place anyone would look for him.

Walking to the Curia of Pompey, Thadius moved up the busy stairs to the door. Merchants, slaves, servants, and guards, mingled with contractors, sales men, entertainers, and tourists; all came and went along the stairs. At the door a guard halted them, "State your business?"

"We're here to speak to Septimus Turinius Catulus," Thadius stated.

"And, who might you be?" the guard said.

"I am Moras Tiberius Thadius, and this is Peresius Albas Dominus."

"He is currently with the Consul, but said that he would entertain written messages if important. You can give me the message and I'll see it delivered," the guard said handing Thadius a wax tablet and stylus.

Taking a moment he wrote a brief introduction and a summary of his visit. Handing the tablet back to the guard the man read it and then handed it to another guard who ran off into the Curio.

"Strange message," the guard commented off handedly while turning some tourists away at the door.

"Stranger then you know," Thadius stated.

After a few moments, Catulus appeared at the door. He looked Thadius up and down. Stepping outside he looked at both men with a wary eye. "Moras Tiberius Thadius?" Catulus said. "You are known to me. It has been many years. What news do you bring of my wife Turia?"

"Can we speak somewhere in private?" Thadius stated.

"Speak here."

"Where is your wife now?"

Looking perturbed Catulus frowned, "What is this about?"

"Do you remember the agreement?" Thadius demanded.

"Of course I do. Now you had better make sense and soon?" Catulus said, his face turning red.

"The document I gave you when at Tolosa. Do you have it?" Thadius pressed.

Dominus looked at Thadius. "What document?"

"My wife has it safe in some strongbox at my villa outside the city. It's protected by my personal guard," Catulus stated.

"Thadius?" Dominus said.

"And your wife is at home now?" Thadius demanded to know.

"Yes."

"You are the last one," Thadius said.

Catulus' eyes went wide, "The last?"

Thadius grabbed Catulus by the shoulders, "Don't you understand? Someone has gathered up all of the Caepio letters. You have the last one. If the letter is at your villa, and your wife is there too, she is in mortal danger. They're going to your home even as we speak. How do we get to your villa?"

"Out the west gate toward Ostia, you can't miss it," Catulus said still not quite comprehending fully what Thadius was talking about

Looking at the door guard Thadius could see he was troubled. "What is it? Did someone come asking questions of the senator's wife today?"

The guard looked forlorn. Shaking his head yes, he looked from Catulus, to Thadius and Dominus. "A young man, an hour ago, said he was taking fresh meat to the senator's wife, and he needed to get it there soon before it spoiled. He asked where the Quaestor's wife was going to be this morning. I told him to try the Senator's villa."

Thadius turned to Dominus, "There's not a moment to lose; we must fly!"

CHAPTER 36

Thadius leapt into the saddle. He shouted back up the steps. "Rouse your guard and send them to your villa now! If we are lucky, your wife is still alive." He drove his heels into his horse and sped away felling pedestrians and dodging carts. Dominus followed closely on his heels.

"Catulus' villa is just a few miles outside the Porta Raudusculanae. Publius has, an hour on us."

"Not if the traffic is as thick at the gates as it is here," Dominus offered.

"True," Thadius said as they wove through the crowds of people and made their way back down the Via Sacra. Thadius took a sharp turn and went along a small and dangerous street of the Subura. He emerged through a vaulted hallway and through a field, past a burnt out house and toward the Porta Raudusculanae.

Moving like a great wave of men, women, and children, the throngs of travelers entering Rome passed around Thadius and Dominus. His horse parted through the crowd and he dug his heels into the beast bolting out the gate. Moving to the side of the road, over a ditch, and into a grassy pasture, he motioned for Dominus to follow. They paralleled the Via Ostiensis, and rode towards Ostia. Finding a break in the traffic, Thadius drove his horse on and dashed across the ditch and onto the wide road. He crouched low in the saddle and rode hard for the entrance that led to Catulus' villa.

A frantic young woman nearly collided with Thadius as she rushed from the villa grounds and through the gateway. Pulling hard to the side he avoided her only by inches. She screamed as she ran, her face covered in what appeared to be blood.

Pulling up on the reins as he approached the outer wall of the estate he slowed then stopped and jumped from his horse. Following suit, Dominus pulled up behind Thadius and dismounted. He came up alongside then checked to make sure his dagger was secure at his belt. Leaning over he whispered to Thadius, "Did you see that slave girl?"

"I almost killed her," Thadius whispered back.

"I think someone else almost killed her," Dominus stated.

Walking up to the estate wall, Thadius noticed the absence of people. Getting closer he noticed the guard post unattended.

"No one seems about. Perhaps Turia didn't come here after all," Dominus said while looking about nervously.

Noticing a pair of hobnail sandals near the gate, Thadius moved in that direction. Stopping at the high cement wall, he could see the sandals still attached to the feet of the guard they belonged to, and the guard was surely dead. A row of hedges lined the path leading from the gate to a short inner wall within the garden and atrium. Ionic columns lined the path, and ivy grew along an arbor above the columns. In the new morning sun the shade over the atrium entrance created dark shadows.

"Well?" Dominus said. "Every second is a second lost."

"Succinctly put," Thadius stated quietly. "We should go around to the kitchen entrance."

"The easiest way in?" Dominus said.

"I'll wager we will be unexpected if we go through the kitchen."

"Good plan," Dominus added. "I hope we're not surprised."

"Me too," Thadius said.

"Publius is just one sickly man," Dominus stated. "He should be easy to subdue."

"I suspect he's not alone. The puppet master is here to collect the letter," Thadius added. "Take no chances."

"About those letters," Dominus began, "what are they and why are they so valuable?"

"The eve of the gold shipment I was asked by Servilius to give out seven letters to seven officers. They were instructed to keep the documents and not open them unless told to do so. Each letter contained one description of a location."

"How do you know what was in the documents?"

Thadius looked Dominus in the eye. "Because I wrote them."

CHAPTER 37

Arriving at the short stone wall that marked the inner perimeter of the villa's yard, Thadius noticed another body lying in a pool of blood. He stepped around the dead man and could see he had actually removed his sword from its sheath before being killed.

He could see a small wrought iron gate kicked from its hinges lying in the dirt. Thadius moved into the yard and towards the house.

Dominus advanced to the wall. Peeking over the top he saw another guard lying in his own blood, the corpse still clutched his neck wound.

"And, all this time you had something to do with the stolen gold, and you didn't tell me?" Dominus whispered a bit indignant.

"I didn't know what it all was about. Not until two days ago."

Pointing down at some bloody footprints leading away from the body Thadius moved down a stone path and around the villa. Coming to another gate he could see it open. He moved into the peristylum, where he saw a pile of coal most likely used for cooking. Seeing an open door under an awning, he motioned for them to move towards it. As he got closer, he could see the door led into the kitchen. He put his finger to his lips as he turned and quickly looked in. Taking in the scene, he noted the kitchen to be rather unremarkable. The iron door to the stove was open and the fire was lit. Yellow flames crackled in the open chamber. A cloud of thin smoke filled the room, and the bloody footprints vanished into another room at the far side. He signaled with his hand for them to enter, and he drew his dagger.

Entering the room he checked behind the door and gingerly made his way to the opposite doorway. He moved into the next room. Dominus motioned with his hand towards the door. Placing his hand against his ear Dominus signaled there was noise beyond the opening. Pointing into the room, where a chair sat near the wall, Dominus slipped into the room and hid behind the chair. He motioned for Thadius to enter. Thadius found the footprints ended at the rug in the middle of the room. The room appeared to be a triclinium and three couches with green pillows were placed at right angles to one another forming an open square. At the other end of the room two doors led out.

A muffled cry echoed down the hall, and Thadius moved to the far left portal. Lying just in the doorway was the body of a female slave. Her golden hair had fallen down about her nude upper body. The tatters of her slave's toga lay about her waist. It was clear she had been stabbed in the back and her throat cut. Blood, covered the tiled floor, and in her hand was a piece of golden material. Taking the gold threaded fragment from the dead woman's hand, Thadius motioned for Dominus to move down the hallway. The sound of pleading caught his attention and he watched with intent as Dominus moved around the pool of crimson fluid and towards the sound at the end of the hall.

As Thadius moved by the slave's body he could see the poor girl's eyes now a dull gray-green. *Sad*, he thought, *they were probably a spectacular emerald color once.* The sound of slapping drifted down the hallway, and Dominus held up his hand to signal him to halt. Pointing he motioned for Thadius to move to the doorway.

"Please, my husband will pay you anything," cried out a demure woman's voice.

Listening, Thadius heard three voices. One was a woman's. Another voice seemed confused and harried. Yet, another voice was calm and soft. "You are doing fine. Don't let that disgusting blight sway you from your task. When you're done we'll go to the fleece," the calm voice said.

"Her eyes, they see me," the confused voice said hurriedly, "Look at her – she's dirty. I can smell her."

"Take your medicine. Give her a taste too. You will both be reborn when all is done."

Thadius looked over at Dominus and shrugged his shoulders. Dominus signaled he was going to look in the room and waited for Thadius to acknowledge his intent.

"She drank it," the confused voice said.

"But, you must do it too. The magic will only work if you both drink."

"My head, it aches, and you never have taken it away," the confused voice protested.

"This is the last. After this, kneel and I shall remove your headache forever. Sleep will come for you."

Dominus snuck a peek and signaled to Thadius that he saw only two people in the room. Stealing himself, Thadius made ready to enter. Dominus nodded his head as if he could read Thadius' mind. Looking at Dominus, he could see the man's eyes change from passive to warrior. Dominus turned the dagger in his hand from pointing down to thrust. He was only waiting on Thadius to move.

Thadius stepped in and saw a woman lying on her back, naked and bound hand and foot. Standing over her was Publius, a surgeon's scalpel in his hand and the blade nearly against the flesh of her left breast. Turia, looked over at Thadius, her eyes filled with terror and pleading.

Publius, seeing him, stood frozen and looked confused. He dropped the scalpel and clutched his head. Falling to the floor the boy jerked and quaked like a fish on the deck of a boat.

"Dominus, free her," Thadius shouted as Dominus headed instinctively to the bound woman. Thadius moved toward Publius, as a steady flow of nonsense flowed from the boy's mouth. "Saturn, Apollo, no, mother, the fleece can make all well, the fleece…" Publius kept repeating.

Something came from the side. Thadius threw himself to the ground, rolled to his side and looked to Dominus. Dominus, still standing, clutched the exposed shaft of an arrow in his chest. Blood dribbled from the wound staining his toga crimson. He swayed on his feet, looked down at the still bound woman and continued moving toward her. Reaching with his dagger for the woman's roped hands, he collapsed and fell to the floor unconscious.

From behind a tapestry an apparition rushed up to Thadius and kicked the dagger from his hand. The blade skidded to a halt against the opposite wall. Thadius stepped to the side, but the apparition caught him by the arm and threw him against a chair, shattering the seat. Stepping back the figure looked down at him. In the lamp light Thadius could clearly see a man covered in shimmering golden fabric and wearing a radiant gold sun mask that reflected all the light in the room.

Publius suffered more spasms. "Stupid boy. I told him to drink only a small amount," the man in the sun mask said. Blood gurgled through Publius clenched teeth and down his chin. He jerked a few more times and his eyes rolled up into his head. "Look what I have to work with."

"Who are you?" Thadius demanded.

"Apollo, or isn't it obvious?"

"You are no Apollo," Thadius said.

"True. But, that's of little matter. I will soon be as rich as Apollo, and as powerful."

Thadius got to his knees, and the masked figure motioned with a gladius for him to stay there. "Not yet old friend," he said in a familiar voice. Reaching up the figure removed the mask.

"Gnaeus!" Thadius said his eyes darting from Gnaeus to Publius then back again.

"Yes, none other," Gnaeus stated. "It would seem that Publius has tortured yet another poor innocent citizen. And, what's this? The great Thadius at work controlling the murderer. Of course it is, for I Gnaeus have born witness to this tragedy. And, as reward, I'll get all your businesses, and property, and prestige. Oh, and the stolen gold of Tolosa."

"I don't get it," Thadius stated.

"Okay, I really thought you were smarter. But, I guess you've aged as I, and things are not quite as clear. I intend on buying a Consulship with the Tolosa gold, then I'll create mayhem on the streets of Rome. The senate will see fit to proclaim me dictator for the year, and I will dissolve the senate, and impose a new golden reign for a mighty Roman king, me. All this made possible by you and that damned gold." He chuckled, "You did hear me say golden reign?"

"I got that," Thadius said. "Clever…"

"It is a shame you were killed while trying to murder the wife of Septimus Turinius Catulus. Thadius the fiend," he laughed suddenly. "Your reputation destroyed in the process. But, I will give you a lovely funeral pyre in the Forum nonetheless. I will of course call for an immediate investigation, and what will be found? You were in every place a murder took place," he smiled. "I still can't believe how easily you were led."

"So all this is just a plot to be made a king?" Thadius stated trying to buy time.

"Not just any king, but King of Rome."

"The boy," Thadius gestured to Publius unconscious on the floor. "Did he do any of the killings?"

"He did them all," Gnaeus said. "Apollo told him that Rome would fall if he did not retrieve the Golden Fleece, hidden by the Seven Sisters of Atlas. We had to get the clues. And now the last of them are in hand."

"How did you know of the letters?" Thadius said.

"How does anyone find out about anything? I was here in the city five years ago when I happened to have a drink with an old comrade of yours. He told me of the Tolosa gold and how he saw you deliver seven letters after it went missing. He mused that they were clues to the location of the lost gold. After some inquiry, I had to agree. The next year I met Malco, and his son. Opportunity met means, and I began down this road to power."

"So, Publius did all the murders?" Thadius pressed.

Limping to Publius, "poor boy." Gnaeus raised and drove the point of his sword into the unconscious man's throat. Publius fell into spasms as his blood pumped out the wound and onto the floor. A sickly choking sound filled the room and the boy clutched his throat, then fell silent and motionless.

"Well, unfortunately not this one…or the next few. In fact, before I'm done, I believe the streets of Rome will run red, but not by Publius' hand," Gnaeus said. Looking back at Publius' body, "The poor sickly fellow has served his purpose," he smiled. "It was too easy to feed you clues, old friend. I'm surprised you didn't see through the plot. It was unbearable as I waited in my cabin on the ship, with you and Dominus just down the hall. I was so tempted to leave you another note, but thought better of it."

"And Eilifr?" Thadius stated.

"A dupe like you. Eilifr just did the transporting. He knew nothing."

"But, why?"

"Because," shouted Gnaeus, "you had everything! The wife, the wealth, the property, and the fame. What did I have? Debt, lament, no prodigy, nothing but loyalty to the Republic. Now is the time for you to suffer as I did, in the shadow of greatness."

"What now?"

"With this one move I shall destroy my enemies, and, erase all the conspiracy against me," Gnaeus said his eyes vacant of empathy."

"I see that you're limping," Thadius added.

"This?" Gnaeus pointed at his leg. "My mistake, I got too confident. Your friend there cut me in the market in Lutetia; though I believe it was by accident." He looked annoyed, "But, now I've returned the favor, many times over." "Would you like me to kill you now, or would you like to watch what creative work I will do to the lovely Lady Catulus here?" He nodded toward the woman.

"She's unconscious and can't tell you where the letter is."

"I already got the letter. And, while she seems unconscious, she can hear everything, and feel everything I assure you. A special potion that I discovered in the hills of Hispania some years ago. Now it's time for fun," Gnaeus stated.

"Perhaps you should just kill me now," Thadius said bending his head downward. "I'm not one for torture as you know."

"Always the weak stomach," Gnaeus said as he limped toward Thadius. "Wouldn't you first like to know where the gold is hidden?"

"I already know where it is," Thadius stated.

Gnaeus looked down at him surprised, "What do you mean?"

"I've always known where the Tolosa gold was."

"You make no sense. How could you know?"

Thadius took in a deep breath. "I was the one who stole the gold."

"What?" Gnaeus stepped back.

"Yes. After the shipment left Tolosa, Servilius and I conspired to kill the soldiers of the convoy, and steal the gold. I commanded a cohort and we ambushed the train. We killed all of them, and arranged them to appear as if attacked by Celts. On that campaign I became so rich with land I didn't know what to do with it all," he mockingly chuckled, "while you toiled for incompetent proconsuls." Thadius shrugged, "True, the gold is still there, untouched. Servilius couldn't get to it after his banishment."

"What? I mean, why didn't you go get the gold? Servilius has been dead for many years now."

"Why? I was already rich beyond any ability to spend it all. I had glory, and rank from all the wars and looting. I had a wife who gave me children who will live beyond me. Why did I need that gold?"

"You idiot," Gnaeus scolded. "Don't you understand what you had?" His eyes flashed rage, "Such a fool, such an arrogant cursed fool!" His hands shook with rage.

Thadius took two quick steps and drove the small hidden dagger that Eilifr had given him into Gnaeus' foot. The man screamed and dropped his sword. Thadius scooped it up. Gnaeus tore free his robe and threw it at him.

A dagger was in Gnaeus' hand and he lunged at Thadius. Thadius countered and thrust his blade. Gnaeus' hit solidly, but the blade did not penetrate to Thadius' skin. Both men tried to grapple, then they broke apart. Thadius spun to the side and leveled a blow to Gnaeus' side. Gnaeus tried to block but missed and the sword blade bit into his ribs. He cried out, and then plunged his dagger into Thadius. Gnaeus tried to grapple. His free hand gripped Thadius' toga and tunic and ripped them exposing the chain mail vest.

"You sly bastard," Gnaeus said angrily. He flew at Thadius who sidestepped.

Stepping around and then into Gnaeus, Thadius kicked up between the man's legs. Gnaeus fell back bent at the waist gasping. Darting in, Thadius tried to drive his sword into Gnaeus. The man spun and latched onto Thadius' chain mail, looking up into his eyes. "It is so unfair that the gods favor you so. I curse you with all my might," Gnaeus said. Thadius shoved him back, brought the sword up and around and severed Gnaeus' hands at the wrist. He stood there, his eyes wide with shock.

"Rome doesn't need a king," Thadius said.

Gnaeus stared at the stumps where his hands used to be. He leered at Thadius, "Rome is a mob that needs to be led." He fell to his knees. Blood began to ooze from the stumps and he looked at them, then up at Thadius again. "You're life has always mocked me."

"Like the mocking you've done to Apollo? Did you think he would take the insult of your mockery so easily?"

The blood pumped from Gnaeus' wounds and onto the floor. "I should have chosen Cupid to impersonate instead..." He slumped to the floor as the blood flowed out in a rhythmic fashion.

Thadius stepped back, then staggered. He braced himself at the wall. Looking down he could see Gnaeus' crimson life force slow. Thadius felt sick. He staggered to Dominus and fell to his knees. His leg was bleeding and he patched the wound with some of his torn toga.

"I see you won," Dominus said looking up.

"By the gods!" Thadius proclaimed.

"By Eilifr," Dominus stated while unwrapping his toga, pulling open his tunic and showing Thadius a similar chain mail vest. "Is what you said true? Did you really steal the Tolosa gold?"

Thadius smirked, "I just said that to drive Gnaeus off balance." He looked back at the still bound unconscious woman. "I did write the letters, but I didn't kill our own soldiers. Someone else did that."

"What are you saying?"

"I assume Servilius needed to be protected in the event he was linked to the theft. I knew only that I wrote seven documents that named seven woodland features. The Legatus who gave me the clues was murdered that night." He exhaled heavily, "I thought all those events most random at the time. But, on the ship I realized they were not."

"Why didn't the seven just put their clues together and go get the gold?"

"I'm not sure that they each knew the other had one of the clues. Servilius instructed that the documents be kept until he came to get them. But, when Caepio was later tried for incompetence and banished from Rome to the hinterlands, the matter of the letters was forgotten. None of them knew what they actually had. Knowing what you do now, would you risk digging up the Tolosa gold?"

Dominus looked up, "If I did it with a trusted friend."

"As soon as you suggested the connection, one of the others would have taken your letter and slit your throat. Besides, that gold belongs to Rome. If the Senate found out, you could be put to death, or made a slave. You know what could happen." Thadius pressed on his leg wound to stop the bleeding. "Nevertheless, the seven all had wealth, and probably like me wouldn't know what to do with the gold if they had it."

"Now, there is only one who knows," Dominus said.

"Well, that does make things awkward," Thadius tightened the bandage around his leg. Examining Dominus' wound Thadius could see the arrow penetrated his armor, and stuck between two ribs, but not deeply.

The sound of running feet echoed in the hallway. Several soldiers rushed into the room. Slipping on the plentiful blood, one soldier skidded out of control and fell in a heap near Publius body.

Catulus entered the room, his face a mask of worry. The other soldiers secured the room and stood watch over Thadius, Dominus and the two bodies. One guard untied Turia. Another guard watched the door.

"Merciful Jupiter," Catulus said.

"These men have saved my life," Lady Catulus groggily stated. "But before I tell you anymore you must call for our personal surgeon and have these men seen to," she demanded.

"As you wish," Catulus stated. Turning to one of the soldiers he commanded the man to fetch the surgeon. Rushing out the door the soldier shoved aside several of the Senator's bodyguards. "What happened here?" Catulus said to his wife."

Stepping into the hall she began to explain what happened to her and her servants. When she finished Catulus turned to Thadius. "And what is it you have to add to this story?"

Thadius told his story, starting with the arrival of the letter and ending with the trip to Rome in pursuit of Publius. Catulus stared, his face a betraying disbelief. "You mean to tell me Gnaeus murdered all those people because he thought we knew where the Tolosa gold was at? He wanted to make himself King of Rome? He must have been truly mad." Interrupting the senator's focus, a man shoved his way through the soldiers.

"Whose been wounded?"

"Over here Opilio," Catulus said pointing at Dominus and Thadius.

The blond haired young surgeon ordered the room emptied, except for Thadius and Dominus. Calling out the door he yelled for water to be boiled. A few moments later, several soldiers came with bowls of steaming water. "Now bring me clean linens and several unused sponges," the surgeon commanded as he removed some small glass bottles with stoppers from his case. Shaking one of the bottles he set it down to his side. Opening one of the other bottles he took out a yellow paste with a flat stick, and mixed it with some water in a small cup. Taking a rag he hastily cleaned Thadius' wounds with the yellow liquid, and dressed it.

"Keep pressure on the leg wound and wait until I can staple it closed. Now, let me get to this man here," Opilio said pointing at Dominus who lay on his back, his face twisted with pain.

Opening a brownish bottle, the surgeon poured a small amount of liquid into a tiny silver cup. "I'm going to have you drink this, it will take away the pain," he said to Dominus. Dominus drank the liquid forcing it through his clinched teeth. Burning as it hit his stomach; he winced for a moment then relaxed, and closed his eyes.

The surgeon cut the flesh on either side of the wound. Removing the arrow he pulled out the short iron point. He stemmed the bleeding with two clamps and sopped up the red ooze with a small sponge. Slowly he checked the depth of the wound with a silver probe. "Your friend here was lucky the arrow didn't penetrate beyond his ribs."

Thadius watched, reminded of the field surgeons who worked on the fallen soldiers in his days of battle. Admiring the man's work he noted the blood leaking from around his own wound.

The young man sutured up Dominus and applied a white paste, then clamped over the wound with some small silver staples. "He'll need to rest for a week, with no movement of the upper body, stomach muscles, or back," Opilio said.

Turning his attention to Thadius he quickly removed the bandage and examined the wound. The bleeding had stopped. Applying a powder to the laceration, Thadius felt the pain ebbed. Opilio took a small needle and sutured the wound's leaking vein, and then applied the white paste he had used on Dominus, and stapled the wound shut. "I'll be back in a day to check on you. If you see leakage around the wound, clean it with boiled water. I'll tell the senator to have you both watched for signs of fever," the surgeon said as he began cleaning his tools and putting them away. "Drink only tea and thin wine, and do not bathe the wounds for at least two weeks."

"Should I worry?" Thadius said pointing at Dominus.

The surgeon shook his head. "That wound will make a scar but won't kill him. Just do as I say and you'll both live." He turned and walked to the door, stopped and spoke with Turia for a moment then left. Turia entered the room and asked her husband to assign two soldiers to care for Thadius and Dominus. Catulus looked down at the two men, "I am grateful for what you've done. You may stay here as long as you need and I'll pay your way home when the time comes." He motioned for two guards to approach. "My soldiers will care for you until I can send some servants from our home in the city. Opilio, our surgeon has left medicine and clear instructions."

Walking to the door Catulus frowned back at Thadius, "I must get back to the Forum."

Holding up a small vile Turia spoke, "Opilio left this with instruction. Take a spoon full and we'll get you to your room." She administered the medicine and then motioned for the soldiers to approach. Thadius felt instantly disconnected. His eyes felt heavy, and he recognized the effect of the poppy extract. In truth, he welcomed it. Poppy had that affect; he could remember it well from years before.

Turia directed the soldiers to move Dominus onto a stretcher and take him down the hall. She helped Thadius to his feet and he limped down the hall to one of the villa's many bedrooms. Once in the bedroom Turia assisted him from his clothes and into bed. The soft down mattress and clean sheets felt good, and the smell of lavender lulled him into slumber. Quickly his eyes fell closed and he began falling, deep into a dark well of dreams.

The mist cleared and Thadius was across the river. In his heart a joyful feeling overwhelmed him. His wife stood before him and smiled, "You've traveled a weary distance. You're tired, and in need of rest. Sleep my love, and when you wake, all will be clear. You are past the point of wishing for me to return. I'm here, well and happy. You'll find another path, and it will speak to you in ways a woman cannot." She began to fade.

Thadius grasped for her, but like a vapor she no longer had form. He looked about, and in the distance a golden glow appeared. It became brighter, and brighter, blinding him with its brilliance. "Do what is right, do what is good," her voice said.

CHAPTER 38

Leaving Catulus' villa, Thadius and Dominus began their journey towards the docks at Ostia Antica. Three weeks had elapsed since landing in Rome and Thadius wondered if they would ever see Herculaneum again.

Riding slowly, Dominus spoke of the travels they made. "It was a full campaign, just as if we were still in the legion. I can't believe how many miles we traveled."

"Or, the women you had," Thadius said. Weaving past the many pedestrians, Thadius made note of their determined faces as the travelers headed towards the Eternal City. "It is certain that the trip home will not take long," he stated as his horse snorted and shoved through the throng.

"Tis true, I did take a few women," Dominus lazily said as he looked straight ahead. "It is for tales best told later, while I enjoy your house wine - in your house. Speaking of which, it's not more than a day's journey from Ostia."

The crowd thinned as they came to the gates of Ostia Antica. Several of the port guards eyed them as they passed but did not challenge them. Entering the town Thadius noted the many travelers wandering the streets, some with packs and others with carts. Bursts of laughter erupted from a tavern and a couple of patrons emerged, one with his arm around the other's shoulders. The two men stumbled drunkenly into the street, made a ninety-degree turn and staggered off together into another tavern down the road.

A smell of the sea and cooking food filled the air. As Thadius made his way towards the waterfront he noted the bland expression on Dominus' face. "Why so glum my friend?"

"I've thought a lot about what you said; that the gold does not mean that much. I agree it doesn't mean that much to you or I who've lived these many years in luxury. But, what about all those waifs out there? What of those free men who make no shadows in Rome?"

"The Senate would only spend it to glorify itself," Thadius said.

"True enough." Dominus smiled. "But, what of Lutetia, or Tolosa? Surely good could be done there, and Rome none the wiser?"

"Dominus the giver?" Thadius chuckled.

"I've given away a fortune by gambling, why not do it in such a way as to do real good?"

"An interesting suggestion," Thadius said.

Coming around the corner, the street widened and an expanse of land sticking into the sea came into view. All around the street were small shops and apartments. To one side appeared to be the beginning brickwork of a theater and to the other side was the Antica Forum.

Looking up at the early morning blue sky, Dominus squinted. "Seems we're in for a fine day of sailing."

"Too bad it will only take us a day to reach home from here. I sure could do with more sailing," Thadius said with a grin.

"Now who's the one wishing for a gamble?" Dominus chuckled.

"I cannot hide the fact that I am saddened that the trip is at an end."

"We're not home yet," Dominus reminded him with a wag of his finger. "Who's to say we shouldn't just take these two horses and turn them back towards Gaul?"

"If I was twenty years younger I would agree. But, I long to see my home," Thadius said with conviction.

"I suppose I do too," Dominus stated. "What was the name of the ship we are sailing on?"

"No name, just a berth; berth eleven," Thadius said.

The port of Ostia Antica appeared busy. Ships of every description lay at harbor and moored at the marina. Long trains of carts hauled goods both to and from the docks.

"Seems like we were here just the other day," said Dominus.

"More like a month ago, now." Thadius maneuvered his horse around a cart carrying a caged leopard. The wild cat moved back and forth in the cage, tilting its black nose up sniffing the air. Another cart passed filled with rolls of cloth, and yet another cart with wooden boxes marked with the Alexandria seal on the sides.

Stopping at the stables, he talked with the owner for a few minutes, haggling over a good price to sell the horses. Settling on twenty silver coins a piece he turned over the animals to the stable owner and bid the man fare well. Taking the blankets from the back of his saddle, he let the bundle drop to the cobblestones of the street. Dominus did the same, and he smiled at the man. "Much lighter than what we started with," he laughed.

"No need for extra clothes or food stocks now," Dominus said. "But I will miss the wine."

"Nonetheless, we'd better find the ship and make ready. Though it will take us only a day, the sea can be unpredictable," Thadius stated.

He and Dominus made their way towards the marina. The way was simple, and the two men only had to cross one crowded street. Finding the marina road, Thadius led the way to the docks and the ships. "Strange," Dominus began. "The ship at birth eleven appears to be of a familiar design."

"Strange indeed. But, we did see another on the river to Lutetia as you remember. Perhaps it is that we have just been too idle all these years and do not know what types of boats now roam our waters?"

Slinging the rolled up blankets onto his shoulder, Dominus sucked in the sea air. The faint odor of sewage wafted to his nose and he laughed heartily at the acrid smell. "Seaside sewage, never a good thing."

"Yet it doesn't stop the trade or tourists from moving through this city," stated Thadius. Stepping down onto the marina road, he moved towards birth eleven. Here the mix of imports and exports moved with great speed. Men rushed past carrying crates filled with vegetables and livestock, others wheeled carts filled with nuts and olives, and yet others stacked lumber and bundles of Egyptian cotton.

Through this confusion a booming voice erupted from afar. At first he did not recognize the voice, but as he rounded a large pile of cotton bales he saw a bear of a man standing up on the rudder platform of the ship at birth eleven. "Good of you little Romans to finally arrive," Eilifr called to them. "I have been waiting two days for you and was not going to wait a day longer."

"Eilifr," shouted Dominus with glee, "you old salt."

"How did you find us," Thadius asked.

"It was easy," Eilifr began. "When I returned to Britannia, the garrison there had some items for me to bring to Rome for Gnaeus. There were not many items, but they were large and cumbersome. We were ordered to make straight for Rome and stop little." Adjusting his brown belt Eilifr stepped from the ship onto the dock. Walking to Thadius and Dominus he opened his massive arms wide and embraced both men at once.

"When we arrived I was told by a man at the Senate that Gnaeus had been killed and my cargo was worthless. Then the man said something that surprised me. He said that a Tiberius Thadius had slain Gnaeus in single combat."

Eilifr walked with the two men towards the ship. "I inquired where I might find you and was told you were at the Villa of Septimus Turinius Catulus. When I arrived at the villa, I was turned away, told that there was no Thadius there. But, when I told the woman that I had sailed with you on your most recent journey, she became most agreeable. That was three days ago."

Lifting the bundles up to Wyglad, Eilifr boasted a tremendous laugh. "She did not invite me in, but did bid me to wait at the docks for you, as you would soon be healed from your wounds and ready to travel to Herculaneum. She paid me a hundred gold coins to wait for you."

"A hundred gold coins indeed," Dominus laughed. "It would seem you've done well."

Thadius, laughing heartily climbed up the gangplank and onto the ship. Wyglad came over and examined him up and down. "You seem no worse for the wound, Gray Lion," Wyglad smiled.

Bojon and Tuturk came over, as did the rest of the crew. Some spoke in their native tongue and others in Latin, and even some in Greek. Handing Thadius a long horn of strong mead, Tuturk smiled warmly, "It is good to have our brothers back with us."

"Yes, yes," called out Bojon while slapping Thadius on the shoulder. "We have many more places to sail and much more to see and do before our eyes darken."

Wyglad laughed and sat down on a rower's bench. "It would seem we have come full circle. Now we take you to the place at which we met. After that, the gods will have something new for us to do."

Sitting down on the rower's bench Dominus admired the ship. Looking at it as one might a woman he spoke, "I hate to leave her again."

"Do not speak foolish," Eilifr chastised Dominus, "we are not gods, nor do we have the right to be sad. You see my ship now and let it be that alone." Pointing at the new morning sky Eilifr chuckled, "A fair day to be upon the sea, now enjoy it."

"And not far to your home," Wyglad said. "By today's end you will see your town and sleep in your own bed."

"Now that it is close, I'm not sure that I want to see it," Dominus stated. "I would much rather sail the seas with you until I am food for the sea beasts."

"And you Thadius?" Eilifr asked. "Do you feel the same?"

"I paid a fare of gold long ago for a ride on a boat, but across a river in the underworld, not upon a sea, and the captain of that boat doesn't command a crew. I think it's time I went home."

"Then, release the ropes, prepare the oars," Eilifr shouted as he climbed up to the rudder deck. "Drop the plank and let's get underway."

"Shouldn't we have to sleep on the boat first?" Dominus said.

"No time for that, we'll have to take our chances that the gods do not curse us," Eilifr stated.

The tempo of the oars hitting the water set the mood as Thadius pulled, recovered and pulled again. Reaching the breakwater of the bay, the ship slipped down the trough of a ten-foot wave. Feeling the sea wind growing strong Thadius heard Eilifr call the command to hoist the sail. Wyglad and Bojon secured the ropes and the great red sail snapped full. Quickly the ship came under speed and Eilifr maneuvered the tiller to direct the ship to its intended course. Dominus and Thadius secured their oars, and stood swaying with the roll of the ship.

"It would seem that our journey is at an end," said Dominus as he retrieved a loaf of bread and a horn of mead from the aft.

"Perhaps," Thadius said a strange lilt was in his voice.

"Perhaps?" Dominus wiped his mouth with the back of his hand. "You're not considering something foolish are you?"

"Is life to be spent digging in the garden and falling to the underworld in my sleep?"

Dominus' eyes went wide with understanding. Laughing loudly he set down his bread on a bench and slapped Thadius on the back. "But what of Simon, your home, and wealth?

"From time to time you say wise things," Thadius said.

"You're joking right?"

"No. You said that the Tolosa gold could do some good. Well, it's true it's doing nothing now. So, what say you, shall we go find some good to do?" Thadius stood.

"I can't be hearing you right," Dominus stated.

"I have left written instructions with Simon that he and the servants shall be paid a sum and be set free if I do not return. Half my treasure will be split among them, and my sons." Thadius pulled down at his tunic and grinned, "I don't think I have any use for all those mortal trappings now."

"You old salt," Dominus chuckled loudly. "I'm ready to go spend Caepio's gold."

Smiling broadly Thadius nodded his head in agreement. Scooping up the bread from the bench, he took a large bite, then took Dominus' horn from him, and quaffed until the horn was empty. "We should see if our captain has better plans than sailing to a resort town," Thadius laughed. "Eilifr," Thadius shouted, "would you take on two little Romans as crew?"

Looking down at them Eilifr burst with laughter. Keeping the rudder on task, he called out to his crew. "Listen brothers, will you accept two small and frail Romans as crew to fight beside you and row to the ends of the world?"

A great cheer rang up from the crew and they raised their fists to the sky and called loudly using the barbarian word for brother in a rhythmic chant. One at a time they came to Dominus and Thadius placing a hand on their shoulder and drinking a toast.

"The crew has decided," Eilifr said. "Now you must proclaim an oath. Do you swear upon your honor as a Roman, sailor, and part of this crew, to fight to your last breath for your brothers, to live by the rules of the sea, and never show fear in the face of the god's challenges?"

Dominus called out for all the crew to hear, "I swear such an oath."

"And, you Gray Lion?" Eilifr said.

"I too swear such an oath."

"Even though we are exiled and a poor crew?" Eilifr said.

"You are rich at heart. That's the only wealth I need now. But, I think I see a golden opportunity coming our way in the not too distant future," Thadius stated.

Eilifr laughed, and then shouted down at the assembled crew, "To your work. We have far to travel and riches to make." Shifting on the rudder he brought the ship about. Turning into the wind he called down to the men, "Drop sail, prepare oars."

Doing as commanded the men assumed their posts. Thadius sat at his oar bench, and untied his oar. Dominus did likewise. Securing the oar through the iron hole Thadius pushed down on the handle and lifted the other end into the air. Holding down the oar he looked over at Dominus. "Here we go," he said.

"To the draw and pull," shouted Eilifr as the ship began its movement into the wind and the westward sea.

ABOUT THE AUTHOR

Lawrence BoarerPitchford ~
Is the author of such works as Tales of Mad Cows and Brothels, The
Lantern of Dern Blackhammer, Sawbones, and In the World of Hyboria.
He's provided royalties to the American Cancer Society, and contributes to
other worthy charities such as the American Society for the Prevention of
Cruelty to Animals (ASPCA), and Meals on Wheels. His motto is "Less
cruelty and more kindness makes a better world."

www.ingramcontent.com/pod-product-compliance
Lightning Source LLC
Chambersburg PA
CBHW030357020726
47493CB00003B/855